DOLL HOUSE

JOHN HUNT

ISBN: 978-1-61296-807-0
PUBLISHED BY BLACK ROSE WRITING
www.blackrosewriting.com

Printed in the United States of America
Suggested retail price $18.95

Doll House is printed in Garamond

This book is dedicated to my wife, Louise.

Special thanks to my sister, Alana, who spent hours of her free time to read and suggest ways in which to make the book better. In general, thanks to all of my family (especially the boy), for their encouragement and support.

Thanks also must be given to my friend, Kyle Grant, who read and offered suggestions for the betterment of the story.

PRAISE FOR *DOLL HOUSE*

- "I was engaged from the very first to the very end." – Linda Strong, *Strong Book Reviews*

- "*Doll House* is a deeply felt and admirably realized tale of an unending real-life nightmare." – *Mallory Heart Reviews*

- "This book seriously blew me away. My head is spinning... I was clenching my hands and biting my nails the WHOLE time. It takes a lot for a book to make me step back and say... woah WHILE I'm reading it but this one did just that." – Brandi Aga, *After the Pages*

- "I absolutely loved this book." – Angela Hunt, Bolton Library

- "From the pace to plot and a kick-ass female protagonist, I found not much to fault in *Doll House*. This novel is out now, so if you want a 'scare your pants off' type horror thriller, then look no further." – Samantha Melonche, *Clues and Reviews*

- "This book is not for the faint of heart. It's deliciously dark and gruesome. Extremely fast paced, yet somehow you feel every part of the girls' pain." – Chandra Claypool, *Where the Reader Grows*

DOLL HOUSE

-1-

"Is Dale okay with the break up?"

Olivia sipped her coffee, licked away the foam moustache and said, "I guess. He didn't pitch a fit or anything. How could he be okay with it? We'd been together for a while. I don't like it, but it's the right thing to do, you know?"

Harry nodded, turning the coffee cup on the table with his fingers. They sat in Starbucks with light music playing in the background, people moving and the rich smell of coffee and chocolate thick enough to touch. They placed themselves by the window because he wanted to keep an eye on his car, amazed how much of Olivia's stuff they had crammed in his Prius. After loading it, he had to lean on the hatch with all his body weight to get it closed. They had stuffed it with all the things she would need for school and items she probably wouldn't need. Olivia was starting university on Monday. It hurt to let her go, a hand squeezing his heart. He didn't like it. But, like she said, even if you don't like it, you should do the right thing. He thought that's what she said. Maybe he paraphrased her a little. Even though he felt the pending empty nest, he couldn't deny the tingle of excitement for her. It was a good time in her life, to leave home for the first time and travel into the unknown. Like going on an adventure with no treasure map to guide the way, armed with good judgement and moral character. It had been his job to equip her with those attributes and he believed he had done well enough. Exceptional young woman. Isn't that what all dads thought of their children? Maybe yes, maybe no.

Harry scanned the coffee shop noting MacBooks, tablets, headphones and ebooks. People isolating themselves in public with electronics. Might as well have stayed home if all they wanted to do was drink coffee and browse the internet. Jeez, he realized he was getting old. It happened quick. One day you woke up, looked around and started saying things like, "It was better back then," or, "Music nowadays is just noise," and when the words leave your lips, you're stunned, thinking, man, when did this old guy appear?

"You okay, Daddy?"

"What? Yeah."

"You were frowning and staring off into space. That thing you do when you're brooding."

"Brooding? I don't brood. I'm more of a pensive person. Brooding sounds negative."

"Brooding is negative. And you look it, when you frown like that."

She was concerned and he knew she had reservations about leaving home as well. It had been the two of them for so long. She could stay at home and go to a local college and maybe not even have to break up with Dale. Everything stays the same. She would do it more for him than herself. And because he knew this and wanted to be a good dad even if he lost a part of his heart when she left, he smiled and said, "I'm just excited for you. This is going to be good for you."

"Yeah, but is it going too good for you?"

"Of course it is. This is natural. Kids grow up, kids leave home. It's the way things are supposed to go. And I'm glad you turned out the way you did. I'm stunned, actually, with all my bumbling."

"You were great, Dad. I couldn't have asked for better."

"Me either, kiddo."

She sipped her coffee and with his words, some tension eased from her shoulders. She smiled and put a hand over his.

He grinned and shook his head.

"What?"

"Remember when I tried to tell you about—" he glanced around the coffee shop and when certain no one was paying them any attention, he whispered, "your period?"

Olivia chuckled and then groaned, "Oh my, that was a disaster. You started sweating and stuttering. Like the time you tried to explain the birds and the bees. I mean, who even says that anymore?"

He said, "I wanted to puke. My stomach flipped around on me and I thought I was going to heave when I took the tampon out of the wrapper and tried to show you where it went. Remember that? Holy Christ on a popsicle stick I sucked."

He sipped on his drink, his face a bright red, a rueful smile dressing his face.

Olivia, laughing at him, drew a chuckle from him. The camaraderie of comedy.

"You didn't suck. You just didn't have a vagina."

"Jeez. Keep it down would ya?"

"You did it all alone, Dad. I think you did a terrific job, cause I am pretty awesome." She grinned, amusement a dancing jewel in her eye.

Beautiful, like her mother. He thanked a God he didn't believe in she didn't take after him. He wasn't ugly but he wasn't good looking either. The crown of his head decided to start pushing the hair out too early in his opinion. He fussed over it this morning, taking care to comb his hair over the growing pink crown without looking like he was trying to cover it which everyone, including him, knew was impossible. He lost the hair on the top of his head where he wanted it and instead it sprouted out of his ears where he didn't want it. What is the evolutionary purpose of growing hair in your ears as you aged? Harry liked that Olivia had been spared any resemblance to him. You always want the best for your children and a daughter with his looks? That would've been less than ideal.

Her mother, Samantha, had been stunning. She was just not interested in being a mother. Or maybe she didn't want to be involved with him. The result was the same either way. After Olivia had been born, she left her with him, said she never wanted a child and left town. She hadn't been heard or seen from again. He got a beautiful daughter out of it, from a one night stand with a woman who had been way out of his league.

He remembered the night he had met her. Flabbergasted would have been an understatement to his reaction when *she* bought him a drink. They moved from the bar to a booth and spoke for most of the night. She laughed at his jokes, reached to touch him with her fingers, punctuating her words with manicured nails. She smelled like strawberries. Not her perfume, her skin. Like goddamn strawberries.

He hadn't expected marriage. He knew he had been a drunk decision of regret on her part. Still, to just leave and never want to be involved with their wonderful daughter? Harry couldn't fathom it. Hard thing to explain when Olivia got old enough to ask where was her mother and why did she leave. A part of him wondered if she sometimes wished her mother would come back and take her away from her awkward father. Maybe she dreamed about it late at night, staring at the glow-in-the-dark stars he had pasted to her ceiling.

"Yeah. You are marginally awesome."

"Marginal?"

"Yes. After strong reflection, I believe your awesomeness is marginal at this point. After university, I'm sure your stock will rise, but it depends."

"Oh yeah, depends on what?"

"On how often you call and visit your father."

"Well, I thought I'd stop by for Christmas, to get presents of course. Oh, and if I run out of money, I may come home. You know, *only* if I need something."

Harry clutched his chest, "My heart! You've broken it! But I will accept those terms."

Olivia laughed, "C'mon Dad. I'll call and visit as much as I can. I'm not even gone yet and I already miss you. I'm going to miss this."

"This?"

"Yeah. This. Moments like this."

"It is a pretty good one. And because I raised you to be awesome, I think you're going to have a great time."

"Thanks Dad. I think I will too."

"Don't get pregnant."

"Dad!"

"Stay away from crystal meth and boys named Andy."

"What? Andy?"

"Shifty little bastards, boys' named Andy."

She laughed and said, "You're so random!"

"Hey!" Feigning offence he said, "These are pearls of parental wisdom. You should treat them as such. Andy and crystal meth? Terrible."

She raised her eyebrows and after a quick glance at her watch said, "It's time to go. I gotta be on residence soon. Where's Uncle Frank? I thought he was helping us."

Such big blue eyes watching him and he remembered picking her up after the first day of kindergarten. She looked at him with the absolute trust particular to children and raised her arms to be lifted up and carried. He never thought he could love someone so much and feel the love in return. He had lifted her off the ground and walked her to the car in his arms. She had jabbered in his ear about her day and the friends she met. Harry, listening and nodding, wondered how much love can a heart hold? Limitless. His heart anyways.

Harry checked his watch and said, "Frank? He's gonna meet us there. You're right. It's time to scoot. We gotta long drive ahead of us."

"Dad. It's an hour. I'm only an hour away."

"Like I said, a long drive. Probably have to fill up twice. On the way there and on the way back."

"You drive a Prius. You won't have to fill it up until next month."

He nodded, "They do get good mileage don't they?"

She stood and he followed her out to the car.

They drove to the university of Guelph from their home town of Hamilton. They talked, comfortable with each other. Harry thought even if she wasn't his daughter, she'd be someone he'd actually like. A good person. Was it parental blindness? Could be. He didn't think so. He could tell by the way her friends greeted her and how Dale had held her in reverence that there was something about her. She was the person people glanced at when she entered a room. She was the person dogs never barked at.

He did alright, as a father. Even the teenage years weren't all that bad. They weren't that good either. A few sleepless nights wishing he had someone to talk to about it. Frank, the consummate bachelor, never had anything helpful to say. Harry had no idea how to talk to her when she came home smelling of dope, giggling at nothing particularly funny. Still, compared to some of the stories he'd heard he figured he survived the years of the teen relatively unscathed.

They arrived in the city and followed the signs posted on the Hanlon Highway to the university. Smaller than Hamilton and less industrialized, Guelph was a pretty city. Old trees, plenty of green-space, a town built around and accommodating to the university, Harry believed Olivia would be safe here. One of the safest cities in Canada according to Statistics Canada. The sprawling university grounds bloomed before them. Older red-brick buildings beside newer glass and steel ones. Long expanses of grass sprouting thick trunked trees with branches drooping from the weight of leaves. Moving-in day, the roads around the campus were clogged with inching cars packed with laundry hampers, lamps, and the detritus of student living. The roads wound around the buildings creating a daunting maze. After many glances at a glossy map in a pamphlet, they found the right building. Frank stood out front, ogling the passing girls.

"Jeez, Uncle Frank, put your eyes back in your head would you? You look like a lion at a watering hole."

"Yes, of course. Should I have worn sunglasses you think? Then, no one can see where I'm looking."

Olivia laughed and said, "You know, you're old enough to be their father."

He waved the statement off, "Nonsense. I'm younger than your dad, you know. By quite a lot. I'm more like an older cousin, handsome, witty and so much more attractive because, as a cousin, I have to be off limits. The risk of birth defects and all."

Harry said, "Alright, alright. Let's get her unloaded and then you two can carry on your conversation about how Frank is a creeper."

"Creeper? Me?" He smiled and wiggled his eyebrows.

Olivia laughed.

They lugged her stuff to her room, weaving and twisting past smiling students, happy to be out from under their parents' watchful eye. Harry noticed a few male heads turn to look at his daughter and a knot of worry tightened in his guts. People put drugs in drinks. He exhaled and reminded himself he trusted Olivia. She knew more about what went on than he did. She would be fine.

After Harry placed the last box in the room, he leaned against a desk drinking a Coke. Olivia drank a Coke Zero. Frank checked his watch like he had somewhere to be.

Harry said, "You need a hand unpacking all this?"

"No."

"Alright. I'll get going then."

Frank said, "Yeah. Cool. I gotta go too. So, I'll leave you two cry babies alone to say your goodbyes." He pointed at Olivia, "I'll expect to see you on Thanksgiving young lady."

"Depends. Are you gonna bring a date? A classic Frank date."

"This should be good. What's a classic Frank date?"

"All looks, no substance."

"It hurts that I'm so transparent. But, of course. I don't date for conversation. I have you and your dad for that. The few times a year I decide to show up anyways. Well, take care. Remember, try out as many dudes as you can before settling for one."

Harry said, "Frank! C'mon man!"

He raised his hands, "It's good advice."

He scurried out the door when Harry's mouth turned into a thin line and said, "See you."

Harry jabbed a thumb at Frank's back and said, "Quite a character."

"Yeah."

He stood and she hugged him and he squeezed her right back. Harry thought, *keep it together! Don't you cry!* She smelled of memories. Her first walk, her first words, her first bike ride, her first day of school, all the images popping through the hippocampus in his brain. Weird, to hold your heart in your arms and know you must let it go. He released her first. Did his eyes have a bit of shine to them? Definitely. Olivia faked not noticing very well.

"I'll be home for Thanksgiving. You'll pick me up right?"

"Absolutely. Let me know the time and I'll be here. Frank's date should be entertaining. Provided she can string some words together to form a sentence."

She rolled her eyes, "Can't wait."

"I know right? At least you know it'll be interesting."

"Frank's dates usually are."

"I'll see you then?"

"Yeah. Drive safe Dad. I'll call you."

"Once a week?"

"Maybe twice."

He pointed at her, "I'm holding you to that."

"Okay, okay. I'll call you twice a week and see you in a month or so."

"Damn right you will."

He walked out, proud and sad, hoping she liked it here and hoping she hated it and wanted to come home.

-2-

Harry sank into the couch with a beer in his hand and turned on the TV. Five o'clock and already dark out. He shook his head. Fucking Canadian winters. He popped the top on the can and flicked through the channels, not seeing anything, just trying to find background noise. Something to dull the senses. Like drinking beer. It served to induce a stillness of thoughts. Since Olivia disappeared five years ago, or let's be real here, since she was taken, he couldn't slow his brain. The gears wouldn't slow, kept clunking along showing him images of Olivia dead in a ditch. When he thought of this, and he often did because of his stupid cruel brain, in his mind's eye it was always raining. She'd be at the bottom, her hair a golden halo fanned out on the dirty mud. Her hands would be taped in front of her. Her fingernails worn down and peeled back as though she tried to escape by scratching through a wall. The rain splashed into her open mouth and plinked into her eyes. She never flinched. She never blinked. That's how he knew she was dead.

Sometimes, he saw her body crumpled in the bottom of an old well. Arms and legs bent at unnatural angles. Bones poking through flesh, her expression a postcard of pain. Again, the rain a humming backdrop falling from the heavy grey clouds. And he'd think, *I failed her.* She'd been taken and he couldn't find her, he couldn't save her and he sure as hell couldn't do the one thing parents are supposed to do: protect her. Now, as soon as he got home from work, he drank until the recriminations in his brain silenced. He had a problem with the drink. He knew it. He knew the people at work knew it. When you come in the morning with red eyes and popping Advil like candy, people noticed.

Good thing he worked like a bastard. Work, he found, also produced a stillness of thoughts. Turning his thoughts and focus to a problem to be solved pushed the images away, put a lid on his worrying for a short time. Working in IT for a big corporate firm kept him busy and he did like it. It was his drinking that had stopped his upward mobility. For as long as he'd been there and with his experience, he should have been a supervisor by now, or maybe in the admin side and be the guy who decided what equipment to buy, what software to acquire, all the fun shit super geeks like him lived for. At least he'd kept his drinking for when he wasn't working. Almost, anyways. There was the one time he came back from lunch with a bit of a sway. He had one too many martinis with lunch, well, probably a few too many. While gulping one down, he pointed at the glass to the bartender, signalling he wanted another with a flurry hands, wanting it in a hurry. His lunch hour wasn't over but it was getting close. The bartender, a young guy with an eyebrow piercing and one ugly moustache, shrugged and made him another one. He knew a drunk when he saw one. Harry liked the warm feeling inside. It settled in his stomach and then reached out to all parts of his body, a pleasant, tingling feeling. Maybe too pleasant. A Martini was not a chugging drink he decided because man, they could fuck you up in a hurry. Returning to the office like that was a mistake. He should have called in sick and went home to sleep it off. But like most drunks, he thought he'd been fooling everyone and like most drunks, he soon found out how wrong he was. He swayed in, talking a little too loud, bumping into cubicles and making a giant fool of himself in front of his peers and supervisors. Naturally, his supervisors became concerned.

They sent Tracey to talk to him. A person he had trained. A person he had been getting closer to before Olivia…well, before he'd lost her. She walked into his office and closed the door behind her. Never a good sign. He remembered his heart sped up a little and he thought, *they're finally going to do it. I'm getting fired.* His stomach rebelled and he thought he was going to puke on his own desk. He swallowed, his mouth gushing with saliva and he couldn't look her in the eyes. He stared at the coffee cup on his desk. It was white and in black lettering across the front it read, *Don't talk to me until I've had my first coffee.* He kept his eyes on it as she approached. He saw the front of her shirt where it met her waist. Black with some pattern on it, were they glasses? Like reading glasses? He couldn't tell. All he knew was that he couldn't look at her. Not at her face. They couldn't make him do that could they? He felt a deep shame then and his face burned with it. But a part of him, the alcoholic part, the greedy little man in the corner of his soul thought maybe it wouldn't be so bad to be fired. It could be a good thing. They'd have to buy him out and then he could get down to serious drinking. Something attractive about the idea, a nihilistic urge to destroy himself. He wanted to find bottom and stay there, where the pain wasn't as sharp, where it didn't have teeth. Then Tracey surprised him. She handed him a pamphlet for

Alcoholics Anonymous and spoke to him about the lunchtime martinis. He had a problem. The bosses knew it and were monitoring him. They were sympathetic to his loss and would support therapy if he wanted it. No, he didn't want it and he raised his eyes to hers. Her face flushed. She had the pale skin red heads have, white as paper that filled with red in embarrassing or awkward moments: like this one. He watched her lips and wanted to kiss them. Did she smell like strawberries? Drunk thoughts. Stupid thoughts. She told him this was his one and final warning. Come back to work drunk again, and he'd be fired. He nodded. He understood. She told him he was to go home now and return tomorrow sober. The company already called a cab on his behalf. And in case he was wondering, it wasn't a suggestion.

He stood, patted his pockets for his keys, nodded and left. He didn't meet anyone's gaze on the way out. He couldn't. And he wondered if he could even return the next day. In the cab as he was passing shops, cars and people walking to anywhere, he realized the break he'd just gotten. He didn't want bottom that bad after all. He needed work to keep busy or he'd go crazy. In the office there, when Tracey was speaking to him and he had the urge to kiss her in the most inappropriate setting, to smell her to find out if her skin smelled of strawberries, in that moment he had a taste of crazy. He thought of that saying, he couldn't remember what it was from but it surfaced in the cab and it played in his brain, like a song on repeat: the centre cannot hold. Dread flooded him. If he kept going like that, without work to act as a behavioural anchor, he'd lose all identity, moving from one drunken fog to another, broken up by the need to sleep or the search for his next bottle. He would be sucked into an abyss that he created, a crazy place with no escape where images of Olivia's dead body kept him constant company pointing accusatory fingers. He didn't want to visit there again.

For a brief moment, in the cab when embarrassment pushed aside his inebriation with a vicious elbow, he told himself he'd quit for good. Better rampant thoughts than facing that type of humiliation again. When he got home and opened the fridge to see a six pack of Labatt Maximum Ice beer on the shelf, he thought, *7.1% alcohol content baby!* And then the drunk's constant lie of tomorrow, I'll quit tomorrow flitted through his mind as he reached for the bottle. From then on, he restricted his drinking to home after work. He ate lunch at his desk in his office so people could see him and let the office spies know he was sticking to the deal. And who knew? Maybe it'd help him quit. He just had to take it one day at a time. He was fooling himself and insightful enough to know it. The best lies, the most convincing, are the ones we tell ourselves. And no one can lie better than an alcoholic.

He turned on the hockey game, slugged back the beer and went into the kitchen for another. He opened the cupboard for a glass and saw a shot glass. He took it down and looked in the liquor cabinet. It stood empty. When the hell did he drink the dark rum? He was sure he had half a bottle at least. *You're a drunk and drunks have no memory,* he thought. It scared him a bit, to think he drank a bottle without remembering it. He put the shot glass back, opened another can and poured it into a glass and took a drink. Have a fear you don't want to face? The ugly truth a little too ugly? Have a beer. The solution to harsh realities. A small smile creased his cheek.

He took another can of beer and brought it back to the couch to watch the Leafs suffer another loss. Goddamn tough to be a Leafs' fan. He sipped at his beer, feeling the edges getting softer, his eyelids drooping, his chin dancing on his chest. He managed to keep filling the glass when it had the nerve to be empty.

The phone bleated, alarming him. Cold beer slopped over the rim of the glass and splashed in his lap, "Fuck!"

Who'd be calling him? It wouldn't be work. They used to call him out for IT problems in the past, but not since he began his love affair with the sauce. He did have friends, once upon a time, but with a combination of withdrawal and liberal self-medication of alcohol, they disappeared along with Olivia. Even his brother Frank barely called anymore. The phone digitally clanged. Probably a jack-ass cold-caller even though he put himself on the no-contact list.

It continued to bray. He stood, a little wobbly, and set the glass down before he slopped more out of it. He walked to the cordless, saw the 'unknown number' display and picked it up.

"Listen, I'm drunk, tired and not interested in what you're selling."

"Daddy!"

His world stopped.

-3-

Olivia hadn't even made it to her first class before being taken. Hell, she hadn't even slept in her new bed at residence. She puzzled over it a long time, in her prison wondering, like most people who have something terrible happen to them, how she could have avoided it. How did she not sense what was bearing down on her? A monolith of menace. How could it happen with such suddenness? Like walking off a cliff having no idea the path ended. One second you're whistling along and the next, you're falling through the sky, your face a study in confusion. No warning, no expectation of disaster. And even after a lifetime of reading or seeing the news on TV, relating the terrors of natural disasters or man-made ones, it never occurred to her that such things could happen to her. It seemed those terrible things happened far away, to far away people with names she didn't know and faces she had never seen. Might as well have happened on the moon. One thing she was sure of, she wasn't a goddamn psychic. No tarot card readings for her in the future.

After her dad left her at the university amidst luggage and boxes, she examined her new home for the next year. More like a glorified closet. She thought if she stretched out her arms she could probably touch both walls. She tried it and she could. Her fingertips brushing the ridged contours of the cinderblock walls, painted a sunny yellow. She began the tedious process of unpacking. She propped open the door so she could hear the students in the hall laughing and moving about backdropped by competing music genres from different rooms. Busy, happy sounds. Olivia decided to contribute. She searched her boxes, found the Bose sound dock and plugged it in. Easy to get lost in the music while your hands busied themselves with onerous chores. Olivia believed music made everything better and once she connected her iPod, the fear of the new, of being alone and reliant upon herself, faded with her immersion in the music. The excitement of this entirely new experience built inside her and she couldn't wait to get to class, meet other people and maybe sit under one of the overhanging willows and discuss life with pedantic boys growing their first beards. Humming, she finished unpacking and folded down the boxes to slip into her closet for later use.

She lay on the bed, congratulating herself on her efficiency and thinking the ceiling could use a poster. Rock band? Or some cute actor? Someone knocked on her open door. A tall guy, lanky, stood in the door with the suggestion of a smile. He had a tattoo on the side of his neck, a symbol, obscured by his hair. He held papers in his hand and said, "Hi."

"Hey."

"I'm the R.A. The uh, resident advisor. Just popping in, saying hi."

She stood and offered her hand, "I'm Olivia."

"Rick. So. Here are some useful pamphlets. Maps of the buildings for the classes. You should wander around tomorrow, find where your classes are. This place is big. It also shows where the cafeteria is and the on-campus pub. You old enough to drink? Probably not. First year, right?"

"Yeah."

"This little booklet contains the rules for living here. It has a list of fines and what not. And the last one there, has the phone number for campus security and all the R.A's and oh, also has admin numbers, like who to talk to and what to do about changing a class."

"Okay. Thanks."

"The cafeteria has a Starbucks now. And a Timmy's. They accept the meal plan cards. They're open late, too. Classes don't officially start until Tuesday. Monday, there is an orientation session if you wanna go. It's like a more detailed version of the stuff I just gave you. Starts in the university Centre, at around nine in the morning. You'll get an event calendar, for frosh week there too. But you can get those anywhere."

"Perfect. Thanks again, Rick."

"No problem. See you around."

"Alright."

He hustled off and she heard him knock on another door down the hall and begin his speech. She sat on the bed and browsed through the pamphlets. The daylight faded and she noticed the sun shone mid sky, outlining the buildings as though drawn in black marker. Maybe she should go for a walk now, browse the campus with a coffee in one hand and a cookie in the other. Early evening, summer warmth still lingering, it'd be pleasant. Besides, what else would she do? She needed to burn off all the energy roiling inside and buzzing under her skin. She should use the energy for an adventure. She slipped on her flip flops, patted the pockets of her jean shorts to make sure she had her keys, student card and phone and after closing the door behind her and using the map to orient herself, she headed to Starbucks, her flip flops flapping on the ground.

She passed by rooms with the doors open and saw students lounging on the bed or in chairs. Bottles of alcohol and mix lined up like sentries on the desk, half empty or half full, depending on your outlook. Some nodded, grinning as though she were part of the conspiracy and others invited her in, slurred speech indicating they already had too much. She smiled to some said, "Another time," to others and left the building to be met by fresh air redolent of barbecues roasting meat and the sounds of laughter dancing to her ears. So busy here and cheerful.

She glanced to the sky, rippled purple like a dark bruise as the sun circled to the horizon. Maybe they'd have a nice September. Could never tell in Canada. Wasn't uncommon to have plus twenty degrees Celsius one day and a snow storm the next. She loved the warmth and endured the winter. She hoped to have a warm autumn. Amazing to her, to feel excited, scared and hopeful all at the same time. Almost like when she got her driver's license. She bounced up and down in front of her dad and thought her heart would explode when he handed her the keys. Everything seemed possible then and it was the same way now. A long road of possibilities stretched out before her.

She walked down a path winding its way through thick trees, drooping branches laden with leaves and into an open area where some students threw a football to each other with red plastic cups at their feet.

Starbucks was in the cafeteria area in the university centre building. She got a latte and a gingerbread cookie. While sprinkling some cinnamon on her latte she spied a familiar face seated at a table. It took her a moment to place him. Then she remembered she'd seen him many times over the years at the recreation centre she worked in while in high school. A big man, strong through the shoulders but always ready with a smile. While the kids swam, he always sat by the pool, reading a book and sipping a coffee. Much like now. What was he doing in Guelph? At the Starbucks on campus? Did he have a kid going here? Seemed a bit too young. She shrugged it off and left the university Centre and continued with her exploration. The sun had disappeared behind the earth. The street lamps hummed above her casting haloes of light at their base and darkness claimed the spaces in between. She didn't mind. She hadn't learned to fear the dark.

Main roads intersected throughout the campus. Olivia preferred to walk along the main roads because they were better lit. A logical precaution that in most instances made sense. Main roads are better lit and frequently travelled.

Olivia's phone chirped. She took it out of her pocket and read a text from her friend, Sara, wondering how the new digs were. Sara was commuting from Hamilton to Western university in London, and was jealous, in a good natured way, of Olivia living away from home. With deft hands Olivia texted back and forth with Sara. She was unaware of the panel van slowing behind. Later, by the texts between Sara and Olivia, police would determine the time of her abduction between 8:45pm and 9:00pm.

Olivia described the social R.A., Rick, to Sara and didn't hear the van creaking to a stop and the door sliding open. She was completely and utterly oblivious of the large man in a gorilla mask coming up behind her until his arms encircled her. She saw the phone slip out of her hands to hit the sidewalk, in slow motion, like when something terrible happened in a movie so they slowed it right down to better witness the tragedy. She was lifted from her feet, carried to the van and thrown inside. It happened so quick and so befuddled her, she didn't start screaming until the door slid closed and the van accelerated into the night. The snatch took approximately three seconds. Police later thought it unusual there were no witnesses on such a busy road. Not unusual, just perfect timing with a dash of bad luck for Olivia thrown in.

•   •   •

She screamed and thrashed her legs, twisting in the grip of the man in the gorilla mask. He punched her in the nose and that stopped her screaming. White spots twinkled behind her eyes. The back of her head clanged against the metal floor. Her eyes teared and her mouth flooded with blood and the salty taste slid past her tongue and down her throat.

"That's a good little bitch. Keep fucking quiet," said the man.

He turned her over and secured her hands behind her with plastic ties. She spat blood on the floor, confused, blinking her eyes to rid them of the bright spots. The gorilla man flipped her on her back and he placed his knees on both sides of her and sat on her stomach. She grunted as his weight stretched the skin on her hip bones and crushed her ribs against her insides. Her breath hitched in difficult gasps.

The driver didn't look back. He didn't glance in her direction at all and she knew there'd be no help from him. Olivia guessed the broad shouldered man would be driving the speed limit, stopping for all the lights and following all the rules of the road. They could not afford to be pulled over. Not with her, their stolen cargo in back.

Gorilla man must have had keys or something in his back pocket because she felt something unyielding grind against her hip bone. The pain took on an immensity of its own and reduced the lesser pains to dim background noise. Her nose throbbed and blood still ran into her mouth yet the grinding pain on her hip overshadowed it. She grit her teeth and tried to move her hips a little, to adjust the angle of her hips to lessen the pain. He must have thought she were trying to buck him off because he put his hand over her nose and mouth, pressing tight. The pain in her nose exploded, needles probing at her brain and the hand tightened, fingers pinching her nostrils closed and cutting off her air. She could see the outline of his mask as the passing street lights glowed on the fur. Her lungs burned. She twisted her head, trying to dislodge the hand. He responded by gripping tighter. The pain of his grip battled against her need to breathe. She opened her mouth and jerked her head and she felt skin against her teeth: his skin. Without thinking about it, knowing she had to breathe, needing air, needing that goddamn hand off her mouth, she clamped down on the skin and crunched through it.

"Fuck!" He lifted his hand and she pulled sweet, beautiful air into her mouth. The air tasted wonderful and her lungs filled with it. She inhaled again and she choked on the blood in her mouth while the man in the gorilla mask examined his hand in the passing lights from the street. The driver never said a word. He picked up an iPod and pressed play. A woman's voice singing *Ava Maria* issued from the speakers. She knew that song from her music teacher in high school. Her teacher, Mrs. Trayne, used to play it all the time and tilt her head listening to it with her eyes closed. The driver didn't look back, unconcerned about his partner's swearing or why he did.

The Gorilla got off her and knelt beside her. In this moment, the removal of his weight equated to heaven. He leaned over her and even though she couldn't see his eyes in the depths of the mask, she felt them roaming up and down her body. Olivia pressed her body into the floor of the van, desperate to create distance, maybe to disappear into the metal floor. He grabbed her nose in between his thumb and index finger and squeezed. She squealed and tasted blood dribbling into her mouth. The pain lifted her hips off the floor. He let go, chuckling. Lights from the street ran across the ceiling, his head a dark, furry blob.

"You and I? We're gonna have some fun aren't we darling? You got spunk. I like it."

Her voice trembled, "Do what you like. Just please. Let me go. I haven't seen your faces. Please. Let me go."

He didn't move. The van rocked gently. He ran his fingers lightly over her cheeks, almost a caress. She flinched and couldn't suppress a shudder. His hand snapped out and grabbed her breast and twisted it, pulling her off the floor with his strength. She cried out and after what seemed a lifetime of pain, he let go. He said, "I'll do what I like anyways. But letting you go? Doesn't matter how nice you play or how great you suck a dick. We're never letting you go. You're ours now. And baby, we're gonna have us some fun tonight! Have to break you in, honey, take that fight right out of you. That's the best part, breaking the new ones in. Woo-hee!"

The ceiling of the van blurred with her tears. Whatever they had in store for her wouldn't be pleasant. And no matter what she did, in the end, she knew they had to kill her. Why wouldn't they? The dead make terrible witnesses. It was clear from what he said, she wasn't their first victim. They weren't bumbling fools. They'd done this before and acted with confidence because of it. How many girls had perished under their cruel hands? Her veins ran cold with despair.

●　　●　　●

Before the van stopped, Gorilla man put a sack over her head and tied it around her neck, taut enough to be uncomfortable. Her hands throbbed from the tightness of the plastic cuffs. He lifted her up and slung her over his shoulder with a grunt. A blood clump fell out of her swollen nose and rolled along her skin and into her hair.

From the van, it seemed a short distance before the sound of boots on gravel turned to the click of tile. She wished she could see inside the house, where they were and what they were doing. Blood pulsed in her head and his shoulder digging into her diaphragm made it hard to breathe. Her stomach roiled and she thought she might vomit in the sack. *No, no, no, don't do that,* she thought, clenching her teeth and swallowed down rising bile not wanting to have her own head and face swimming in her own puke.

A door creaked and heavy feet clomped on wooden stairs. She could tell they were descending because each step dipped down. The stairs went on forever, every drop a fresh dig into her stomach. Her knee cracked on the corner of something hard and she yelped. She felt the blood clot roll against her cheek. It was cold.

"Shut up. That was nothing. You don't know what pain is."

Her world had been reduced to sounds and battling the urge to vomit. She heard a clinking of metal and a door scraped open. His steps thudded forward. He let her slide off his shoulder and she knew he was going to drop her like a sack. She managed to turn her body before she hit cold concrete. Her right shoulder and hip took most of the impact and an expulsion of air hissed through her lips. Her hip and shoulder throbbed, pulses of pain in a universe of pain. The plastic ties on her wrist bit into the flesh when she hit the floor and a warm trickle of blood slid along her tingling thumbs and palm. Her head clipped the ground and her teeth clacked together. Winded, she curled on the ground waiting for the pain to subside. Steps receded and the heavy door clanged shut. The rope around her neck dug in, cutting off the carotid and dimming her vision until she lifted her head for relief.

"Hold still, honey. I gotta cut the string. You wouldn't want me to nick ya."

Metal pressed against her ear, down her jawline, playing along it with patient pressure. The string cut with ease. He yanked the sack off her head, getting a few hairs in the grabbing and she gritted her teeth against it wondering how many hairs he got in that grab. Bright light stung her eyes. She blinked and sniffed back blood leaking from her nose. She moved to wipe it away but her hands couldn't comply. She felt the numbing sensation moving up her forearms, an intense tingling, like a buzzing under her skin. She'd read one time that lack of oxygenated blood killed cells. Would they keep her trussed up long enough for her hands to become useless? Now what were they going to do to her? Nothing pleasant, nothing she'd laugh and blush about, that's for sure. Something terrible. Something cruel enough she had to be snatched and hidden so they could enjoy their prize and do things to her where she could expect no help and her screams wouldn't matter. Except to those who caused them.

Her head flicked around the room. Cinder Brick walls like her dorm room except pink. A Pepto Bismol eye stinging sort of pink. The floor was concrete grey. A pink metal dresser against the wall. She later learned the dresser was bolted to the floor, like everything in the room and the bolts were melted at the seam, impossible to remove. Her eyes took in an open shower with pink tiles and a heart-shaped mat outside the stall on the floor. And next to the stall? A pink fucking toilet. And behind her, she had to crane her neck to see, a cot, frame painted pink, bolted to the floor covered in pink blankets and red pillows. The room measured two, maybe three times bigger than the one she'd moved into at the university, which seemed now a lifetime ago.

The Gorilla man squatted before her, "Welcome home!"

Another man stood in the corner, wearing a jackal mask. Must be the driver, the one who didn't speak or turn to look all the way here. Where-ever here was. His arms crossed over his chest, he had broad shoulders and the muscles rippled along his forearm. The dark pockets of his eyes devoured her.

The Gorilla man stood unbuckling his belt, casual, as though he were getting ready to climb into bed after a hard day.

"Nice place isn't it? Warm," he gestured to the toilet and shower, "private amenities," he tossed the belt behind him and started kicking off his boots, "and best of all: rent free!" He slid his pants down and his erection bounced above her. "Well, not really free. We all have to pay in some way, I suppose. Sometimes, paying can be painful. Yep. It sure can be. How painful this gets is completely up to you...kind of mostly up to you. If you misbehave, I'm not accountable for my actions. Sometimes I just get carried away. All of a sudden I'm covered in blood and my poor date? Well, she barely looks human anymore! And for what? I'm gonna get what I want in the end anyways. I always do."

He grabbed her shorts, fumbling for the button and she squirmed, scrambled and kicked out with her foot. He caught it effortlessly. She bucked and twisted and kicked out, trying to get loose of him.

He held on, his grip tightening and he said, "You're gonna wanna play nice."

He spoke over his shoulder, to the Jackal, "A little help here."

The Jackal walked over. Olivia could see a bulge in the Jackal's pants and knew there would be no help from him. She knew she should just listen to him, give in, give them what they wanted and maybe, just maybe she could figure a way to get out of here but she couldn't. She didn't have it in her to quit like that. Couldn't give in to these fuckers! Amazing, how similar terror and rage were to Olivia. Rage made her forget about how much her shoulders hurt or how her hands tingled for lack of blood flow. Olivia thought, *Fuck them! Think they can just scoop her off the street and she'd be their plaything for nothing? Everything has a cost and they were going to pay it.* Her nose didn't bother her at all in the moment the Jackal grabbed her feet and the Gorilla started tearing at her shorts. Instead she screamed, a piercing scream, warbling in pitch and echoing in the small room. She kicked out, twisted, squirmed, screaming and snarling and fighting them. Gorilla man grabbed a fistful of her hair and punched her in the face. Her lips mashed against her teeth and her head hit the floor, again! The ceiling spun, the long tubes of light fading in and out. She tried to scream and instead choked on blood. Coughs wracked her chest and she spit out blood onto the grey floor.

"I like this one. I really do, but she's gotta learn. You got them shears on you? Good. Now hold her tight. She's not going to like this."

Still dazed, the word "shears" reached a part of her brain telling her she should be concerned. She lifted her head and frowned at what she saw. The Jackal sat on one of her legs and held the other by the ankle, his grip tight, his biceps bulging. The Gorilla held shears. Garden shears, the type she'd seen her dad use to cut thick branches. She read a brand name on the blade, CRAFTSMAN and knew he bought them at Canadian Tire, the same place her dad bought all his tools.

She whispered, "Hey now! Hey! What's going—" The shears snipped cleanly through her small toe. The toe jumped into the air, spun and hit the cold floor. A dash of blood punctuated where it landed. A red blot on grey. What the hell just happened? She couldn't believe it. Was that her toe? Then the pain hit. They'd cut off her toe alright and instead of screaming, she yelled, "You motherfuckers! Cock-sucking shit-bags! Let me go, let me go or I swear to—" Gorilla squished her cheeks with his hand, fingers digging in deep. Her jaw bone creaked under the grinding pressure. It cut short her cries.

He said, "Shut. The. Fuck. Up!" He shook her head and she could feel the grinding pressure on the bones in her skull. He leaned in close and said, "You want me to keep going? You want me to whittle down every toe? Then what? Start on your fingers? After that, an arm? Is that what you want?"

She shook her head. Her courage faltering under the images he presented.

"I'm gonna cut those ties off your wrist. Then, you're going to take off your own fucking clothes and lie down on that bed my partner took the time to make all nice and pretty. I don't want no more shit from you. Not one fucking word or whining or 'please don't,' crap. You got it? One more sound out of you, and you lose your other baby toe. We understand each other, princess?"

She nodded. He held the shears up to her eyes and clicked them shut. She flinched. He turned her roughly by the shoulder and snipped through the plastic ties.

Blood rushed into her hands, tingling life fluttered in her fingers, another location of pain on a body wracked with it. Blood dribbled from where her toe had been. It ached. Intermittent shards of pain made her wince and suck in air. She saw her disembodied toe on the floor by the metal leg of the bed. She'd painted the toe nail a bright blue. She thought it cute at the time.

She stood, being careful to go easy on the foot, snot, drool and tears a shiny line hanging from her chin. Under the gaze of the Gorilla and the Jackal, she undressed. Her entire body trembled and the toe on the floor kept drawing her eye, as though tethered on a line. When she pulled her shorts off the fabric brushed against the red nub where her toe used to be. She sucked in air and almost fell over, stumbled and she stifled a sob. How to fight men such as these? They'd whittle her down, piece by piece and in the end what would be left? A torso, maybe. They wouldn't need a room to hold her. All they would need is a box. They were going to do what they wanted and there was nothing she could do about it. Tears shined on her cheeks. Fully nude, she hobbled to the bed and sunk into it, staring at the ceiling wishing she were anywhere else or anyone else.

The Gorilla sighed, rubbed his hands together and said, "My! That sure is pretty."

The bed creaked under his weight.

-4-

Five years. Although she'd lost more parts of herself over the time, the first night remained the worst. Maybe because such cruelty was unknown to her she questioned whether it was really happening. Even though it kept happening, over and over. Those things happened only in those horror movies Dale tried to get her to watch but she never would. She wasn't into that sort of thing. She told him once the world didn't need more horrors, even for entertainment. She didn't know anything of real horror then and spoke of it from a protected person's perspective, confident those terrors would never visit her in her suburban home with a full belly and clothes on her back. Now, she lived those terrors. She became a meat puppet, her strings played by two masked men, evil in their own ways.

Quite a contrast between the two men. The Gorilla enjoyed giving pain. The more she squealed the more excited he became. One time, while he was using her, he stabbed her shoulder with a knife. She imagined she heard the skin split as it slid in and ground against bone. Oh, how that hurt! How she bled! She freaked out! Squirming, kicking, screaming and the Gorilla man yelling, "Fuck yeah! Like a goddamn bronco!"

The Jackal barely touched her. He would always be in the room though. They always came into her cell together, always wearing their masks. The Jackal never spoke to her. Not once. Afterwards, when Gorilla man got too enthusiastic, the Jackal would carry her to the shower, clean her wounds, dress her in a fluffy robe and comb her hair, never saying a word, the dark eyes behind the mask enigmatic and more than once she hoped to find some humanity in their depths. There never was. He would play *Ava Maria* on his iPod attached to portable speakers, on repeat, the same fucking song over and over. He would paint her toe nails pink (the toes she had left anyways) resting her foot on his knee, always gentle and relaxed. He would clean her room with some sort of polish, mop the floors and spray the room with freshener before they left. He liked the scent of lavender. The Gorilla man would snore on her bed or wait, pacing in the room, anxious for the Jackal to finish his ministrations or his labor. It was the Jackal who would show up after one of their 'date nights' and made sure she took the morning after pill, the Gorilla man sighing theatrically in the background. No need to threaten or force her to take the pill. She didn't want a child by rape.

The Jackal proved inscrutable. She didn't know what he got from all this. He never used her. Not that way. The Jackal watched, moving around the room for better angles, an almost forgotten shadow seen over the Gorilla man's shoulder. She thought maybe, just maybe, he felt sorry for her or there was some connection she couldn't see that prevented him from participating. Maybe he cared for her. She wanted to believe it, she wanted to think he would become an ally. After a brief time, she dismissed the idea. He never shirked from helping Gorilla man punish her. She sensed he even liked it. He got right in there and she could hear his breathing get faster when he held her down for the Gorilla.

At first, she fought every time they entered the room. She had once removed the shower curtain rod, hid behind the door and when the Gorilla's giant head appeared beyond the door, she struck it, gritting her teeth and screaming, her arm a relentless blur. Problem was, the rod had been hollow. A light weight, piece of shit aluminum. The Gorilla man laughed at her, his arms crossed above his mask and his eyes peering out from the protection of his forearms. Then he took the rod from her hands. Like it were nothing, like *she* were nothing. And then he punished her, laughing sometimes and other times, his voice a growling rage. The Jackal stood by to clean her up after. The Jackal was there to watch.

Over the years, she examined every inch of the room. Everything had been bolted down. There was nothing sharp in the room. The corners of the dressers were rounded. It had been built and designed with soft edges. The mirror, made of hardened plastic, would not break. They had suspended pink curtains on the wall. Nothing behind it, certainly no window just more cinder block pink. It was a decorative curtain, suspended by string. She considered choking someone with it, but they were never alone and to think she could overpower even one of them enough to get a string wrapped around their neck seemed a ludicrous idea. Even if she managed to somehow get the string wrapped around a neck, the flimsy thing would probably snap with the slightest pressure. And she remembered what happened after she tried to ambush them with the curtain rod. There was nothing she could do.

After some time, believing this horror had become her life, she didn't want to keep on living. For what? To be those sick men's plaything? Getting whittled down when she dissatisfied or angered them in some way? What would be left of her at the end? A torso? Helpless in bed, unable to defend her self in any way? What would her life be like?

She fought for the sake of fighting. She couldn't stop herself. When they walked in, expecting to take from her, she shook with anger. Why should she make it easy for them? After a time, the uselessness of her actions took a toll on her. All she ever got for her efforts was punishment. More pain, more degradations. She never got out of the tiny cell, hadn't even seen beyond the door. So she would fight, she'd get hurt, the Gorilla would rape her and then after her wounds were tended to, they would leave. If she didn't fight them, she would be raped. If she did, she would be hurt (maybe get her nose cut off) and still raped. What was the point? They made it clear to her she no longer had control over her life. Her life belonged to them. They could take it at anytime. Before they did though, they could make it hurt. They were masters of pain.

She wanted to die. It was the one decision left to her, one she could contribute to, at least one thing she had control over. How could she get it done? There was nothing lethal in her room to do anything to herself with so instead, she made the decision to do nothing. She would starve herself. She wouldn't eat any of the food they gave her. It was hard at the beginning. Her stomach rumbled and complained and she ignored it by sleeping, turning her back to the plate of food on the dresser calling to her with its smell. She thought of flushing it down the toilet but didn't trust herself to get too close to the pancakes, eggs, or whatever else they had made for her. The two men would come into the room, look at the untouched plate and remove it. Sometimes the Gorilla would chuckle and say something like "How's the hunger strike going?" or "Don't get too skinny, I may not want you then and wouldn't that be a shame?" She felt herself shutting down, despondent and indifferent to everything, living in her mind. She moved to use the toilet and the water in the bowl tempted her. She was so thirsty and look at all that water, right there in a bowl for her and all she had to do was dip her head in it and lap it up. The sink didn't tempt her near as much. She would have to turn on the tap to see the water. In the toilet, it didn't hide, it was right there and she was surprised that water had a smell. Now, a chlorine pool she could smell from quite a distance but she never considered water, out of the tap or in the toilet had a scent to it. The longer she didn't drink, the stronger the smell became. She ignored it and letting the thirst build and the hunger carve out a hollow hole inside her, she felt her energy sliding away. Weakness allowed her to ignore the hunger and the thirst, well, to a certain extent. So, to keep it at bay, to force herself not to give in, she slept and when she wasn't asleep she travelled into her own mind. She stopped using the toilet. She went in her bed although she was amazed at anything coming out of her since she stopped giving her body anything that could create waste. Maybe it was her own body eating itself. To give her energy. And the waste was the dead parts inside getting out. It didn't matter. In her mind she was already dead.

Hours passed in a slow, grinding fog. She developed skin burns from the urine and crap and although a part of her was disgusted, it was a small part with no real voice. That annoying voice couldn't overcome her lack of nutrient induced lethargy. She hoped to eventually blend into the background so they'd forget about her. Meld with the sheets on the bed and disappear into painless oblivion, a place where cruel men couldn't take you apart piece by piece. Stupid, but at the time it wasn't. To her, it was a way to escape them without having to physically escape and face punishment. She pictured them coming into her room, their masks twitching here and there in panic when they couldn't find her even though she lay right on the bed, giggling into her pillow, or more accurately, the pillow giggled because she had fused with it. She believed in this idea the way a young child believes in Santa Claus. A belief sustained by faith and hope. Like all her hopes since she had been imprisoned, they were shattered with careless ease.

The Gorilla and Jackal creaked open the door and the Gorilla said, "What the fuck's that smell? Did she shit her bed? Is that what that is? Jeeeeesus!"

He stomped over to her. When he kneeled before her, his dark angry eyes boring into her, she knew he saw her and that her illusion was just that; not real. She didn't disappear at all. Stupid, stupid girl. She cried.

"You better fucking cry. What is this? What do you think you're doing here? Not eating and now shitting in your goddamn bed! This isn't no hospice! When you're no use to me, you'll get hacked up and hung in my freezer! I'll toss your fucking guts into the woods for the animals to eat. And then I'll cook you on the skillet with extra virgin olive oil and some spices, maybe with a bottle of white. When I have a bit of your meat beside some mashed potatoes and carrots on my plate, I'll think of all the good times I had with you. Goddaaamn, that sounds good. You know what, that idea is making me hungry." He canted his head towards the Jackal and said, "You hungry for that Jackal?"

No answer from the Jackal. He never answered anything.

The Gorilla stood and glared down at her. He waved his arm at her, "This, whatever it is you're doing, doesn't make you useful to me. It makes you more work. I got enough work to do as it is and I don't want anymore. Now, this shit is gonna stop. You're gonna clean yourself up and eat the fucking food I take the time to cook for you."

A razor blade, the old fashioned kind with a handle, danced before her eyes. "Or I start using this. I'll cut off your fucking nose. Then I'll pop it in my mouth and eat it in front of you. And honey, you know I will." He ran the back of the blade down the bridge of her nose. She shivered.

Her gaze shifted to the Jackal. There must have been a pleading in her look because Gorilla chuckled and said, "You looking in the wrong place for help, girlie. There's no help for you here. Not in this place." The truth of those words gutted her.

The Jackal stood against the wall, his arms crossed over his chest. Even if she couldn't see his face, his posture was a description of indifference. No help for her from him. So why try to live? To be raped, left alone to heal and then raped some more? Death would be a blessing. It would be a merciful end considering the alternative. She hoped at one time the Jackal would help her. He had looked after her. After she bled from orifices, legs trembling and too weak to stand, he helped her to the shower with great care. He applied ointment, he gave her pain medication and never, ever tried to fuck her. He'd been gentle every time. Taking care to clean the wounds with a light touch and whenever she hissed in pain, he'd pause until the pain subsided. Why would he be like that if he didn't, in some fucking-crazy-psycho-man way, care for her? There was no reason for it. She had hoped to seduce him into friendship, help her get out of here, but realized now how foolish that idea had been. It could be part of the Jackal's whole fantasy to care for a damsel sorely wounded, even if it had been him that did the wounding in the first place. They never visited her alone. They were careful. And for many reasons. Safety a primary one. What if, by some miracle (up there with Moses parting the red sea type of miracle) she did get the upper hand on one of them? She might escape. And say, by coming alone, one of them actually developed real feelings for her? Got to see her and know her out of the rape context and saw her as an actual person and not their personal Barbie doll? But they never came in alone did they? Their policy of always visiting together had a purpose. A clever one. To prevent feelings from building and to diminish the possibility of her getting the better of one of them. There'd be no escape. There'd be no help. It was meant to discourage hope. It worked.

She turned her head away, expecting the cold razor against her neck before the burning pain of the slice bore her to nothingness. A part of her hoped for it. He didn't cut her neck. The Gorilla stuck a knee into her side and leaned on her, pinning her to the bed. He pinched her nose and she thought, *he's going to do it, he's going to cut off my nose,* then he let go of her nose and pulled her right ear so hard it hurt and then the razor cut into it. He sawed and cut off her right ear. Oh how she screamed and bucked! Her legs kicked out, her arms pressed against his legs and punched at his sides. Nothing stopped his sawing motion or the feeling of blood flooding her ear and the sound of her own tearing flesh as he pulled and sawed, pulled and sawed. At the back of the room, as always, the Jackal watched.

Afterwards, the Jackal carried her to the shower, her trembling legs too weak to sustain her. Blood ran down her shoulder, back and legs. So much blood. She wanted to touch where her ear had been, to make sure it had happened. It throbbed with pain, the air even hurt it and she didn't want to know for sure, not really. All this can't be real, can it? Abysmal cruelty swaddled her in despair. The Jackal, with gentle hands, cleaned her, bandaged her and combed out her long hair. Gorilla man changed her sheets, complaining and swearing the entire time. He muttered to himself, "I got carried away again didn't I? How is she supposed to clean this shit up when I cut off her ear? I suppose we'll need a new mattress and sheets. And I'll have to go get it, as usual."

The Jackal bandaged her head over the spot where her ear had been. They sat her in a chair, left the room with the mattress and sheets and returned with new ones a short time later. They must have a stash of stuff somewhere, for when their charges mess up or when they mess up their charges. After the mattress was down and the clean sheets put on the bed, the Gorilla raped her. They were making a point. It can always get worse. They educated her on that. She had earned her Ph.D in the theory of how-things-can-always-get-worse. Her life, what consisted of one, became a regular routine of irregular rape and torture. What she did do though, after the Gorilla took her ear, was eat the food they brought her and shower with almost consistent regularity. She never knew when they would show up. There was no schedule she could figure out. Her aches would disappear, she would have read three or four of the books they left for her and for moments, she could imagine she were at home in her room with her dad downstairs surrounded by books and awaiting a phone call from a friend. Peaceful and quiet and then the door would creak open and two masked men would enter to damage her for their own amusement and destroying any illusion she had built in her mind. Time passed, marked by a different depravity, a unique indignity she would be forced to suffer. Usually with that fucking *Ava Maria* playing in the background, a soundtrack to her captivity.

She had been cured of suicide. A sharp razor took care of that. She hadn't been cured of depression. A dark cloud hovered over her. Sometimes, she would think of her dad. She would cry until her stomach cramped and her eyes burned. Other times, she sat in her reading chair, open a book, and hours would pass without a page turned or a word read. She'd lose hours in a haze. Her neck, arms and legs would groan from the sudden movement of startling awake. She wouldn't kill herself. It wasn't because she harboured hope of escape. It was because she feared their lessons if she failed. She had lost three toes, two fingers and an ear. They told her the next time, she would lose her leg. And Gorilla man promised he would feed it to her. After all she had been through, she believed him.

-5-

They always entered the room together. The Gorilla man first and then the Jackal. She would hear the deadbolt turn and the squeal of the hinges as the door pushed open, a heavy door, displacing the air before it and there would be a breeze on her face. The Gorilla man would offer a greeting in a happy tone, as though he was asking how your vacation had been but the words belied the joviality of the voice. "How's your snatch? Ready for another round is it?" He would put the key in his pocket and take off his clothes, folding them neatly and placing them on the floor. Strong shoulders and a broad chest suggested an athletic youth. The years added girth to his waist and even though he could lose a few pounds, he was fast. With his giant hands, he would reach for her, pinching her in the sensitive spots to make her cringe and squeal. It had been that way since the first night. A routine she could count on. That's how they treated their prize.

So when the door opened, announcing its intention to admit her tormentors, she pulled the blankets up to her chin even though she knew it would not protect her. A reflexive reaction to fear developed in childhood, hoping the blanket would hide her from the red-eyed monster breathing in her closet. A shiver coursed through her and she grit her teeth against it. Olivia prepared her mind. She had healed nicely, physically at least, from the last time and felt anger she would be messed up again. Anger felt better than fear even though they constantly fought for ascendance within her. Getting hurt and then healing just for them to come along and hurt her some more was getting to be a tired fucking routine. Split lips were the worst because it was hard to eat. Everything stung. Especially when she would be chewing along, mind on something else, and she would crunch into a scab inside her mouth, pulling it open again. That hurt a lot. Her mouth would fill with salty blood and mixing with the food, the combination made her want to gag.

She told herself this time, just maybe, he might be gentle. He might be nice.

Illusions and lies were all she had left to indulge in, like she did when she'd read and imagine herself back at home. She wasn't back home. She constructed the illusions expertly.

The door clanged shut. The lock clicked. The Gorilla man stood alone. No Jackal. The blankets dropped from her hands. Her mouth hung open so wide a bird could have fallen in it.

"Time for a private session, my love. I've had enough of holding back."

Holding back! Was he fucking serious?

He unbuttoned his shirt, folded it, and placed it on the dresser.

"I never liked an audience. His fucking rules though. 'Do this, don't do that.' A man can get tired of that shit."

Olivia had no idea what to say or even if she should say anything. He looked agitated. Nervous. She wondered if he had killed the Jackal, but dismissed the idea. Somehow, she knew the Jackal to be the dangerous one. The one to come out on top if they ever had it out.

He kicked off his shoes. He dropped his pants, folded them and slid off his boxers and put them in the pile. He didn't take off his socks. He never did. Probably because the floor was always cold. His penis hung limp. Also out of the ordinary. Maybe he didn't feel as brave as he pretended.

He stepped towards her on the bed. She pressed herself back. His penis stiffened.

"You know what? I hate this fucking mask! Can barely see! Fuck this thing!" He unlaced the back of the mask and tore it off his head.

Oh fuck! He's gonna kill me now. Countless times over the years Olivia prayed for death and now, faced with the certainty of it, she found she didn't want it. Why else would he take his mask off? That night long ago, when she had been taken, even though they told her they would never let her go, a small part of her believed otherwise. Of course she did. What is life without a spark of hope? Wearing the masks helped her sustain the hope. If she were never to escape, why bother wearing the mask all the time? With the mask on, escape or even more ridiculous, release, was a possibility. Another constructed lie, sure, but she fluctuated between wanting to believe and thinking it foolish to do so.

When the mask dropped to the ground terror squeezed out a scream. A short bark, window dressed with hysteria.

He pointed a finger at her, dark eyes blazing, "Shut up, bitch!" Spittle gathered at the corners of his mouth. The Gorilla was scared. It didn't make sense. Yet she knew it to be true. She knew he was breaking the rules and feared the Jackal.

The first time without a mask made a huge difference. The masks infused them with an inhuman quality, monstrous and unreal. His face humanized him, still a monster, but terrible because it made the nightmare all the more tangible. Dark hair, dark eyes, someone she might have considered, in a different situation, middle-aged handsome. Now the mask on the floor was all she could focus on. The rubber, hairy gorilla mask she had hated all this time. The cause of so many nightmares and real life horrors, discarded on the ground because now was the time for her to die. No more fucking around. After a bout of raping, beating and maybe, if he's feeling frisky, some digital amputation. Maybe her nose this time. Or her lips. A bloody gash for a mouth is all he would leave her. Then he would cut her throat. She shivered on the bed and pointing at the mask, begged, "Please. Please put that on. You have to."

He stopped, a confused eyebrow climbing his forehead. His face bloated red. She knew he thought she were insulting him, telling him to put the mask on to hide his ugly face and she wanted to tell him that wasn't the reason and she opened her mouth to say it and instead, his fist connected with her forehead and the ceiling undulated and spun and time passed in flashes.

He grunted above her. She tasted blood in her mouth. A back tooth wiggled in the gum. Her breast hurt and there was dampness there, slick on her stomach. A slapping sound with every thrust. Was he sweating on her? The bed springs creaked. He buried his head in the pillow above her shoulder and kept going. He must have kept hitting her after the first punch. She must have blacked out. It didn't worry her. It had happened before. Her breast hurt. What did he do to it? Her vision cleared. She could see the lights, recessed in the ceiling behind unbreakable plastic. A collection of dead flies pooled on the bottom.

A vein jumped in his neck, next to her cheek. She clenched her legs around him. He moaned, surprised. She ran her hands through his hair. He tried to lift his head but she held it down, firmly and he responded by moving faster and moaning some more. She focussed on the vein in his neck, pulsing under his skin, jumping fast. She put her mouth on the vein and he paused, maybe sensing the danger. She bit into his neck. Ground her teeth together until they met. He screamed and tried to stand but the bed made it awkward for him to get his feet under him and all he could manage was to get to his knees with his butt on his heels. Intwined upright, she locked her legs around him and squeezed his head to her as she ground her teeth into his skin. Blood spurted into her mouth and jetted down her throat. She gagged but didn't release her hold on him. She held his head to her shoulder, keeping him close with her arms. Her legs tightened on him. He jerked up but still she clung to him. Warm blood, almost hot, ran between them.

"Fucking bitch!" He growled.

He snaked his arms in between them and Olivia could feel his hands on her stomach moving up to her chest. He pushed with his hands and pulled with his back. She strained to hold him. To let go meant her death. She could feel them separating despite her straining to hold them together, her muscles tight with tension. His hands slid along her skin, slick from the blood. She couldn't hold him much longer. With a tremendous heave, he pushed her down. His strength pulled her hands from his head and he reared back with a wet, slipping sound. Her teeth still gripped a chunk of his neck and when he reeled back, the flap of skin stayed with her. The wound pulsed an arc of blood across the room. It splashed on the pink tile of the shower.

His mouth opened in an 'O', his eyes bulged and for a satisfying second of time, she saw panic in them. Honest to God, gonna shit himself type of panic. With a mouthful of his meat, a blood bib on her chest, she smiled and spat the excised meat on the pillow.

He clamped his left hand to his neck and made ready to step off the bed until he saw her smile. He turned back and struck with a hammer fist. Used to his rages, she saw it coming and raised a forearm to block it. His fist crashed through her hand and bent her left index finger back. She heard it crack before the pain hit her and his fist sank into her stomach. The air whooshed out of her and she curled into a ball, holding her injured hand against her chest as she gasped. He lifted his arm to strike her again and he weaved drunkenly, eyes rolling up into his head before he could bring them to focus. He grunted, stumbled and almost fell on the floor. Blood covered the left side of his body, all the way down to his feet. He staggered, righted himself and took tentative steps to his clothes. His chest heaved and his legs shook, like a toddler taking his first steps. To Olivia, he looked drunk. The hole she excised from his neck was too big and he couldn't stop the blood running out. It seemed incredible to her that he might die here. She hadn't thought he could die although she hoped for it with all her heart on many occasions. To see him stumbling, then going down to a knee, his hand falling from his wound, a gush of blood hitting her dresser, she stepped from the bed, her tingling finger forgotten. He swayed on one knee and then fell flat to the floor, his head striking the concrete. It made a thunk sound, like dropping a coconut on the floor. The room was suffused with the scent of blood, coppery and cloying. Olivia crept closer. Was he dead? Could she dare to hope?

She cradled her injured hand against her stomach and moved closer. Small spurts of blood drooled from his neck wound. His socks remained startlingly white considering all the blood. She edged closer to him on her tiptoes afraid she might wake him. Did a finger twitch? She couldn't see the rise and fall of his back. Was he still breathing? She nudged him with her toe. He groaned and she jumped back. Takes a fuck of a long time for someone to die. He didn't move. His flesh so white and porcine. Spattered in blood with white socks, inert on the concrete floor lying in a spreading pool of blood, he didn't look real and none of this seemed real until the blood touched her toes. Warm and then cool. So quick to lose its warmth.

The blood oozed out and then stopped altogether. Fucker must be dead. She felt numb, dazed. Everything took on great detail. She could see the pores in his shoulder and the individual hairs sticking up. His sagging middle aged ass appeared sunken and for once in her miserable time spent here, she didn't feel afraid of him. Because he was dead! Disgusting piece of shit! Rapist! Torturer! How she hated him! She hit him with her healthy hand, punched him right in the back and the impact sent ripples through his flesh. She stood and stomped on his head. She hated him and thought hate such an inadequate word for what she felt for him. There was no word to describe the depths of her abhorrence for him. She wanted to crush his head into the ground. She hauled her foot back, aiming for his head and she connected alright and it bent her toes back and stretched the tendons running along the top of her foot. Her other foot slipped in the blood and she fell back, putting her hands out and her injured finger struck the floor with her hand and the pain was like lightning under her skin and she yelped and cursed under her breath.

She crawled out of his blood, eyes blinded with tears and wondering if she could have fucked that up even more. Now her foot and hand ached and she was sitting in a room with a cooling corpse. Still stuck right where she was before and suffering new injuries she caused. While the pain receded from sharp stabs to an ebbing pulse, she glanced around her prison. So much blood! Glaring contrast of dark red and bright pink. Some of the blood appeared black. She stood, struggling to get her feet under her and wavered above the dead man. Naked, she felt vulnerable. She limped to the dresser and struggled into underwear and wincing, pulled a tank top over her head. At the closet she selected the two items of clothing they allowed her. Track pants and a sweatshirt. No strings in any of them. If they wanted her in something nice, they brought it with them and waited for her to put it on under their salacious gazes. The Gorilla man would rub a hand along his crotch, watching her. How she fucking hated him, both of them! Once dressed she noticed the salty taste of blood in her mouth. Knowing it was his blood almost made her gag. She wanted nothing of him on her or near her. He revolted her.

She hurried to the sink and sucked back water, swishing it around trying to keep the nagging thought of what the Jackal would do to her if he returned at that moment to find his companion dead on the floor. Everything had been bolted down, no weapons for her in here to help her. She was stuck here and her hands palsied as she tried to wipe the blood off around her mouth. The thought of the Jackal returning quivered her stomach. She had to get out of here before he returned! How to do that now when she couldn't do it before?

The key! When the Gorilla came in to her room, she watched him put the key to her prison in his pocket! That's what he always did! She gasped seeing his pants in a neat pile on the dresser. She could get out of here. And with some luck, and by God it would be about time she had some, she could get out of here before the Jackal returned!

Leaving the faucet running, she hobbled to where he had folded his clothes, her foot throbbing with every step. She tossed the clothes on the floor in her scramble to get his pants. She saw him put the key in his pocket, she knew it, yet still, a nagging fear persisted. What if it wasn't there? After all this time, escape couldn't be this close could it? She felt the hard outline of the keys through the pocket and her heart tugged at the arteries in her chest. She dug her hand inside and pulled them out. She held them up to her blurring eyes, peripherally aware of her missing middle finger from the middle knuckle up. She used her thumb and ring finger to hold the keys. They had taken her index finger too, from the same right hand. The smooth pink end grotesque to her. Her lip quivered. They had taken so much from her. She inhaled and pushed down the sadness. Time to get out of here. She stepped over Gorilla man, fumbling through the keys, her concentration down to a narrow point. A handful of keys on the ring. Which would open the door? She tried, three, four, no luck. Was the Jackal pulling in the driveway right now while she stood here messing with keys? A key slipped in and turned. She exhaled a deep breath and it shuddered in her breast. She pulled the door open. For the first time in five years, she left her prison.

Wooden stairs in front of her led up to another door. A hallway extended to her left and right. Narrow, the hallway walls were painted white with a dim bulb in the ceiling. There were three doors on her left and one to the right. Heavy metal doors, painted pink, just like her room. Were there more women like her down here? Toys for the demented? How is this even possible? She should go. Right now. Get help and return. It'd be the smart thing to do. She wasn't equipped for a rescue mission. She took a step towards the wooden stairs and paused, her foot in the air. But then, what if the Jackal returned in her absence and decided to get rid of the rest of them? Could she live with herself knowing she could have saved them? The rooms were probably empty though. How many people could you abduct and not be found out? Maybe they were just supply rooms and she should get the fuck out of here while she still could. Lying to herself again. The rooms weren't empty and she knew it. There were others like her, abused and tortured waiting for an escape that might never come. Olivia had to do something. Either way, she should at least check. She held up the key ring and they jingled before her eyes. Lot of keys here. She moved to the door on the right, listening intently for any sound of movement from upstairs. What would she do if she heard a front door open and heavy treads on the boards above? Probably have a fucking heart attack, that's what. Whatever happened, there was no way she was going back into that room. No goddamned way in hell.

The key slipped in on the first try. She pushed the door open and faced a room identical to the one she'd left. A young woman sat on the bed, clad in track pants and a sweatshirt, like the ones she wore. Probably got a deal in bulk, the sick fuckers. She pictured them pushing a cart around Costco, wearing their masks, holding up clothing and nodding as they tossed it in the cart.

The girl hugged her knees, terrified eyes peering out through strands of hair. Olivia thought she could be looking in a mirror. She resembled her so much except, after a quick glance, Olivia noticed the woman wasn't missing any fingers or toes. The girl, lifted her head with raised eyebrows, confusion and hope warring in her eyes.

Olivia said, "Let's get out of here. We gotta go."

"Who are you?"

"Someone like you. Someone who wants to get the fuck out of here!"

The girl bounced off the bed and reached Olivia in an instant. She appeared healthy and strong and Olivia thought she must be a new addition here. She didn't have that worn down look.

Olivia said, "There are more doors. This way."

They moved down the hall. Olivia's hands shook at the door. The keys rattled in her hands. Fear and pain exhausted her, making her movements clumsy. The girl put a hand on Olivia's, steadying them and said, "Here. Let me do it."

Olivia let go of the keys.

"I'm Lucy."

"Olivia."

Lucy opened the door on the second try. Another pink room. Another prisoner on the bed. Startlingly similar to Olivia and Lucy except this one appeared as lifeless as a mannequin. Her eyes followed them as they entered the room. Despondency showed in her gaze. She didn't have any clothes on and it didn't seem to bother her. She didn't try to cover herself at all. Books were scattered on the floor. The rest of the room appeared neat.

Lucy said, "Oh my God! Her hand. They cut off her hand!"

Olivia gasped. Her right arm ended at the wrist in an angry red stump, covered with scabs. A fluid-sopped bandage sat discarded at the foot of the bed. Her eyes regarded them with disinterest. Olivia knew this girl had been here a long time. Maybe even longer than her. She had that look to her, like just a part of her were here. The rest of her had escaped inside. Olivia knew all about that. She had tried it herself.

In a soft monotone she said, "They ate it, my hand. They brought it in here on a plate after to show me. Only my bones were left. They said it tasted delicious. They said my flesh was delicious."

The girl turned her head to the wall seeing things only she could see.

Olivia said, "We're getting out of here."

Still facing the wall, the girl said, "No one gets out of here. They told me that."

Olivia, voice hardening said, "They were wrong. We're getting out. You're coming with us."

The girl didn't move. The wall held her complete interest.

Lucy took clothes from the closet. Track pants and a sweatshirt. Must have been easy to shop. Same clothes, same sizes.

Lucy said, "Let me help you. C'mon. Put these on."

The girl moved mechanically. Lucy manipulated her arms to get the sweatshirt on and pulled her off the bed to get the pants on. The girl lifted her legs to help when directed to do so with a tug or a touch. All the while, Olivia's heart pounded, punching against her ribs. They were taking too much time. They have to go.

While dressing the girl, Lucy said, "How'd you do it? How'd you get out."

"I killed him."

Lucy's head whipped around, "Both of them?"

Olivia shook her head, "No. Just Gorilla man."

"The other guy wasn't with him?"

"No. Just him."

"But they always come together. Always."

"Not this time."

"How'd you kill him?"

"I bit his neck open."

At that, the girl with no hand smiled. A small smile, but it was there all the same and it gave Olivia hope.

-6-

The next room: empty. Pink and identical to the others except lacking a victim.

Lucy said, "I don't like the other guy still being out there. He could show up any second."

"I'm trying not to think about it."

"What's with the pink? It's like a fucking unicorn puked in here."

The girl with no hand said, "They see us as toy dolls. We're in a doll house. *Their* doll house."

Olivia said, "What's your name?"

"Jen."

"I'm Olivia. This is Lucy."

Jen moved a strand of her hair out of her eyes with the stump and said, "Thanks for not leaving me here."

Olivia said, "You would have done the same."

Jen shook her head, "No, I wouldn't have. I would've run for the hills. I'm getting out of here."

Jen turned and with careful steps, walked up the stairs.

Olivia and Lucy glanced at each other, wondering if Jen had the right idea. How many doors would they open? What type of chance were they taking staying around for so long? There was one door left. The last one. What if there were a whole slew of them upstairs? A giant house full of pink rooms with tortured dolls. What then? Olivia exhaled, knowing she could only worry about one thing at a time. Like the door ahead of them. They didn't know what waited upstairs. No point in concerning themselves with that until they had to. But there could be one more girl like them, huddling in there, maybe pieces of her cut off, hoping for something, anything to vanquish the horror of being imprisoned here. Olivia said, "Just one more door! Then we all go together. All of us."

Jen paused on the stairs, her thin shoulder bones trembling through the back of her sweater. Lucy said, "Hurry the fuck up, then!"

Olivia said, "Bring the keys."

The last door was different than the others. Thicker, with a rubber seal along the bottom. Olivia put a hand on it, "It's cold."

Lucy slid a key in, turned it with a click and pushed the door. It hissed open. Cold air plumed out. Olivia and Lucy took a step back as frosted air billowed into the hallway.

Lucy saw them first. She yelped and gasped at the same time. A unique tittering sounding of lunacy and desperation. Lucy's hand tightened on Olivia's arm. The smoke cleared. Shadows became visible. Two girls were suspended from ceiling hooks with their stomachs hollowed out, resembling flesh canoes. One girl was minus a leg, the other one lacked an arm from the shoulder down. Cold storage for their food. Even death didn't offer an escape. Olivia's stomach gurgled. Sweat beaded her brow as a chill, originating in her bones, shook her entire body.

When Lucy spoke, Olivia jumped, "Let's get the fuck out of here! Like now!"

Olivia backed up, her injured hand and foot a low throb in the background of this horror. That's where they were supposed to end up, all three of them, in the meat fridge awaiting a gruesome dinner. The Gorilla and the Jackal, seated around a table alight with candles and napkins on their laps, wearing tuxedos and their masks. In her mind, they weren't masks. They were their real faces and on the table by their plates, were human masks. Hearts in blood sauce from the stock in their secret freezer dressed their plates. Someone's daughter, someone's loved one. They'd toast each other with glasses full of red wine and dig in. The image conjured bile. She swallowed it and when she felt more in control she nodded at Lucy. Time to go.

Jen led the way upstairs with Lucy in the middle and Olivia at the back. The stairs creaked under their weight. Olivia worried they were making too much noise. Enough noise for a person to hear them coming, right outside the door at the top of the stairs. A person wearing a Jackal mask and holding something deadly, like an axe, sweaty hands gripping the handle as they approached, breathing harsh behind the rubber mask. Her eyes focussed on the door knob. Nothing to do about it. They had no weapons and they were not going back. Not alive anyways. She couldn't shake the image of him waiting for them beyond the door. Her heart trembled and her mouth cottoned. She couldn't be steps away from freedom. This isn't how things happened. Not in real life. The

Gorilla and the Jackal taught her all about the real world. They cut away her optimism with a few snips of garden shears and a sharp razor. They showed her in real life, more often than not, the monster gets his meal and the bogeyman claims another child. Olivia found it hard to press forward, as though she trudged through a swamp. She wanted to be sure. Lucy reached to grasp the handle and Olivia said, "Wait! Do you hear anything?"

Alarmed, Lucy said, "No! Do you?"

"Just listen at the door."

Jen said, "There's nobody there. I'd feel him."

Olivia stared at Jen and thought, maybe she would. Jen had most likely been here the longest. What provided for the longevity? How did Olivia and Jen placate the two men to avoid ending up on the hook in the freezer? It was obvious Lucy hadn't been here that long. She didn't have the look to her, that look of placid desperation she and Jen shared, the haunted look seen in old photos of Holocaust survivors. She hadn't lost an ear or a hand or some fingers and toes. She had all her fingers. She'd been through some terrible times, that's for sure, they all had but there were varying degrees of it weren't there? Sure there was. Getting your hand cut off and having it returned to you minus flesh was pretty fucking terrible. On the barometer of awfulness, it sat right at the top. Those atrocious moments can shape you, mould you into someone you no longer recognized. The Olivia who had been thrown in here so long ago is vastly different to the Olivia standing on the stairs in the dark hoping murder in a jackal mask wasn't waiting on the other side. They've all been changed. So maybe Jen, who'd been here the longest, could feel him. Maybe her senses had been so sharpened she picked up the ability to know when a visit was imminent. Maybe. Olivia did know the soft assurance issued by Jen served to quell her fear and still her doubts.

"Alright," said Olivia, "open the door. Let's get out of here."

Jen turned the knob and when the door didn't open Lucy sighed and said, "It's locked. Of course it's fucking locked."

Olivia said, "Try one of the keys."

"Yeah. Right," sounding surprised, as though she'd forgotten all about them, she tittered, "I still got em' in my hand."

Jen stepped to the side and Lucy, after finding the right key, pushed open the door.

Olivia saw a kitchen over the shoulder of Jen and Lucy. Stainless steel appliances, granite counter, white cupboards and a wooden sign above a light switch reading, *Bless this Mess*. Olivia, struck by the ordinariness of the scene, paused on the stairs. They all did. Olivia didn't know what she expected but commonplace domesticity with a hint of religion wasn't it. She expected more…chains? Hooks? Something indicative of the evil personalities living here. Jen, crouched low, moved ahead first, head swivelling like a deer approaching a watering hole. On the island in front of them, Lucy plucked a knife out of the set in a block. She paused, considering, and then grabbed another one. Olivia crept in to do the same and her eyes were drawn to the cordless phone, sitting there on the counter. She didn't remember crossing the distance from the doorway to the phone. It was like the phone materialized in her hand. She pressed the talk button and the numbers back lit a pleasant green. The dial tone droned in her ear. Had there ever been a more beautiful sound? Her fingers flew on their own. She should have phoned the police. Called 911. That would be the smart thing to do. Instead, the image in the forefront of her mind was her father's face. She could still hear his voice in her head, telling her it was okay, she would make friends on that first day of school when the yard of screaming kids overwhelmed her and weakened her knees. The person who checked her closet and under her bed because she was too afraid to. The man who read to her when she was sick, keeping a cool cloth close to hand making sure she took the medicine at the right times. His calm assurances when he was teaching her to drive after she reversed into a light pole in an empty parking lot when the jumping car scared her heart into her throat. He had been her rock. The one person she could always count on. It didn't occur to her he wouldn't answer, or that he moved and his number had changed. He would be home because he wouldn't be anywhere else. So that's who she called and when his voice came on the line, it felt like sunshine on her face, the sweetest music in her ears. In a voice soaked in tears and hope, she cried the name of the person who had always been there and would always be there. She cried, she couldn't help it, as her dad screamed her name back to her.

-7-

The Jackal tapped the steering wheel to the Steve Miller Band singing *The Joker* on the radio. He attempted to sing along but he didn't know the words and tended to mumble them. He knew himself to be a terrible singer. The worst. Still, it put him in a better mood. Music could do that. And he knew what else lifted his mood: a visit with his girls. What were they up to now he wondered? Especially his favourite, Olivia. His beautiful angel. Soft skin, eyes made for pain, large liquid pools of despair, he yearned for her. How he loved her the most.

The truth is they saved him from normalcy. They allowed him to stand out from the herd of boring conformity. With them, he could remove his carefully crafted mask and put on his true one. In many ways, he was grateful to them. They made him free. They made him exult in the freedom their pain and death provided him. The freedom to indulge in his fantasies. How many people could say they did that? Maybe a handful of people? Maybe less? Unless you were some fascist dictator, the person who created the laws, no one possessed real freedom to do what they want. With every action accompanied by consequence, true freedom couldn't be achieved. In theory, it could never be achieved but it didn't hurt to strive for it. In order for him to pursue the freedom he wanted, he had to fool the world. Fool everyone that knew him. He had to wear the face that said 'trust me', or, 'I'm safe.' He hated that face and if he had to wear it all the time, he would go nuts, like the shooter in the bell tower kind of nuts. He preferred his own type of crazy to that. And it was the girls who gave it to them. Against their will of course and that made it more precious to him.

He glanced at the time on his dash and nodded. He had time. He could pop in for a visit. It would serve to keep Grady on his toes. Even better, he could spend time with Olivia. Grady could just sit in the fucking corner for all he cared. Pouting under his mask with his arms folded across his chest like some sulky teenager. No need to hurt Olivia tonight. Tonight he would be gentle.

Maybe paint her nails or French braid her hair. He liked the French braid on Olivia. She looked like royalty after he finished. His erection pressed pleasurably against the front of his pants.

He grinned. Only Olivia had the power to do that. To cause him an erection without the thought of violence entwined. Imagine when he took her, made that long awaited decision to partake of her. It would be nothing short of glorious. He could wait a while longer yet. Without her, what would he have? The other girls, although wonderful and very similar to Olivia, were missing that something. They were cardboard cutouts of Olivia. Strange, to feel this emotion for a person. What is it that he felt? Love? He smiled at the notion. Would you want to destroy the thing you loved? He didn't know. He changed the song to *Ava Maria*. It boosted his excitement to see her. A thing he didn't believe possible. It scared him a little to feel this much. It gave the other person a certain power over you and it was both terrible and scary. He would have to destroy her sooner or later. He knew that.

-8-

"Olivia! My God! Where are you, honey?"

Crying on the other end, "I don't know. Daddy, you have to get me out of here!"

"Okay! Okay! Where are you?"

"I uh, I don't know! In a house! Daddy, they did things to me!"

He squeezed his eyes shut tight. White motes danced under his lids. He didn't know it, but his free hand was in his hair, tugging at it. If he caught a glimpse of himself in a mirror, he would think that's what insane looked like. Don't think about that right now. Help her. Help your daughter. He paced the floor. His thoughts twisted and swirled, refusing coherence.

Focus. You need to focus. His guts felt loose, almost liquid inside. Harry dug the nails of his fingers into his palm. The sharp pain brought clarity.

"Okay, um, is there any mail lying around. Something with an address on it. Bills."

She spoke to someone and then a drawer opened and he heard something metallic hitting the floor.

"Olivia? Who is with you?"

A wetness to her voice, thickened with tears when she replied, "Others like me."

"Dear God."

Others like her. More fathers and mothers waiting to hear, to know something about where their daughters went. People living in constant hope and despair. Hope to learn their children were safe, despair to learn of their death. Plastic smiles covering up the urge to scream, to cry, to tear out their hair and wish it were someone else's child they were reading about. Someone else's baby who had been ripped violently from their life.

"Okay. We got something. A hydro bill? I don't know. It says the address is 87 Alice Street. In Erin."

"Erin? You know how close that is? Jesus, you've been so close all this time."

"Come get me Daddy!"

"I will, right away but I need you to hang up and dial 911."

"No, no, no. I don't want to. I need to hear you."

"I know. It'll be hard for me too. Real hard. You have to do it. They'll get the address from the phone call but if they don't you at least know it. And then, if you can, run out to a neighbour's house and wait. I'm going to call them too. From my end. Just to make sure someone's coming. I'm coming too. I'm leaving right now. I'll be there as fast as I can."

"Daddy!"

"Call them, honey." His voice broke, "You have to call them."

"Okay. Hurry. Come take me home."

"I'm coming! Call them!"

When she hung up, he released the phone, his hand an aching claw from holding it so tight. Olivia! Alive! He snatched the keys and cell phone off the table, grateful to be only two beers deep. He could drive. He ran to his car, and yanked on the door so hard it peeled the nail from his index finger back. He cursed, realizing he hadn't unlocked the door. He depressed the button, got in and sped out of the driveway, typing the address into the GPS as he went. He white-knuckled the steering wheel, his face glowing in concentration. He muttered under his breath and called 911 from his cellphone. With luck, Olivia had already called and they were almost there.

An operator answered, "Police. What is your emergency?"

Harry told them.

-9-

Olivia called the police. At first, the operator's voice resonated indifference, but that soon changed. The operator told her the police were on the way. Could she make it out of the house, maybe go to a neighbour's? Olivia didn't know. She had no idea how far a neighbour was. Could be right next door or it could be through a field in the deep snow. The operator asked Olivia to stay on the phone until the police arrived. The calm, professional voice soothed her rattled nerves for the moment. Jen and Lucy stayed near her with widened eyes searching out every part of the kitchen.

Olivia said, "Okay. I'm going to try to find the front door."

The dispatcher said, "Are you sure the other one is not in the house?"

Olivia remembered what Lucy said earlier, how she knew he wasn't here because she couldn't feel him. Olivia thought she was right about that. She knew what Lucy meant. The Jackal and the Gorilla carried with them an air of oppressive menace and tangible doom. The house felt empty, devoid of them, a vacuum bereft of evil.

"I'm sure."

"Then get out of there. Our officers are about five minutes out."

"Okay, okay."

Barefoot, she moved out of the kitchen into a hallway. The front door awaited them. Stairs curved upstairs. She ignored a dimly lit room branching off the hallway. She focussed on the front door. It offered an exit from this hell house. All she had to do was open it and walk out and keep walking and she would be free. Tears spilled down her cheeks unnoticed. The aching in her fingers and toes a distant hum. The two girls following behind her, companions in misery were nothing to her at that moment. All she cared about was the freedom on the other side of that door. A mountain lion could be on the porch and Olivia would kick it aside to escape this house. What was a fucking cat compared to the animals who imprisoned her?

Olivia said, more to herself than the operator, "I'm at the door. It's right there."

"Good, good. Get out of there."

"I'm going, I'm going."

She reached for the knob and frowned. The door didn't have a handle. Just a deadbolt lock right where the knob should be.

"Fuck!"

"What?" The operator sounded alarmed.

"There's no latch or doorknob. Just a lock. You need a key to open it."

"Do you have one?"

Lucy squeezed up beside Olivia and holding up the keys Olivia took from the Gorilla said, "How about one of these? One of these should do it."

To the operator, Olivia said, "Maybe."

Lucy gave Olivia one of the knives she took, the smaller one, and held the keys up to the light. Olivia had no idea what she was looking at. They were keys for fuck's sake. Just pick one and get on with it.

Olivia glanced back at Jen. She held her stump to her stomach, bent over, peering at a picture in a frame on a dark table in the hallway. She turned her head to Olivia and said, "Fake. Like the picture came with the frame or something."

Olivia didn't answer, though what could she say? Who gave a shit what picture was in what frame? They were still trapped in this house. They didn't know where the Jackal was and they didn't even know if they had the keys to get out. Olivia trembled so much her teeth chattered.

In her ear the operator said, "Is everything okay?"

Olivia said, "I don't know yet."

Scrape of keys and breathing.

Lucy said, "Goddamnit! None of them work!"

"Should we look around?"

Lucy held her arms out, exasperated and said, "Where? I mean this isn't a small fucking house. They could be anywhere."

Jen said, "Just break a window," in the same tone someone would say pass the salt.

Olivia said, "Fuck it. Let's do that then."

The operator said, "The police should be there any minute."

Olivia said, "I'm not waiting any longer."

Heavy footsteps crunched gravel outside. A porch plank groaned.

Lucy backed away from the door, knife held out in front of her.

Olivia whispered to the operator, "I think he's back!"

The operator, caught up in the moment, lost her professional demeanour and blurted, "Fuck!"

•   •   •

The girls backed up from the door. Something sharp poked Olivia in the back. Lucy muttered, "Sorry," and Olivia realized Lucy's knife must have jabbed her. Olivia didn't respond. She held the phone against her ear and held the knife in front of her. The pitiful little knife, pointy end towards the door. What the fuck would it do against the Jackal? He'd take it from her and carve her up, piece by piece. No window in the front door so she could not see who stood outside. It had to be the Jackal though. She should have known better. There was no escape from this place or him. He'll open the door any second now and yell, "Honey! I'm home!" and then whisk them away to another hidey-hole to stock up another meat freezer. She sucked back a sob. It wracked her bony frame. Would he have a gun? Would he even bother taking them someplace new? It would be smarter to execute them all and torch the place.

"It's an officer!"

Olivia jumped and glanced at the phone, surprised she still held it in her hand. She'd forgotten all about it.

"What?"

The operator said, "At the door. It's a police officer!"

"How do you know?"

"We're talking to him, over the radio. There are three of them there. Two are at the back of the house."

"Tell him to break down the fucking door!" Lucy said.

"They can't. It's a steel door."

Olivia said, "Windows."

The operator said, "I'll tell them. Stand back from any windows."

The girls glanced to the living room off the hallway. A shadow passed in front of the window. A flashlight beam circled the room. A loud snap and the window shook in the frame. Another snap from the back of the house and then a cacophony of sound as officers tried to break the windows.

Jen said, "Some sort of safety glass. It won't break."

Lucy snorted and said, "You gotta be fucking kidding me! Cops can't get in and we can't get out!"

Jen said, "We weren't meant to get out. No one was."

Olivia said, "Give it a rest, Jen!" She said it harshly and wanted to take it back after Jen cringed from her with her stump raised to ward off a blow she thought coming. Only, it scared her, what Jen said. It scared her even more because she was thinking the same thing. The Jackal owned them. He had proven it to them over and over. He would never let them go. No matter how many cops surrounded the house. Stupid thought, paranoid even. Didn't make it feel any less true. Her dad should be here soon. Please get here soon.

The operator said, "Tactical officers will be there soon. They have a ram, something to break down the door. Hold tight. The maniac won't come back. Not with the place surrounded by police."

-10-

The Jackal saw the swirling red and blue lights reflecting off windows and colouring the night sky with undulating waves. He knew what it meant. The show was over. They had found his girls. He felt gut punched. The floor he thought so solid underneath him disappeared. He floated over an abyss.

He had to see. Dangerous and against everything he had taught himself about self-discipline yet the compulsion would not be denied. He made the turn towards the house, his sanctuary. Nearing Christmas, the suburban homes glittered and flashed at him. A neighbour with grey hair and large framed glasses hugged his arms against the cold staring down the street towards all the flashing lights. Where was the Gorilla? He would be the weak spot. Even after all his careful conditioning of him he knew staring at an infinite life sentence could change any man's mind about loyalty.

He slowed as he passed the house. Three police cars spaced out on the street, lights cycling through the colours. He squinted and saw an officer on the porch. The doors and glass were keeping the officers out...for now. Three cops? He knew most of the officers in this town rode around solo. Could be more though. If not, the rest would be here soon. He felt a sudden surge of rage at the sight of them, standing there like they belonged, like they were invited! Nosing around, talking to his girls, judging him as though given the right to. What did they know about him? Nothing! Did they know how many hours he spent caring for his girls? Bandaging them, showering them, cleaning up after them after they pissed the bed in fear? They had no right to take from him. His knuckles cracked as they tightened on the steering wheel. He could pull over right now and get his carbine from the trunk. He could get pretty close since they were so distracted with trying to get in. He could take them out. He knew it. The police don't train that often and the one fat cop on the porch looked like he would faint if he ever faced danger. And the Jackal was dangerous. He could empty his magazine into them all before they even drew their guns. He could get his girls. He figured the rifle rounds would penetrate the vests they wore. He could do it. He could get Olivia back. His foot lifted off the pedal as he spied an empty driveway. He exhaled, the air expelling shakily and thought, and then what? Kill the cops and get his girls? For what? To be hunted all over the province, the country? Stupid. Right now, he was free and unknown. He could stay that way if he continued driving. Let his tires eat the road and lay low. Spend some time in a hotel and check the news. See what happened to the Gorilla before he decided what to do next. Right now, his obscurity afforded him time. He would waste that if he went in guns blazing. Better to be the unknown. It hurt to do it, to give them up. He would miss them terribly. Especially Olivia. He didn't know if he could bear to live without her. He would worry about it later. Right now, he needed to get out of sight.

He turned right and headed towards the highway. His stomach felt hollowed out and his eyes burned. Why did his heart feel like it had sunk into his intestines? He had been thinking of Olivia. She was gone from him now and it fucking hurt. He would rather have needles pressed into his eyeballs than feel this loss. Is this what love felt like? He could think of nothing else and no one else. It angered him to think of the police officers helping her and comforting her. He did that! That was his job! He showered her, braided her hair and painted her nails! He didn't do it because it was his job. No. He did it because he cared for her and needed the connection to her and he did feel connected. He would say they were fused at the soul if he believed in that nonsense. How could they appreciate that? They couldn't and they wouldn't. They would be hunting him forever. His lip trembled. Olivia was gone from him now.

-11-

Bam!

The door shook in the frame and bulged when struck. Olivia cringed thinking it might fly off the hinges and crack her one. It didn't. The door stubbornly remained closed.

Lucy said, "I feel like I'm in one of those cromedies."

Olivia said, "Cromedies?"

Lucy said, "Yeah. A crime-comedy. Where the cops can't get a damn door open at a crucial moment in the storyline. The camera would show them all standing out there, rubbing their chins, discussing whether or not to blow the door open."

"They wouldn't do that would they?" Olivia said.

Lucy shrugged.

They all moved further away from the door, staring at it with suspicion. Olivia would have asked the operator but she had put the phone down when the Tactical Officers showed up.

Bam!

The frame cracked the plaster.

Bam!

The frame warped and the door limped open, squealing on bent hinges and the crooked frame. Standing in the doorway, Olivia saw a Tactical Officer holding the ram, his eyes wide, surprised he breached the door.

Three men, clad in black and wearing helmets and goggles charged in with machine gun sights held up to their eyes. Everywhere their eyes moved, the barrel followed.

The first one in said to Olivia without looking at her, "Anyone else in the house?"

"No."

"You sure?"

"Pretty sure."

"Okay. Go with them."

Officers in regular uniforms rushed in and ushered the women outside. They squinted against the flashing strobe-lights and felt as disoriented and bewildered as cavemen leaving their dark home. Ambulances were parked in front of the house with crews standing outside, heavy bags slung over their shoulders. Seeing the girls emerge the crews hurried over to them. The porch was freezing under Olivia's bare feet. A blanket was thrown over her shoulders as she was bombarded with questions. A CTV news van parked tight beside an ambulance. A man with a camera on his shoulder argued with a paramedic. Olivia's eyes followed the elongated tower protruding from the roof of the news van. It scraped the night sky and then she noticed it. A real sky with real stars. A cold breeze ruffled her hair and she gloried in it. Out of the house. She was out of the house. Liberating and terrifying at the same time, so much space, and not enough space. Her eyes darted everywhere, so much happening, lights flashing, faces crowding into her space and a tiny part of her wanted to be back in her room where it was, for the most part, quiet.

A hand pried the knife out of her hand. An older man, a paramedic with silver hair and kind eyes behind glasses said, "Come with me, dear. You're safe now."

Olivia burst into tears.

-12-

The reunion with Olivia overwhelmed them both. He rolled up in his car, panicked because no one told him anything on the phone. He called the police, asking for updates and they brushed him off. He didn't know what that meant. Were they intentionally keeping him in the dark because they weren't ready to give him terrible news? When he got there, would an officer with stripes on his sleeve meet him there to tell him they had been too late? Sorry about your luck Mr. Barnes. We found your daughter. She's dead. Was that what awaited him when he got there? Goddamn he could go for a drink right now. A little nip, to get him through this, something to bolster his courage. He didn't believe he could take a blow like that. To hear Olivia's voice on the phone which he thought was impossible, a goddamn miracle, really, he was terrified to believe it was her and terrified to doubt it. But he knew. It was her alright. His golden heart, calling for him, wanting her daddy to bring her home. He couldn't fail her. Not again. It would kill him. The urge to continue living would dissolve as sugar in water.

After she disappeared, the first few months, hell, the first couple of years, he believed she would return. Some people would call that denial. He preferred to call it hope. She would walk in the door with some temporary amnesia story that would make any soap opera writer proud and he would believe it. Why wouldn't he? He just wanted her back. When the couple of years turned into three, then four, the reality of Olivia never coming home sunk in, albeit, slowly. The not knowing kept him up many nights sucking back the contents of any bottle left in the house. Was she alive? Was she dead? What the fuck happened to her? He needed to know something. He couldn't make any life decision because of it. His life on pause.

It got to the point he would rather know she was dead than to continue living in this fugue of indecision. It was the not knowing that corroded his soul. And still he looked for her even though the little asshole voice in his head kept telling him she had to be gone, gone for good. Time to quit jumping up whenever the phone rang and to stop checking the door every time the house settled thinking it might be her footsteps on the boards. Forget spending his weekends cruising the university searching for her blonde head, waiting for her to turn, see him and smile. Time to stop chasing ghosts.

He hated that voice. With every day that Olivia didn't return, the whispers grew more insistent, refusing to be ignored. The practical side of him, telling him his hoping for her return was a foolish, childish idea and not fit for his adult mind. He drank to silence those whispers. He preferred drunken oblivion to those dark fears. Some hope, even if based on a stubborn refusal to believe her dead, was better than despair. If he got there and she was dead, it would be the end of him. He knew it. It would be too cruel.

He listened to the GPS voice directing him where to go, determined not to miss a turn and he pulled onto Alice Street almost running over two people standing in the road. His tires slid on the icy pavement and he turned the wheel and bumped into the curb. Three police cruisers, a large black van, three ambulances and a CTV news truck crowded the street. An elongated antenna protruded from the roof of the news truck, reaching for the bloated grey clouds in the dark sky. Flashing lights illuminated people, curious neighbours and those who monitored police scanners holding conferences in the street, pointing at the house and talking with serious tight lipped expressions. He turned off the car and left it parked against the curb and got out. The cold wind tore open his coat. He squinted at the house, the one the GPS led him to. Was she there? In the house?

He strode across the street, parting onlookers with his arms. An officer ran crime scene tape along the front of the house, looping it around fence posts. He quickened his pace to get inside the scene before the officer taped it off. The house's front door was missing. Warm yellow light slanted on the snowy lawn. On such a well kept home, the lack of a door was as incongruous as a dark gap in an otherwise white smile. The officer stringing the tape noticed Harry beelining it behind him and shouted at him but the words were lost because he saw her. Olivia, flanked by two paramedics, limped out the front door with a shiny silver blanket, similar to tin foil, hanging across her shoulders. She glanced down at her footing and when she raised her face shiny with tears, she saw him. Her face melted and Harry was sure his features did the same dance, oscillating from relief to fear and fighting to hold back tears that couldn't be restrained. He rushed over the snow feeling the hard icicles slide into the tops of his shoe. He heard someone yelling at him to stop but it didn't mean anything to him. That voice was coming from another planet as far as Harry was concerned. Only Olivia mattered. Olivia fast-hobbled down the stairs and noticing her bare feet he put a hand to his mouth as they sank into the snow. He wished he had brought boots for her.

Something stopped him, something pulling on his arm and his feet almost slid out from under him but whatever had stopped him kept him from falling. He glanced down at his arm, saw a gloved hand on it and followed the arm to the face. The police officer, the one who had been running the tape, curled his mouth into a grim line. His daughter, his beautiful girl screamed, "Daaaaddy!"

The officer looked from Olivia to him, opened his mouth to say something and instead the officer let him go. He made it to the porch and scooped up his daughter and sobbing into her shoulder he felt her ribs through the blanket. A bag of bones crying into his chest. He dreaded learning what happened to her. The fear of it grew in his stomach like a malignant tumour. Five years of horror, melting the flesh from her already thin frame. He would worry about that later. Right now, all that mattered was Olivia, alive in his arms.

Olivia wouldn't let Harry leave her side and he didn't want to. He wanted to soak in her presence. He kept reaching out to touch her, a pat on the leg, a brush of fingers on the shoulder, amazed and grateful at the physical reality of her. He rode in the ambulance with her to the hospital and when they got there he stood in the corner of the room as nurses and doctors busied themselves around her, beeps of machines and the drone of conversations the background orchestra. He noticed the spot where her ear used to be and his stomach clenched. When he held her hand, he felt the empty spaces where her fingers once were. When the nurses covered her in a warm blanket, Harry's eyes took in the missing toes on her feet before the blanket floated down to cover them. He wanted to vomit. That would be for him though and not for her. Time enough to agonize over what she must have gone through these past five years when alone and Olivia wouldn't have to witness anymore pain. Turning into a blubbery mess wouldn't do her any good. She needed her father to be strong for her. Later, alone in the dark, maybe then he could give in to the anguish and fear of what she lived through. Not now. Now was the time to hold her hand, smile when she turned her trusting eyes to him and tell her everything will be alright. Because that's what parents were supposed to do.

Police detectives paced out in the hall wanting to talk to her. She didn't want to speak to them. Not yet. She just wanted to rest. When Olivia fell asleep,

Harry left her side to collect their business cards. He would contact them when she woke up. The officers said they would wait and offered to pick him up a coffee. Harry declined. Harry returned to the room and studied Olivia. Thin, haunted, she twitched in her sleep. Her eyes were deep pockets. So different from the last time he had seen her. Five years is a long time. Longer still for one who suffered so much. She couldn't be the same person he had last seen standing in a room full of boxes ready to unpack. Those injuries to her turned his stomach. She lived through his worst nightmares. He would do anything to help her. Whatever therapy she needed he would take out a second mortgage on his house to make sure she would get it. Man, could he go for a drink. Why is it that he still wanted a drink so bad? Is there a more selfish creature on the planet than an alcoholic? He didn't think so. It wasn't a matter of wanting a drink, he needed one. He stuck his hands in his armpits to stop them from shaking. Harry stood at the window and glanced down. News trucks continued to pile into the visitor area. He spied FOX news down there. American news stations were in it now. Cameras and commentators all took up position in front of the hospital, hoping to learn more of this macabre tale. Mass murderers? Rapists? Abductions? A house of horror in a quiet community? A reporter's feast and the vultures had descended en masse. These sort of things didn't happen in the town of Erin, Ontario. A small town where the big stores have yet to gain a foothold. No Wal-Mart's here, just a Timmy's, but then Timmy's were everywhere. There were mom and pop stores, family owned and family run, lining the main street. Everyone knew everyone else's business and murmured them to each other over coffee and at church gatherings or maybe at a local garage while they waited to get their brakes done or at the hair salon with the click of scissors and the offerings of gossip just as loud. Point being, no one had secrets in this town. Someone, somewhere knew your business and told it to their neighbours ad infinitum. It was how small towns operated, or so Harry thought. Except for this. No one knew about this and the community was not only stunned, they were flabbergasted, knocked down on their collective asses. Right in their town by one of their own. A quiet neighbour sure, but their neighbour. For more than five years two men had been keeping stolen women in their basement. Abusing them and when they no longer continued to please, they killed them. Even more incredible, the men ate them. How could this be? How could the gossips in this town not know? Sure, there were more than a few in town, rocking on their feet in front of some news camera, offering a knowing look and saying, *I knew there was something strange about him*, or *I had my suspicions about that place.* Even still, there were more questions than answers. And one of the killers was still out there. Before exhaustion pulled Olivia into a deep sleep, she spoke enough to the detectives to let them know she had no idea who the Jackal was. Had never seen his face, just his hands. As far as Harry knew, none of the poor girls had seen his face. An unknown. A shark swimming in a sea of people, no one ever realizing how close the danger circled them. He could be anyone. He could be anywhere. He could be wandering the hall in a nurse's uniform, carrying a needle filled with 'nothing good.'

Fuck, he could do with a drink right now! Sweat beaded his brow. Maybe he could sneak out for a quick nip of something. He remembered seeing a pub just down the street. Of course he noticed it. Alcoholics made it their business to make note of such things. An internal GPS of places to get plastered in. He could walk outside, tilt his head, sniff the air and follow the scent to the nearest bar.

Olivia frowned in her sleep. What was she dreaming about? Was he considering leaving her alone so he could go get his drink on? She means so much to you that you can run off after waiting five years for her to return to get a fucking drink? He started drinking after Olivia disappeared and he thought he had every right to. Well, if not a right, it was an excuse anyone could understand. But now she had been returned to him. Safe and alive. So, why did he still want to drink? What was the excuse now? The self-loathing returned. The familiar cycle, so easy to recognize yet always feeling powerless against it. If he drank, he didn't like himself. He didn't like not liking himself and the introspection it brought on, so he drank. So stupid. Just stop and be there for your daughter.

He straightened, resolved to do right by her and for himself. She would need a lot of support from him. He needed to be sober to give it. He could quit for her, right? His drinking got bad after she disappeared, so now that she's back, he should be able to control it right? A niggle of doubt surfaced in his brain. An errant thought suggested he could quit tomorrow. Right after a few drinks tonight. He pushed it away. He had to do this. He would do this. He lasted a day.

-13-

The Jackal lay on the bed flicking back and forth between news stations. They were everywhere. He and his partner had made quite a splash. Olivia killed the Gorilla, also known as Shawn Grady. A cheek creased with amusement, proud of her even though it meant she was gone from him. His Olivia. He sighed. He already felt the loss, the separation from her as distinct as a knife grinding into his guts. Shawn ruined everything they worked, no, what he, the Jackal had worked so hard to build. He paid the price though, didn't he? He sure did and he got what he deserved for being a selfish idiot.

The Jackal knew what had happened as though reading it from a script. Shawn had slipped before and visited one of the girls alone. He'd returned to their place (well, Shawn's place according to the mortgage and bill payments, the Jackal didn't appear on any documentation anywhere) and sensed something off kilter. Usually a TV or radio could be heard somewhere in the house but the house was silent. Shawn's truck was parked in the garage so he knew Shawn to be home but he didn't see him and he didn't hear him. And then the Jackal knew. Shawn had to be in one of the soundproofed rooms. His heart jumped, thinking he might be visiting Olivia without him. A jealous anger fired in his chest. He snatched the keys and sailed down the basement stairs. He stuck the key in the lock, set to turn it and pulled it out with a panicked flick of his wrist. In such a goddamn hurry, he forgot to put on his mask. His heart punched his ribs. So worried about what Shawn was doing and who with and he hoped to a God he didn't believe in it wasn't Olivia, he forgot the one thing he should never forget. The goddamn mask. It provided anonymity and would keep him safe. A careful man, he read about the blunders of other adventurers, hunters of the most interesting game. Potential victims escaping by virtue of luck or the killer's complacency and reporting them to police, able to identify them, some of them even able to point out the house or apartment. That's what got Jeffrey Dahmer arrested. Something similar got Ted Bundy caught too. The possibility existed for one of his charges to escape. Very narrow, yet such things have happened before. To limit it, the Jackal had rules. Always wear a mask and always visit in twos. That way, if one were overpowered, the other would be there to help. Two to one. Always two to one. The safety ratio. And even if by some fluke the person made it out and went to the cops, neither one could be identified. Fairly simple rules. Even an idiot like Shawn should have no trouble following them. Clearly he did.

After he got the mask on, he returned to the door and opened it. Olivia, seated on the bed with her knees drawn up to her chest, tensed when he peered in. He closed the door. Shawn wasn't in there. He checked on the newer girl, Sandra? Fuck, he couldn't remember. Sandra, Sandy, whatever. That's where he found Shawn, rutting on top of her while she cried, his mask forgotten on the floor, his sweaty ass cheeks clenching like a fist. The Jackal closed the door, Shawn unaware of him even entering, and waited for him in the kitchen.

After some time he heard the heavy door clink shut and then heavy tread on the wooden stairs. Shawn paused when he saw the Jackal sitting at the kitchen table, a bottle of water in his hand. A twinge of fear flickered on his face, there and gone. He smirked to hide his fear. Shawn opened the fridge, took out a bottle of beer and drained half in one swallow.

"Thirsty work, that one." He acknowledged the Jackal with a tip of the bottle and drained the rest.

He leaned against the counter, preparing for whatever the Jackal had to say to him. The Jackal stood, swinging the keys around his finger. He plucked a knife from the rack before trotting down the stairs.

"Wait! What are you doing?"

"You didn't wear your mask."

He left the door open for Shawn to hear her screams, to let him know he fucked up and they just wasted a girl they could have kept for a good long while. The Jackal made quick work and had to restrain himself. Blood always excited him. The smell and the warmth of it. He wanted to bite into her when he saw the blood shoot from the cut in her neck. It splashed on his face and into his mouth. The blood was so warm and his erection pulsed wonderfully and he just wanted a bite but thought this was supposed to be a lesson to Shawn about self control. It wouldn't do if he lost control. He left her with a sigh. The gash in her neck resembled a bloody trench. Blood continued to spill in small spurts as he held her in his arms, looking into her eyes. He watched her go and whispered to her it was okay, it wasn't her fault, it was Shawn's. She gurgled and closed her eyes. What a waste.

He returned to the kitchen, blood up to his elbows, red gore glistening on his chin. He tossed the knife into the sink and studying Shawn said, "You wanna do this on your own? Go solo?"

Shawn looked down at his feet, a submissive gesture and said, "No."

"Maybe change the rules, then? Tweak them a little? Seeing as how you can't control yourself it might be a good idea to change them."

The Jackal sucked blood off his fingers waiting for Shawn's response.

"I can control myself."

"Really? So you meant to go down there and fuck her without me there? Without your mask on? You meant to do all those things, did you?"

Sulking, Shawn said, "It, uh, just happened."

The Jackal laughed. A short bark, bloated with incredulity.

"It just happened? That's what you're going with?"

The Jackal crossed the space between them in a flash, gripped Shawn around the neck with his hand and squeezed. Shawn's eyes bugged, surprised at the strength of the Jackal as he lifted him onto his toes. Shawn pulled at the Jackal's wrist and succeeded in lessening the pressure of the grip. The Jackal wouldn't let go. Not until he wanted to.

"I am not an idiot. It would be a mistake to treat me like one. Do we understand each other?"

Shawn gurgled and offered a weak nod. The Jackal released him leaving a red smear on his neck.

"I found you. I brought you in to this. In order for us to continue working together, to our mutual benefit I should add, you need to control yourself from reckless impulses. The *rules* are there to protect us. The *rules* will keep us out of jail. So, I'm going to ask you again. Do you want to go out on your own? Now's your chance if you do."

Shawn pouted at the floor.

"You going solo then or what?"

Shawn's lip protruded. God, what a fucking kid. The Jackal could read the idiot's thoughts on his face. Even as stupid as Shawn was he had to know he wouldn't get out of here alive if he wanted to go on his own and so he was weighing his chances against the Jackal and wondering if he could take him. He could see the slow thought process in Shawn's body language and his blinking eyes. The Jackal almost wanted him to try it. It would be interesting for the short time it would take for him to kill the asshole.

It would ruin this set up though. He would have to leave the house and burn the evidence and the girls with it. Except for Olivia. He could always take her with him.

He said, "No. I don't want to go solo."

He pointed at Shawn, a bloody finger inches from his nose and said, "Good. Then follow the fucking rules! And prepare her for the freezer."

It was good to get it out in the open. For Shawn to acknowledge the Jackal ran the show. Shawn was the perfect front to pin all this on if the Jackal ever needed to. As long as he maintained the power structure, he could manipulate as needed. For Shawn it must have been a painful realization to learn you are not the baddest wolf in the forest. The Jackal thought he took it well, although in retrospect, he may have been wrong. He thought he cured him of the need to disobey. He should have taken the opportunity to reinforce the need for rules. The resentment must have been building in Shawn for some time. Feeling inferior in every way a man could feel inferior, following rules he longed to ignore. Must have been eating him up inside and the Jackal had failed to notice it. Because of that, Shawn went after his beloved. His Olivia. Olivia killed him for it. He smiled again. That is why, my friend, we always visited in twos.

Now the house was gone. His girls were gone. No one for him to visit anymore. He would miss them. Especially Olivia. The smattering of freckles on her nose, man, delightful. The angry glares she delivered whenever they entered her room. Had there ever been a docile glint in her eye? None that he ever saw. They could never tame that one and they had tried. That was where the fun lay. Trying to take the resistance from them, to make them accept and believe their life was no longer theirs to control. Everything about her radiated exquisiteness. She even tasted like heaven. Her ear tasted sweeter than the thighs of any girl he had eaten before. A tear slid down his cheek.

He brushed it away with a surprised frown. What was this feeling? Why did he feel so hollow? So empty? Oh god, how he missed her! Fucking Shawn! Stupid, impulsive Shawn robbing him of Olivia because of his stupid, selfish act! It didn't matter that he knew he would have to kill her someday. He wanted to spend every available moment with her, smelling her skin, counting the freckles across her nose and just being with her and knowing he could do whatever he wanted to her and she couldn't stop him. And then, when he couldn't control himself any longer, when the need overtook control of him, he would take her. He would use her in ways that would make Shawn seem gentle. It would have been a glorious time, if it hadn't been for the fuck-twit Shawn. He wanted to be the one to destroy Olivia. To cut her, slice her open to feel her guts squirm in his fingers. Cover himself in her blood from head to toe so she would be a part of him, bonded by blood, to wear her most intimate essence. Break open her chest to yank her heart out from the roots and tear into it with his teeth. To witness the strength of her life ebb from her dying gaze. To finally take her, without his mask, without hiding. Such bitter exaltation. He would destroy something he loved. Was there anything better in all the world? His heart ached. It was all gone from him now. Five years of foreplay and then to have his moment stolen enraged and hurt him. How long would this agony last?

He glanced at the news again hoping to catch a glimpse of Olivia. The camera angle focussed on the house. Cops in uniforms, hands clasped in front, stood guarding the tape running around the property. There would be plenty of his DNA in there. Though that would only ever matter if he got caught. He had never been arrested or charged with any offence requiring the submission of his DNA. He had read there were certain offences, if convicted, a judge had the option to order a sample of your DNA to be obtained. He hadn't been arrested for anything at anytime in his life so on that front, he was safe. For now, he was free. He had never taken off his mask. The smart thing to do was to simply disappear. Put away his mask and forget all these wonderful games and ply out his remaining years in tedium with only the memory of these deeds to sustain him. He walked away from that place without being identified or being in handcuffs and he knew he was lucky to have done so. What if he had walked in for a fun-time visit with his girls just before the cops showed up? He had been on his way to see Olivia. If he had gotten there sooner, he would be a goner right now. Rotting in a cage he didn't build with bad food and stupid cops for company. It had been a matter of minutes that had kept him free. It would be idiotic to spurn such luck. He would have to let her go. Or would he? Or better question, could he? He could feel the tug from her, the pull on the rope binding them together. He had waited a long time to take her, waiting for her to mature into a woman. And he had had her! For five glorious years! Painting her nails, braiding her hair, laying out comfortable clothes for her on the bed. Could he let her go? The Jackal stared at the TV. Olivia's picture flashed on the screen. He began sobbing. It hurt so much to have her taken from him and he was mortified at his weakness yet helpless against it. He asked himself again, *could he let her go*? He honestly didn't know.

-14-

Olivia flicked her hair to cover her missing ear. In doing so, the gap where her fingers used to be seemed more pronounced. *Face it kiddo, you're a goddamn mess.* She sighed into the mirror, pushing down the impulse to cry. Ugly. They had made her ugly. Her eyes shiny, she swallowed and summoned other thoughts, innocuous, safe thoughts like teddy bears and puppies. She had been home for a week now and being back in her bedroom took some getting used to. She dreamed of this, of being home with her father when she had been in the basement but it felt more real to dream of it than to experience it. Justin Bieber smiled down at her from her wall. She smiled. Was he still cool? She had no idea. And that, too, was a foreign feeling but she found she didn't care. After what she had been through, who was on the top of the charts and what a celebrity did on the weekend, or who, didn't matter at all.

The interview with the police took four days to get done. They gave her plenty of breaks, driving her to and from home each day and when it was all over, Olivia was drained. They said the further along the investigation went, there could be more questions and they asked if they could call her again if that happened and she said sure, but she wasn't sure. She wanted it to be over. When she arrived home after being released from the hospital and before the formal police interviews, the media had crowded the front of her house. They patrolled the sidewalk, jockeying and pushing each other around trying to get the best position to yell their questions at Olivia. They were rude and avaricious. They cared not at all about her. She was a story to exploit. They yelled at her, pushing microphones in her face and forcing shoulder mounted cameras in her way. They tried to block her path to more effectively surround her but the police and her dad shoved them back and the one officer with a port wine stain on his neck, visible above his collar, told them to act like goddamn human beings for once. She thought the experience was like being a celebrity. The weird kind though. Not famous for any sort of talent, musical or otherwise. No, her fame came from surviving five years of rape and torture that left her a mangled, terrified young woman. After passing through the rude people desperate for a sound bite, she stepped into her house with her dad at her elbow.

It was like walking into the past. A past that had nothing to do with her. She felt a stranger in a familiar place and to the pictures of herself smiling from frames hung on the wall. Like going to the wax museum, seeing a celebrity you recognize, but still, after all the work and attention to detail, there was something off. The connection to the real subdued and lacking any shine or soul. The girl in the silver picture frame wearing a black graduation gown and cap didn't exist anymore. That girl had attained honours in high school. She had had friends, a future, something to look forward to, expectations of normality and a feeling of entitlement to happiness. She also had both ears and all her fingers and toes. She had never been raped. A naive girl who didn't believe in the bogeyman. Who could she be now? Free from the pink basement of horror but now a different person to when she went in. She pushed her hair back, exposing the nub of flesh that marked what little remained of her ear. She tied it back in a ponytail, not caring how it looked in this moment. This is who she is now and there was no use hiding it. Especially in the privacy of her own home. If she went out, then that would be different wouldn't it? She didn't want people to stare at her. She wanted peace.

In the kitchen, her dad hovered around the stove. The smell of frying eggs, bacon and toast hung thick in the air.

Harry, with his back to her said, "You want it scrambled?"

"Yeah. That would be great. You got coffee brewing there?"

"Uh, no. I'll set that up."

"No. I can get it."

"Alright."

The kitchen overlooked the front lawn. Yellow curtains brightened the dreary, winter daylight filtering out the grey. Out on the road parked in front of their house were three news trucks idling with the plumes from their vehicles chugging into the air.

"Those idiots still here?"

Harry said, "They showed up thirty minutes ago."

"No wonder so many people hate the media. I almost feel bad for those celebrities, always with their picture in those tabloids. Must get exhausting. I'm exhausted just thinking about them."

Harry patted her shoulder. Since she got home, he always found some way to make physical contact. Almost like he were testing if she were real and not a fantasy. She knew how he felt. None of this seemed real. The basement, the pink walls and the bolted down furniture felt more tangible to her. She could envision a spot of blood on the floor under the bed when the Gorilla had snipped off her index finger with those fucking shears. He loved those shears. He commented on them all the time about how great they were. How easily they clipped through bone. The finger rolled under the bed after it sailed through the air. They couldn't reach it, not with the bed bolted to the floor. She remembered the Gorilla complaining as he lay flat on his stomach, using a broom to snag her index finger and draw it in towards him. Pissed about having to get the finger and not being able to clean up the blood. The ever silent Jackal later bandaged her hand with care. How she hated those fuckers. And one of them was still free. Why couldn't it all be over? She escaped and she just wanted it to be done. Isn't that how its supposed to work?

Harry said, "You okay?"

She flinched, drawn out of her memories, gave him a tremulous smile and said, "Yeah. I think so."

His eyes slid to her ear and he pulled her into a quick hug. He said, "Why don't you sit down. I'll make the coffee."

She pulled away, "No. I got it, Dad. Really."

"Alright."

She put the filter in the coffee maker, scooped in the coffee, filled it with water and turned it on.

"See? Not so hard."

"You forgot to plug it in."

She frowned until she saw the plug in the outlet and said, "Har-d-har, Dad," and playfully bumped him with her hip.

Out the window, the sliding door of one of the news vans rolled open. A man in a red toque and a dark blue jacket waved at her. She scowled. He raised a camera with a huge lens and snapped pictures of her.

She moved away from the window and sat at the table.

Harry closed the curtains and said, "Those people," he shook his head, "have no souls."

Harry clicked on the iPod and with music riding the air around them, he finished making breakfast and poured them both coffee. Sitting at the table they were initially silent while eating and content to be in each other's company.

Harry said, "So, we gotta discuss what we wanna do here."

"About what?"

"Well, about living here for one. Also, I'm going to have to go back to work next week and you're going to be here alone and that other guy is still out there."

"The cops are pretty confident he won't come after me. And they gave me that alarm thingy. That push button thing."

"The one you're supposed to always have on you?"

She pulled the alarm activator out from under her collar. She had attached it to a leather string. "It's right here, Dad."

"Good. I'm glad they gave that to you. Still, it's not like he couldn't find out where you are," he jerked a thumb at the window, "not with those jerks out there."

Olivia suffered the same thoughts. Last night while trying to sleep, she kept glancing at the window expecting a Jackal head to appear. He would turn to her, hands pressed against the glass and his excited breath would fog the pane. Needless to say she had trouble sleeping. Silly considering her room was on the second floor. He would have to be able to levitate or use a ladder to see into her window. And he would have to drag the ladder through the crusted snow past the well-lit yard of their neighbours. Still, once the thought took root in her brain, it became impossible to yank out. At night, when the moon shone bright in the window and the wind pushed against the house creating noises you never noticed before, silly ideas become plausible. Dark thoughts grew teeth and bared them from the recesses of imagination. Even though the police and her dad took steps to protect her, she didn't feel safe. Before she even got home from the hospital, Harry had someone install an alarm. And the police gave her the plunger alarm too at the time. Usually reserved for victims of domestic violence, the alarm wasn't bigger than a lipstick container and easy to use. Depress the button at the top and the signal would be sent to the police to respond to her home as a priority one. Lights and sirens all the way. Even if pressed by accident, the police were obligated to see her in person to make sure she wasn't being held hostage and being forced to lie to them over the phone telling them everything was alright. Police regularly patrolled her street. She would see them pass, twenty, thirty times in a day. The Jackal would have to be crazy to come after her. And he was crazy, a loon, but not the uncontrolled impulses type of mental illness. To come after her, he would almost have to want to get caught. She couldn't see that in him. He had been the controlled and quiet one. She had too much attention on her now. It would be too dangerous for him to come after her. Especially with the news vans parked out front.

They wouldn't be there forever, though, would they? Something worse would happen and she would be old news. Then, at some point, with no action, the cops would stop driving by and maybe, if enough time passed, they would ask for their alarm back. Then he would be there, waiting for her under the bed, ready to snatch at her passing feet.

She would rather be dead than spend another second in a prison constructed by the Jackal. Moving and disappearing from sight might be the best idea. She would be hiding, which wasn't an ideal way to live but she at least would be alive. She wouldn't be a prisoner in a pink cell dreading the screech of a metal door opening and admitting two animals meaning to devour her. After some time, she might be able to breathe again. Being home while knowing the bastard still stalked the streets and might show up at anytime made her feel like she had been holding her breath, waiting for the worst because the worst is what she had gotten used to wasn't it? Five years of it. Hard to shrug off the chains those years had created. Would she ever feel safe again or would she always be looking over her shoulder? If the Jackal were dead maybe it would be a little easier to breathe. Maybe she could finally exhale.

Olivia said, "Moving could be a good idea. We'd have to wait for those ass-clowns to leave. I'm sure they'll find some other misery to circle over."

Harry smiled, "Ass-clowns? I like it. You have a way with words my dear."

His expression darkened and he said, "Would you want to have a gun around? We could both get a licence. Practice at the shooting range, you know, so we can both be comfortable with one."

"I don't want to think too much right now, Dad. I'll consider it."

"Okay. No problem."

She had thought of it though and then researched it. She wasn't sure how she felt about it. Unless she carried it with her everywhere it wouldn't be much use. In the house the firearms would have to be secured in a locker. The ammunition would have to be stored in a separate place and the firearm couldn't be loaded. She could imagine it. The Jackal shows up and she kindly asks him to wait while she unlocks the gun locker, takes it to where the ammunition is stored, loads the gun and then shoots him. All in all, not a realistic expectation and not worth the effort to get one. It wasn't like she could take the gun out of the house either, not in a way she could access it quick if she needed to. There were transportation requirements. You're not allowed to carry them around outside just under your coat or something. She wasn't living in Texas.

She would think about it though. Might be some extra insurance in it. Hell, she might just have one loaded by her bed and fuck the law. It wasn't like the law rescued her from that basement. She did that all by herself. Something to consider anyways. She did have another idea about protection though, but it wasn't the first on her list. The cops were still vigilant about patrols and with the alarm around her neck, they were a quick press away. That part of her plan could wait for now. There were other things to get done first. Like getting her dad to an Alcoholics Anonymous meeting. She had seen him in the evenings, drinking until he slurred words and walked with unsure steps like the room had tilted on him. She didn't like it. He wasn't the dad she had left behind. Her absence had left scars on him too. Her return hadn't magically healed them either, but why would it? He developed the addiction in her absence and after all, it was an addiction.

It concerned her at first. She didn't think it was as bad as it was but she hadn't been home all that long. Only then she noticed he drank every night and not just a beer with dinner either. By the time he went to bed he was usually six to ten beers in. She saw the stack of empties growing in the garage each day. Even this morning, she saw him toss a couple of Tylenol in his mouth and dry chew them. A stale smell of alcohol hovered around him all the time. Even after a shower. His eyes were puffy and red for most of the day. He hadn't drank like this before she had been taken. She knew that. This was something new. Well, new to her. To him, it seemed a well-practiced routine. He sipped on his coffee and touched her hand. A reassuring touch. A good dad. It hurt her to see him suffer. He wouldn't have started drinking if she hadn't been taken. Not that it was her fault or that he blamed her but his addiction was something she had inadvertently helped to start. For five years he had no idea that she was alive and what was his coping tool for that? Alcohol. He wanted a drink right now. Two broken people. Maybe they could help each other. Maybe they could heal each other. The thought pulled her lips into a smile. She reached out and held her dad's hand. His lips trembled and formed a smile. They could get better.

After clearing up the dishes, Olivia retired to the living room and turned on the TV. She curled up on the couch, her knees up to hold the iPad on her lap. The TV droned in the background. Her dad sat in a chair across from her, a book open in his hands, stealing glances of Olivia every once in awhile.

Harry said, "Frank should be back next week. He called a few times, you know."

"Where's he been?"

"Some conference. Big important contractors conference where the only serious work getting done is drinking."

"Why didn't he want to talk to me?"

"He sounded in shock. Kept asking if you were really home. I told him yes, you know, asked him if he wanted to speak to you and he was like, 'No, no, no. Just tell me how she is.' Like if he spoke to you it wouldn't be real anymore."

"What do you mean?"

"I don't know. I guess like when you get someone to pinch you to make sure you're awake when something incredible happens. With Frank, hearing your voice might wake him from the dream of your return. Something like that anyways."

"Huh. I never saw Uncle Frank as that way."

"What way?"

"It's gonna sound mean."

"I'm sure I can take it."

"Caring."

Harry laughed, "Yeah. I guess I can see that. That's just his way. But he does care. He never forgets a birthday does he?"

"I always thought that was because of you and his administrative assistant."

"That's all Frank. Anyways, he'll be by some time next week, for dinner."

"Alright."

She returned her attention to the iPad. Touch screen. She kept wanting to use her index finger but just a nub remained. She stared at the pink scar tissue over the remaining bone. Shiny pink, twisted skin. Deformed. How she hated those bastards! It burned inside her and at times, palsied her hands. The most dangerous one got away too, and from the sounds of it, would probably get away with it. The cops had fuck all. She asked them about it, after the interviews were finished. The lead detective, a bald guy with dark rimmed glasses avoided her eyes when answering, giving her the same platitudes he had given hundreds of other victims as their world dissolved around them. Using lines from TV shows about cops. He said to her, after a nervous clearing of his throat, "We're following up a number of potential leads and still have to process all the evidence collected. We'll let you know." Blah-blah-blah.

He did say something though, something she couldn't stop thinking about. He repeatedly questioned her about the two men. And when she told him about the roles of the two men and how the Jackal never touched her sexually and had never spoken to her his brow creased and his lips pursed, like he didn't believe her, like she was making this shit up. She bristled and said, "How many times you going to ask me the same thing? I'm telling you, not once did he touch me that way! Not once did the fucker even talk to me! God! Why do we keep going over this?"

He reddened, the scant moustache dancing as he withered under her anger and confusion. Didn't he believe her? She didn't mean to get so mad but how many times could she say the same thing though? And when it seemed like the cop was fucking sceptical about her version of events, like she would make this shit up for amusement, she wanted to explode, rip the ugly little moustache off his face. Didn't he know no one wore those anymore? Even ironically? They were old news before she had been taken. She could feel the veins in her eyeballs pulse, that's how mad she had been.

His hands fluttered about his tie, a nervous tic and he stuttered out, "Look, I'm sorry if it looks like we're going around in circles here. I can't even comprehend how bad it must've been for you. Your story is like the other girls', Lucy and Jen, except for a huge detail."

"Oh, yeah? What's that?"

"This Jackal character? He uh, raped the other two girls, with Shawn, the Gorilla. He also spoke to them all the time. Giving them orders on what he wanted done to him and what he wanted done to his pal, Shawn. They both punished him. Never so gentle with them as you describe he was with you. Never painting their nails. And, yeah, he did the bandaging on the other girls, just with no kindness? If you can call anything they did as kind. So you see, it's odd. I, mean, why didn't he ever touch you? I'm glad he didn't. One asshole would be enough for anyone. I'm asking all these questions, and yes, they seem repetitive, but I just wanna know why? Why not you? Why didn't he even talk to you? Curious, don't you think?"

Stunned, she said, "Downright fucking weird, is what I think."

And it was weird, totally insane. She continually questioned the motivations of the Jackal. What did he get from it all? Never touching, never abusing her the way the Gorilla did, or even speaking to her. He was no friend to her. He wouldn't have helped her to escape. She figured he liked to watch. With the detective's revelation, it now appeared to be something else. A sickness only the Jackal could understand. Why not her?

The thought squirmed like snakes in her stomach. She leaned back appraising the detective. Not as stupid as he looked. Well, maybe he was. One good question does not a genius make. His sceptical tone had rankled her.

Sitting in her living room, eyes vacant on the iPad screen, she couldn't get the thought out of her head. It popped up, unbidden, pushing out any good feeling she might have had, fleeting as those moments were. She knew the Jackal felt something special for her. Whatever it was, it prevented him from raping her and from speaking to her. She didn't know what it was or why it existed but it was there. As tangible as his touch. Did she remind him of someone? A mother he loved and hated? A sister? If so, why weren't Lucy and Jen spared his touch? They were all very similar. Height, weight, hair colour, hell, line them up and you might think they were related. Why not her then? It scared her and in a guilty corner of her soul, she felt relief. She hadn't been subjected to the tag-team horrors. The Gorilla was bad enough. But what did it mean? She could talk to the other girls, ask them about it. Should she though? They had just been through it with the detectives and from what it sounded like, they had it even worse than her, if that could be possible. Olivia didn't know if she wanted to revisit it either. Talk about it all again as though they were some women in a book club, saying shit like, *So what did it mean to you?* No, she was so not ready for that nonsense. Not yet. It was all too fresh, like pulling off a scab before it healed.

She fingered the little bit of cartilage of what remained of her ear. Why had they taken it again? So many slights, so many punishments. It could have been for the time she played nice, acting provocative until the Gorilla got close enough for her to kick him in his hanging bits. How he howled! He even puked on the floor! She was positive that behind the mask, he was crying. Hearing him sob and watching the puke leak out of his mask, she thought whatever the punishment was going to be, still, it was worth it. Until they took her ear. No wait, that wasn't it. They took the ear for not eating and messing in her bed. Time blurred the events. Cruelty merging with other acts of vileness. For the kick in the bits, they took her big toe. A secret part of her maybe wanted to get them mad enough to kill her, like when she wouldn't eat or get up to go to the washroom. They would release her from prison in the most permanent way. Otherwise why provoke them like that?

Two days later they returned. The Gorilla still hobbling a bit as he approached her. Those Craftsman clippers appeared in his hand and she knew beneath the stupid mask of his he was grinning from ear to ear. The Jackal held her down, pinning her head to the cold floor with his knee. The room itself had been warm, comfortably so, but the floor had always been cold. He placed his other knee in the small of her back and held her arms on the other side of his body so they were pulled straight out and she thought her shoulder would pop out of the socket and flop loose under the skin. The Gorilla straddled her legs, his weight grinding her bony hips against the floor. He said, "Punishment time!" He clacked the clippers together, so she could hear it and he grabbed her foot. She kicked out and the Gorilla lost his grip. He slid further down her legs, onto the backs of her calves. She couldn't lift him. He grabbed her foot and she tried to move it. Too strong, all she could do was wiggle her foot. She stopped wiggling when she felt the cold blades on either side of her big toe. The clippers crunched through her skin and stopped at the bone. She screamed. The Gorillas said, "Hold still would ya? Just one more clip." The Gorilla grunted and she heard the click as the blade bit through bone. Her toe popped off and the Gorilla said, "Got it!"

The pain! Her body convulsed with it. The Jackal held her down. She screamed until she thought the inside of her throat must be bleeding. The Gorilla laughed. He picked up the toe and held it before her eyes.

He said, "Another part. Gone forever. Whittling away at you dear, one piece at a time. Soon there'll be nothing."

He dropped the toe. It bounced and struck her nose, leaving a red splotch on the floor. No longer a part of her. Afterwards, the Jackal tended to her with gentle ministrations. Yeah, he felt something for her. Olivia could never manipulate whatever it was he felt to her advantage. There had always been two of them in the room and the Jackal was the leader. She knew it with certainty. And she meant something to him. More than the other girls. Some connection the Jackal believed they shared and not to be spoiled by a sordid romp. What did he see in her? She hugged her arms to her chest. He was still out there, biding his time.

Like the detective, she thought it significant the Jackal never touched her. Would it reveal his identity somehow? Maybe point them in the right direction? Olivia *should* talk to Lucy and Jen. Some questions needed answering and maybe, those two had the answers. She wasn't ready to do that yet. She could wait. Even if Lucy and Jen were ready to talk about it to another survivor, Olivia needed more time to be comfortable enough with all that had happened to her before she could discuss it. She never did feel comfortable discussing her emotions and talking about it again, so soon, would be too much. She tapped a button on the iPad, her missing fingers as noticeable as neon. It made her feel ugly, deformed and she hated being reminded of it.

-15-

The Jackal's stomach clenched. He felt anxious a lot of the time now. A master at blending in, no one noticed the anguish he suffered. A smart man, he knew it would be folly to contact her or try to get her again. The play that made sense was to start again somewhere new. Work alone this time. It had been convenient to have a helper, someone to live in the place, to keep an eye on the girls as long as the person didn't visit the girls on their own. To find such a person again would be challenging. No, it would be next to impossible. He knew how rare it had been to run across a man like Shawn. Chances of finding another were slim to none and slim had left town. Besides, Shawn was the reason it fell apart. His foolishness had brought it all down. That and Olivia. His penis throbbed at the thought of her. She killed Shawn. The news people confirmed it although they didn't have to. He knew it had been her because Shawn had wanted to hurt the Jackal and that was the best way to do it. To be intimate with Olivia when he wasn't there. Shawn had paid for it and it wasn't him doing the punishing this time. He would love to have seen it. Seriously, how could Shawn not realize the danger? It had been her who had kicked him in the balls so hard he was bruised for days. He smiled, thinking of it. He had grinned under the mask when Shawn crumpled and triumph shone from Olivia's face. So pleased with herself. It took a lot of restraint for him to not laugh out loud. He would have to stop thinking of her. The memory of her face! Torture! He couldn't stop himself from turning on the TV hoping to see her on the news. He would lean towards the TV burning for a glimpse of her leaving the police station under guard or running into her house and scowling at the cameras while making sure her hair covered her missing ear. It excited him to see Lucy and Jen too, just not nearly as much. Olivia. She inspired him. The smell of her, the feel of her skin and the golden tints in her eyes. He wanted to take her and use her and watch the fire, the strength drain from her eyes. He wanted to crush any hope inside her in his hands and when all her light had been extinguished, he would kill her. He wanted to taste her and take all of her inside him, absorb her very essence through her flesh. They would be together always then. What better way to do that than to consume her? He frowned. Those thoughts were dangerous. He had to forget about her and move on. Everyone, the cops and Olivia were on high alert. To go for her again would be a Shawn type of move. The move of an idiot.

The best way to get over her would be to find another pet. Another obsession. He decided to scout for new locations tomorrow, find a new base of operations and figure out how to make it untraceable to him. He needed to keep busy. He was developing a junkie fixation on her. He supposed he always had it, this unhealthy need for Olivia. And time apart wasn't making it any easier. If truth be told, it was making it worse.

•   •   •

The next day, while scouting for new locations, he looked up and noticed he had gravitated closer to Olivia's house. Driving down streets thinking about nothing, his brain in idle, he noticed he was circling closer and closer to her. He cursed himself. Not a good idea. Shit like this could get him caught. Maybe she would be at the kitchen window as he passed. He was close to her now, might as well take advantage of the situation.

A cop car drove by. Outwardly, the Jackal appeared unconcerned although his heart tried to climb out of his chest with its pounding. Jesus man, you need to let her go. Find someone else. A whole harem of others. He could glory in pounding them with cock and fists, tenderizing them until they landed on his plate. He needed to stay away from here, away from her. The Jackal drove away, glancing in the rearview mirror to make sure the cop hadn't turned around. The cop car kept going and the Jackal released a whistle of air. He stopped at a red light, thinking the red was the exact shade he had painted Olivia's nails once. He sighed. If he was making the right decision, then why did he feel so bad? He would have to give it time. What was that stupid saying? Time healed all wounds? Hippy nonsense. He needed to find some other distraction. Most definitely of the female variety.

-16-

Olivia's predictions proved correct. It only took another week for the media to be distracted with some other inanity. A city council member taking bribes or some such nonsense. They still reported on the house of horrors and the two men in masks because it was one hell of a story and they loved to play backseat investigators. Most of their attention focussed on the police and their lack of progress in the investigation, insinuating police incompetence without coming right out and saying it. It served their agenda of creating fear in the community. Scaring the public witless improved ratings and circulation sales. With headlines reading, "Jackal still at large! Police are clueless," Olivia felt sorry for the detective with the terrible moustache. He must be under enormous pressure and he didn't appear equipped to deal with it. The main reason the media vans left was simple: Olivia wouldn't give them an interview. She hid in her house most of the time so she imagined the powers that be thought their resources could be better spent elsewhere. Lucy didn't have the same reservations about speaking with the media. She had already been on one local morning show. Her light coloured hair, wonderful almond shaped eyes and slim figure made for a beautiful heroine and the public ate it up. Olivia suspected Lucy was being paid to appear on the shows and had ambiguous feelings about it. She thought Lucy was at least making something positive out of a negative. Maybe talking about it would even help her recover. But then she thought it wasn't just her story though was it? It belonged to Olivia and Jen too.

Still, just because Olivia wanted to put it behind her by not discussing it with the media vultures didn't mean Lucy did. Olivia believed it dangerous to keep stirring it up instead of letting it fade away. Dangerous for all of them. Her appearing on the talk show circuit might renew interest from the media. Olivia liked not having the media camped out on her lawn. It helped her breathe a little easier with them gone. Less media cover, less exposure and less chance of the Jackal seeing her on the TV and inciting him to visit her one night so he could finish what he started. Olivia wanted the media to leave her alone so she could have time to think without the talking heads pressuring her to discuss what she went through in gruesome detail. When it all faded into black and white memories where their power to hurt had diminished, then maybe she could talk to Lucy and Jen about it. Funny. It was okay to yap about it when she felt it was okay? She shook her head at herself. Still, she would need to talk to them eventually. All those nagging questions. Why not her? Why didn't he try to rape her or speak to her? Not that she wasn't relieved. The Gorilla had been more than enough. It made her think she might know him. If he had spoken, would she have recognized his voice? Her arms rippled with goosebumps at the possibility. With thoughts like that, how could she ever feel safe again?

Her dad told her the cops had investigated the hell out of Dale. She had just broken up with him before moving into the university, he was an ex-boyfriend, he was upset and obviously the prime suspect. The ex-boyfriend always is. In the end, they had nothing to go with. At the presumed time of her abduction he said he had been home, watching a movie he rented through YouTube. He provided them with an online receipt indicating the date and time he rented it. It matched up. Although, didn't you have twenty-four hours to watch it? There was some sort of time constraint on it. Didn't mean he couldn't have grabbed her. Thinking Dale could be the Jackal was ridiculous to her. They were the same age, grew up together, had the same friends. So, how did he meet Shawn Grady? How did he become the leader of the torture duo? She could tell, by the body language and deference shown by Shawn that the Jackal was the leader of their little torture club. Besides, the Jackal looked a lot bigger than Dale. It's possible her projection of fear made him seem bigger but Dale had always been kind, gentle. The Jackal's kindness came at the expense of her pain. Without her pain and torture he wouldn't bandage her or paint her nails or comb her hair. Dale had been kind because he couldn't be any other way. Dale couldn't be the Jackal. It didn't make sense on so many levels. An absurd idea with the power to niggle at her brain. Then why did the Jackal never talk to her? Why did he never rape her? He may have been saving her for something or he could have a scar or tattoo she might recognize. For whatever reason, he had fixated on her as someone different than the other girls and didn't want to ruin the fantasy he concocted in his head. But if he never intended for her to get out of there (which she knew he didn't) then what would it matter if she knew him? He would get what he wanted from her and kill her. Hang her on a hook in his freezer to dine on later. Fuck! Why couldn't she be some Zen master that could let this shit go and walk around with the gentle smile of inner peace etched on her face, happy to be alive and not a corpse on a hook in an insane man's freezer? Instead, she huddled in her house terrified, expecting a shadow wearing a Jackal mask to walk past her window.

She had taken to carrying a knife around with her. Ever since her dad went back to work and she had been left alone in the house, she was afraid to leave her room when he wasn't home. Every creak menaced her. The wind pushing and pulling at the house jellied her legs. A dog barking in the distance had her peering out the window expecting to see the Jackal's tall frame moving down the side of the house. She wanted to get through it. She knew her dad had to go to work and couldn't stay home forever. If he did that, they would end up living in a box in an alley. She fought the urge to call him although the fear sometimes paralyzed her to the point she wouldn't even leave her room to eat. She knew he set the house alarm before he left. Knew he walked around the house to see if there were any new footprints in the snow. He called it 'checking the perimeter' and he would flash her an extravagant salute. He did everything he could to make her feel safe. He even called the police station to make sure the patrol cars would cruise by their house in case their vigilance began to lag. Even with this knowledge and the firm belief the Jackal would have to be a complete idiot to try and nab her the pressure continued to build inside. She used the washroom with the door open. She wanted to close it but what if she opened it and there he stood, reaching for her, his breath sounding forced from behind the mask. Irrational. She knew it. But how to suppress it? No idea. She lasted two days before she called her dad at work, voice condensed into a terrified whisper, asking him to come home while hiding in her closet. He did and he brought with him a knife. A six-inch bowie knife complete with sheath and attachable to a belt to hang at her waist. She liked it. A lot. The blade gleamed. She studied her eyes in it and the wide-eyed terror she normally saw staring back was gone.

Most of the time she wore track pants. They were comfortable and who the hell did she have to impress? She didn't want to acknowledge she got used to wearing them in the room she had been kept in and wore them out of familiarity as much as anything else. She wore a belt over them so she could attach the knife to it. She patted it throughout the day, reassured by its cold weight. She still hid in her room most of the time (there were too many windows downstairs in her opinion) and only darted out to use the washroom or make something to eat. Day by day the terror lessened its hold on her. So she thought. She would be reminded of how the fear controlled her when her dad came home and the relief at the sight of him trembled her body. She knew it would get better with time and she would have to be patient. Five years in a basement taught her all about patience. One step at a time. Quite the misfit family. Her dad the alcoholic and she, the terrified, scarred girl imprisoning herself in her house. Now might be the time to focus on something, get her mind occupied with something else. Like helping her dad and maybe they should move somewhere else now that the media had lost interest. Both of them could get a fresh start. For the first time in a long while, a faint stirring of hope fluttered in her chest. A fresh start had a nice clean ring to it.

-17-

Harry didn't like going to work. No surprise. Most people don't. There are a lucky few who have found their dream job and for them, work became playtime. Playtime you got paid for. Harry didn't mind his job and before Olivia had been taken, he sometimes enjoyed it. When he got to use his brain and solve a problem no else could, it provided him with a sense of satisfaction. After she had been taken, it prevented him from going crazy with worry. It gave him something to think about other than what might be or what had happened to his daughter. Even after the embarrassing incident when they sent him home, he didn't mind going there day after day. It helped him keep some sort of handle on his drinking. Then Olivia came home and going to work terrified him because now he feared she wouldn't be there when he walked through the door. He feared her return had been a dream. A remarkable dream in which the impossible became reality. How many parents still waited for some word of their missing children? He had been one of those. Fighting to breathe with such a heavy weight on his chest. Imitating life while drifting through a fog. In the space between thoughts, terror's fingers would crush his heart and he would want to call her, to hear her voice and know her return was real. He worried it would cause her to fear more if he did that. He couldn't imagine how she functioned, escaping such an insane situation and being thrust back into a world where beds weren't bolted to the floor and men with animal masks no longer visited her room on a whim. Instead, he called the detective almost daily to check on the status of the investigation and to see if officers were still driving by his house. No new updates and yes, they were driving by. He loved it when she called, asking him to come home and felt guilty for loving it. He shouldn't be happy she was so scared at home she called him, should he? It did mean he could go home to her. It meant he could know her return hadn't been a dream. His boss had been very accommodating. She had two kids of her own and understood his need to leave when Olivia called but at some point it would have to stop. Olivia knew it too. Her calls came less frequently and he found himself spending entire days at work without a call from her. It nagged at him and he lost time wondering what she was up to and if she was okay.

Harry called Olivia before leaving work everyday to see if she needed anything for him to pick up on the way home and if he had been running low on booze, he would make a quick stop to resupply. He knew his drinking worried her. He noticed her watching him when he got up to get another beer. He worried about himself too. Since she returned, he had been getting carried away with his booze intake and couldn't even explain to himself why he continued. She was home right? There should be no reason to keep drinking. Most times, he would be pissed halfway through dinner. Slurring his words and staggering to the washroom and confused as to how he got so drunk so fast. Olivia's eyes would remain on him, a concerned frown drawing lines between her eyebrows. He wanted to stop. Oh God, how he wanted to stop! It amazed him, the level of self-deception required to keep going. To lie to yourself and to know it yet still convince yourself you'll quit tomorrow or the next day and that all you need is just one more drink, one more taste before you shut it down for good. It never was one more taste. One more taste became one more bottle became one more case became I'm still a goddamn drunk! How is it a person can hate themselves in one moment and cheers themselves in the next with a bottle of booze in the hand? Truth is, Harry loved to drink. That simple. That's what made it so scary. The alcohol hitting his lips soothed the anxiety he lived with. It turned ocean waves of fear into gentle ripples. It made his mind empty. It erased every fear and amplified self-deception.

When he called Olivia before going home, she sounded nervous, as though she had spent it in the closet again. He hoped she hadn't. He swiped a hand across his lips. Something he knew he did when he felt like a drink. Was there any beer in the fridge? He couldn't remember. He thought there might be some but his memories of such things tended to blur together and become an amorphous blob. He would pick some up on the way home. He logged off the computer, threw on his coat and nodded and smiled his way to his car. His busy hand wiping at his upper lip, anxious for a cold bottle to press against it and let the amber liquid flow into his stomach, satisfying his need. Yeah, he should stop for a case. Didn't matter if he had too much beer in the fridge but it did matter if he didn't have enough.

-18-

"You think this will work?" Frank said.

Olivia had called him earlier in the week, planning an intervention for her dad. Sounded lame, even in her own head. Sounded so…dramatic. She preferred to think of it as a life assist to stop the slow self-immolation her dad seemed hell bent on.

When she let Frank in the front door she knew his question referred to the intervention she was planning. She responded by engaging in an awkward hug. She saw he noticed the knife at her waist. He had always been reluctant to touch her, as though it would lead to caring or something. He cared about her in his own way, a familial obligation that dictated some interest in her well-being, she knew that, but she never depended on him for anything before. They had never been really close and their pattern of amiable acquaintance would take awhile to reassert itself. Olivia found herself reluctant to let others in. She trusted her father and he needed help. It was the reason she asked Uncle Frank to come over. Because she wanted Harry to get better. She offered Frank coffee. He accepted and then she placed herself on the couch, the crease in her brow deepening with the passing of every car.

"It has to," Olivia said, her arms hugging her knees as she peered out the window waiting for her dad. Her hand strayed away from her knees and a finger played about the remaining tissue of her ear. She pulled her hair down over it.

Frank stood, leaning against the wall, looking almost bored.

He turned the coffee cup in his hand and said, "I could really do with a beer right about now."

She rolled her eyes at him, "Not funny."

He shifted his gaze from the window to her and said, "You're right. Sorry. I'm just not comfortable with this…this whole intervention thing."

"He needs it."

"I don't see it. I mean, sure, he has a drink now and then but don't we all?"

"Of course you don't see it. You're never here."

"Don't turn this around on me."

"I'm not. This is not about you at all. I'm stating facts. This is the first I've seen of you since...you know."

"I wasn't in the country!"

"You were supposed to come over for dinner that one time and cancelled, remember? But that doesn't matter. Point is, you're not here. And if you're never here you can't see what I see everyday. I'm telling you he needs help. He drinks himself stupid every night. Not one or two nights a week. Every night. I want my dad back. I need my dad back. If you don't want to help, by all means, leave."

"I never said that!" And then, "I'll do what I can."

The key turned in the lock. Harry walked in, saw Frank and smiled. It made him look young. He was carrying a case of beer in his hands.

"Frank! Holy shit! When did you get in?"

Frank shuffled his feet, his lips jerking into the semblance of a smile and then it faded away. Harry snapped a look at Olivia, confusion fogging his eyes.

"Dad. It's time we talked."

"About what?" But he knew. The panic flared his nostrils and without realizing it, he hugged the case of beer to himself, protecting it the way a running back would a football. For Harry, it was going to be a long night. The hard part wasn't accepting that he needed help. He knew that ages ago even though he preferred to ignore it with the help of copious amounts of alcohol and a strong deflective shield called denial. The hard part was giving it up. Not drinking anything. Sweat dotted his brow. He wanted to turn around and run into the night. He even glanced back over his shoulder. The door was closed.

Olivia took the case from under his arms. He clenched his hands, refusing to let go but only for an instant. He released it and Olivia exhaled, relieved. She handed the case to Frank as he stood against the wall, his mouth a tight grim line.

His voice wavering, Harry said, "Now what?"

"Now we get you some help, Dad."

She hugged him and his body trembled.

• • •

That night, Harry attended his first Alcoholics Anonymous meeting. Olivia sat on one side and Frank, looking equally bored and embarrassed, sat on the other. The stories, all different yet disturbingly similar fell on Harry's ears and he listened. They affected him deeply. His eyes glistened and his lips wiggled tremulously throughout the meeting. These men and women were him. The self-loathing, the hatred, the nights choosing a bottle over a loved one, they were all him. Externally, they appeared different. Some looked homeless with their dirty clothes, unwashed scent and unshaven countenances. Others could be dock workers, truck drivers, nurses, doctors, lawyers all varying in education levels and income yet all the same in one way. Alcohol ruled them. Alcoholism could decimate and humble anyone. The great leveller. Like any disease, it chose whom to infect indiscriminately. And the person carried it like a black mark for the rest of their life. There was no 'just one drink' with people such as these. One drink lit a fire in the dark part of the soul that needed to be continually fed. One drink led to waking up in prison with a vomit bib on their shirt or a night they couldn't remember lying beside a person they didn't know, head throbbing and still reaching for the nearest bottle just to take the edge off. Had Harry been as bad as that? No. But on more than one occasion he dangled over the precipice, one foot on solid ground, the other, wavering over a dark hole, hungry for him, desperate to grind him up. Now Olivia had returned and she pulled and tugged him away from the gaping maw of oblivion. She wanted her father back. She deserved him. And he agreed with her.

Every night for two weeks they attended a meeting. Not Frank. He had enough the first night, saying he was busy at work, blah-blah. They were not always in the same meeting room or even the same building and so new faces showed and new stories were told.

Harry never considered himself a spiritual person. The twelve steps, written in 1952, contained a lot of references concerning God and surrendering to Him. It made Harry uncomfortable to read them over or even repeat them to himself in the quiet of his room when the thirst came upon him and soaked his sheets with the desire to give in, to give up. He sometimes dreamed of drinking from a river of alcohol filling him with equal parts guilt and immense satisfaction and woke up wanting to shred the twelve steps book with his bare hands.

He spoke to Olivia about the religious aspect. Nearing the end of the second week, they sat about the kitchen table each with a cup of coffee before them. The steam snaked into the air.

She asked him about the process and how he felt about it.

He said, "Sometimes it's hard to take it seriously, even though I can't imagine anything more serious. The God stuff. I've never been a big believer. One guy told me it helped, to read this out loud whenever the urge to drink came on." He patted his pocket, "I carry a copy of it with me. The Twelve Steps. And I do read it out loud and, for some reason, it does help. It could be the repetition of the words, you know, is kind of like meditation. It calms me so I like that part of it. It's the God part I have trouble reading. I stumble through it." He held up the book, "It feels outdated. A manual from another time."

She said, "Can I have a look? I'd like to read them."

"Sure."

She flattened the pages on the counter. He inwardly cringed every time her scarred hand appeared, doing normal everyday things. If she noticed, she never gave any outward indication.

The coffee steamed before her concentrated brow. In silence, she read.

Finished, she said, "It's not outdated. It's exactly what you need."

"How so?"

"The repeating theme in the steps is powerlessness and admitting you have no control over alcohol."

"Yeah."

"So, the way I read it, it's like you can't turn to yourself for help, because you've tried and failed every time. So you substitute yourself with something better, something that loves you even though you so often hate yourself. Something that truly sees you. It encourages you to stand before this other, being, God, whoever, completely naked, with all deceits stripped away. It forces introspection."

"So the God thing?"

"It doesn't matter, not really. The point is, people lie to themselves all the time to rationalize bad decisions or to keep drinking or whatever. This other, you can't lie to because it sees all. So, you're not praying to God, you're praying to the self inside you, the other that sees past all the bullshit and won't let you pull the wool over your own eyes. It's always been there, it's just been hogtied and shackled by the need for alcohol. You're providing it with the key. And if you do happen to believe in God? The easier it is to submit. You shouldn't struggle with something so inconsequential. In the end, the purpose is truth. To find out why you drink. Then you can heal. And if you're lucky enough to understand it, you can share the knowledge with others."

He felt better after that conversation and every time he read the twelve steps after, he never stumbled over the 'G' word again. He felt well on his way to recovery and had to caution himself each time to take it slow because alcohol addiction wasn't a beast easily tamed. Olivia provided him with the motivation and although he knew it'd be a lifelong battle, there was wisdom in the advice to taking every day one at a time. Sometimes, he would go a whole morning without even thinking about drinking and it would surprise him into smiling. He looked forward to going a whole day, hell, a whole week, without rubbing his hand over the upper lip, imagining the bubbly suds breaking over his tongue. That would be a time to celebrate…with coffee. Maybe even a fancy mocha! Yeah-yeah!

Three weeks into the program, Harry considered a sponsor. He was told most successful recoverers all had one. They would be someone to call, an alcoholic like him, when the urge became too strong and the demons pressed against his window at night, complete with frosty mugs of beer in each hand. Having someone to talk with, who has walked the same road as you, increased the chances of recovery and abstinence. Maybe Olivia could act as a surrogate sponsor. Smart kid, that one. She had plans for them. He already knew she wanted to move. They had been looking for places, not too far from his work yet far enough where they would both feel they were doing something new and of course, so the Jackal would have a harder time finding her. Making life changes while in the early stages of recovery was discouraged but he could tell Olivia couldn't wait any longer. She prowled the house, glancing out windows, always tapping the knife at her waist. Terrified the bad guy knew where she lived and would pay her a visit. To tell the truth, it scared the crap out of Harry. Every time he walked into their home, he called out to her and for the split second before she answered, his guts coiled in turmoil, expecting silence in return. Compared to her, after what she had been through, his fear paled against it. This realization did nothing to lessen his own terror. Feelings were hard to compare between people because they were so personal and subjective. So they were going to move and he would just have to deal with it. He reviewed the real estate sites on his lunch hour. He hoped to find a place in his price range and not too far away from his work. The idea of a long commute fighting traffic wasn't appealing to him. The move was the second part of her plan.

They talked of it one night after Harry, unable to sleep with sweaty and palsying hands, crept to the kitchen for a glass of water to clear his head. If there had been a bottle of anything lying about he would have downed it in one go. Before his first meeting at Alcoholic's Anonymous, Olivia had him walk her all around the house to collect all the alcohol he had hidden. Every cache had been found. She even found the small bottle of whiskey he put in the back of the toilet. His emergency stash. Even though he would have loved to have a nip of anything, there was nothing left. Olivia had seen to that. And he fought the urge to buy more every day when leaving work. It lessened every day, but sometimes the urge to drink tackled him and held him down like a bully as if it were saying, *thought I was done with you punk? Not by a long shot. You and me are welded together at the soul. Go ahead and have a drink. You know you will so just give in.* So, that night, he went to get a glass of water because there was nothing in the house and the stores were all closed and lucky for him that they were. He would have crept out to get a bottle of something, of anything. He was sweating about it in the kitchen and didn't notice Olivia walk in and when he did, her presence startled him and his face reddened with guilt. Being Olivia, she didn't comment on it. Instead, peeling an orange, she smiled at him and said, "Couldn't sleep either?"

"No. Don't know why. What about you? What woke you up?"

"The night. The wind. Snow pellets tapping at my window. Take your pick. All noises are scary at night. I'm so tired Dad. Tired of being scared most of the time."

"I'm sorry."

She shrugged.

"Is there anything we can do about it?"

She nodded, popping a slice in her mouth. When she finished chewing she said, "I'm working on it. Part of a three-step plan. To help me feel safe. Well, safer anyways."

Harry, with water in hand said, "Three-part plan huh? What are all the parts?"

"Part one: Operation get daddy sober. Part two: Give the bad guy the slip by moving. Part three: It's a secret."

"Even from you?"

"Oh, I know what it is. I'm ready for it and not ready for it, you know? Like looking through the tops of your skis before going down that giant hill. Exciting, scary and still unsure if you want to go through with it."

"Really? Now, I'm intrigued."

She winked.

And that was the last they talked of it. Curious. Very curious. He was anxious to get the move done so he could see what step three was.

The move would be a big change and any change was to be avoided on the journey to sobriety. He would have to give the sponsor idea a little more consideration. For now, he would be there for Olivia and that would have to be enough. On the computer screen on a real estate site, a house caught his eye. A smaller house. Still, the two of them didn't need a lot of room. And it was close to work, hell, really close. He could bike to it in the summer. Even better, the house was situated a block from a police station. Why was it so low priced in the city? A fully detached bungalow? Must be something wrong with it. He perused the upbeat description and saw the problem. The classic fixer upper. The house needed a lot of work. Over eighty years old? No telling what problems were there. Harry and home renovations didn't do well together. He once stapled his thumb to a baseboard. Frank still laughs about it. What about Frank? He's a handy bastard. Hell, he has his own contractor business! He would help wouldn't he? Harry would have to pay him and not just for the materials. It wouldn't surprise him if he had to pay Frank for his time the frugal jerk. Frank made Scrooge seem generous, but c'mon! After what Olivia's been through and the fact they are related, that ought to count for something, right? Hmmm. Maybe, maybe not. Frank was a cheap bastard. Harry sent the link to Olivia's iPad. He had sent her about twenty so far and everyone sent a trill of excitement through him. Who knew he wanted to move so much? Maybe the idea of a fresh start appealed to him. The problem lay in the fact that although the place may be new, the same old asshole (him) was moving there. The thought did nothing to diminish his excitement. He glanced at the clock. Time to go. Leaving the office, he couldn't wait to go home and discuss the potential homes with Olivia. A house by the police station. He liked it.

-19-

He had seen her. So beautiful. How could he hope to stay away? Like bugs under his skin, he had to scratch. The itch wouldn't go away by ignoring it or trying to find someone new to fill the void. No one could fill it. He would have to accept it. Even before he had taken her, the other girls he took were identical to Olivia and that was no accident. Early on, he recognized he would have to grab her and make her his. All those other girls, delightful distractions they were, yet they weren't Olivia, not even close. Everything about her touched something inside him. He tingled everywhere, thinking about her. He couldn't stay away, couldn't think of starting another place without her. She was the key. She was his palpitating heart. He needed her. Her movements strummed the music of his soul.

He turned down streets, gripping the steering wheel until his knuckles turned white and his jaw ached from grinding his teeth. The familiar street. He was near her. He felt her pull on him, like a black hole sucking in matter. He couldn't resist her. He had to see her.

He circled the block, wary of the police although he knew he needn't be. They could not allocate resources to the girls' protection indefinitely. Especially since they believed the Jackal had moved on. They couldn't conceive of a reason of why he would return to Olivia or the other girls. Considering all the steps he had taken to remain anonymous, he knew the stupidity of his actions. Even though the police hadn't identified him he was taking a needless risk. A stupid move. He berated himself to get the hell out of there! Terrible idea, even being in this area. The Mount Everest of idiocy. Why did he even come this way? Time to go, time to get out of the area. He decided to do just that and surprised himself by parking out front of a house two doors down from Olivia's. Even worse, he got out of the car and patted his pocket to make sure the stun gun was there. The hard shell reassured him. Was he doing this? Completely crazy. Still, his feet crunched in the snow, toes pointing inexorably towards her front door, the light above the door spilling across the front step like a golden welcome mat.

-20-

Winter in Canada brought the darkness of evening early. Olivia could go into the kitchen, the soft light of day a pleasant backdrop framed by a frosty window, fill a glass of water and when she looked up, stars studded the black sky. It seemed that quick to Olivia. And she noticed the night now. She was attuned to it. Night brought the fear. Night hid the devils lurking beyond the brightness of her window, or the men wearing animal heads wanting to take her and sneak her away like a princess in some twisted fairy tale. A fairy tale where the currency was an ear, some toes and fingers as well.

The worst time of her day was waiting for her dad to get home. Sitting in the living room, the street outside situated in her peripheral vision, the glow of the iPad in her lap, she waited for the headlights of his car to announce his arrival. She used one finger to tap the screen while reviewing the properties her dad sent her when he was supposed to be busy at work. Her other hand trailed fingers over the handle of the knife. It had become a part of her. She couldn't imagine being without it. And she wouldn't ever be. Not if she could help it.

When the doorbell rang, to say it startled her would be an understatement. She jumped enough the iPad popped off her lap and landed on the carpet. Her entire body shook as shots of adrenaline raced through her. She hadn't noticed and hadn't been alert enough to see someone walk up to her door. She had placed herself by the window for that purpose. So she could see outside and be prepared for anything. She feared getting complacent. Complacency could get her killed. The relative safety of the past month must have softened her defences. She touched the knife at her hip. She unbuttoned the tab around the handle and slid the knife out to make sure it was clear of obstructions. From her position on the couch, she could see someone approach up until they reached the front door. Once the person arrived at the door, a bush and pillar blocked her view. She didn't see anyone walk up to the door. She missed that initial sight and again became disturbed by her lack of awareness. Who was at the door? She patted the knife at her side and noticing she had been holding her breath, exhaled to calm her jerking heart.

Her feet touched the carpet. She stood, listening. On silent feet, she crept toward the front door. She would be able to see who stood there through a small window, but then the person could see her too. Angling herself, she continued to the door. She spotted an exhale of cold breath. The Jackal wouldn't stand there would he? He wouldn't be this obvious after being so careful for so long. Didn't make sense. Always better to be safe. No need to rush. Caution was now the rule. She knew who it wasn't. It sure as shit wasn't her dad. Her dad would've just walked in and she would have seen the lights of his car pull in. She wasn't expecting anyone else and she could think of no one she wanted to see. She could ignore the doorbell and wait for the person to go away. Staying in the shadow of the hallway, Olivia leaned her head closer, to see who stood there. When she got a glimpse, her gaze took on the aspect of someone who had been struck with a hammer. Her mouth lost moisture and her lips stuck to her teeth. The person turned to leave and Olivia rushed to the door, unlocked it and swung it open.

• • •

"Dale?"

"Hey Olivia."

They stared at each other, time and circumstances making them little more than strangers. Olivia flicked her hair to cover her ear and then shoving the missing fingered hand in her pocket, offered a shy smile.

Dale said, "Sorry, I should have called. I didn't have your number anymore."

"No, no. That's okay. You wanna step in?"

"Yeah. Just for a second. I've got to get home."

She moved back so he could squeeze in the small foyer and he shut the door behind him. Talking at once they said,

"How have you—"

"It's good to—"

Olivia, smiled and said, "Sorry. Go ahead."

"It's, uh, good to see you."

"Yeah, you too. It's been so long ago since I last saw you."

"Five years. It is a long time."

A pause in the conversation gave Olivia time to study the bunny ears that paralleled her shins. Jeez. Wearing her bunny slippers. Nice one. She lifted her eyes and noticed Dale hadn't changed much. Except for the beard. He never had a beard when she knew him but he was a kid then. He was right. Five years is a long time. The eyes were the same. Kind eyes, full of compassion. She felt her own welling up. He adored her upon a time. He would have done anything for her. How could he like her anymore? Mangled, ugly, used and abused, what did she have to offer him or anyone? What was he doing here? To remind her of what she lost? Petty thoughts and she knew it. He came to see her because he cared. He always cared. He had always been kind to her and to everyone he met. To see him reminded her of all she had lost. It hurt her and she projected her own insecurities onto him. She exhaled, not wanting to lift her head and reveal her shiny eyes even though she stood in shadow. The doorbell rang again and she emitted a little yelp. Her hand gripped her knife. Dale noticed the movement and his eyes bulged. For a moment she felt ashamed.

The door opened behind Dale and Frank paused, sensing the awkward moment.

He said, "Why's the door unlocked?"

"Hey Uncle Frank. You remember Dale?"

His dark gaze eyed Dale with suspicion. "No. I don't."

"I dated him. A long time ago."

"Oh. Hi, Dale."

Dale nodded and said, "Sir."

"Sir? I'm not in the army. You can call me Frank."

They crowded each other in the small foyer. Olivia wished Frank would just spit out what he came for.

Olivia said, "Dad's not home yet."

"What? Oh. Yeah, I noticed his car wasn't in the drive."

To Dale, Frank said, "Is your car on the street?"

Dale said, "Yeah. I didn't want to block the driveway."

Dale handed Olivia a piece of paper.

"Here's my number. Please call me. I'd like it if you would."

"Okay. I'll do that."

Dale smiled, "Great. That's…really great. Best time to get me is in the evenings. During the day, I'm in class and I have my phone turned off."

Olivia said, "Class?"

"Yeah. Second year of law school."

"How's that going?"

"Good. Good. A lot of work, a lot of reading. But interesting, for the most part."

Frank stood next to them, frowning, watching the exchange with squinted eyes. Dale glanced at him and turned to Olivia. "Well, I better get going."

"Okay. I'll call you."

"Great." He turned to the door. Frank already had it open for him. Dale stopped at the door and said, "You look great Olivia. I hope you know that."

He continued out the door and Frank closed it behind him, a little too hard for Olivia's liking.

She said, "What's your problem?"

"Mine? What's yours?"

"Staring him down like that? Really?"

"Um, excuse me. Do we know who the other kidnapper is?"

Olivia rolled her eyes, "Please! Dale's not the Jackal."

"How do you know that?"

"I just do."

"Very scientific of you. You should join the police force."

"What are *you* doing here?"

His mouth clamped shut and his eyebrows dropped. "I left my hammer drill here. Just came by to grab it."

The doorbell rang.

Olivia twitched and her hand drifted to the knife.

Frank said, "Jesus. Relax would ya?"

Frank opened the door. A Swiss Chalet delivery driver stood on the stoop. He wore a ball cap and held a bag of steaming food in his arms. The pillar cast a shadow on the front of his body. Steam from his mouth billowed from the darkness of his face.

He said, "That'll be $34.50."

Olivia said, "I didn't order anything.

"What number is this? Eighty-nine?"

"No. That's the next house over."

"Huh? Which way?"

Olivia pointed to her left.

"That way."

"Thanks. Sorry about that."

"No problem."

-21-

The next day, the Jackal lay in his bed staring up at the sun cast pillars where the light snuck through the curtains on his ceiling. He didn't want to get out of bed. The covers were warm and besides that, he couldn't summon the energy. His stomach clenched like a fist. He glanced at the bedside clock. It read 1:37pm. He had been up since 4:00am. Thoughts of Olivia tortured him. Her beauty broke his heart. He had missed his opportunity. He could've taken her away and they could be together for as long as she would last. Only there had been a fucking party at her house last night and he didn't even make it onto her lawn before bolting away. There was no way to do it without witnesses. Too much risk and now, after the moment of seeing her, his pain waxed stronger. The very thought of leaving his bed sapped his energy. This must be what they called depression. He had always thought depression affected the weak-minded, those who perpetually wallowed in self pity like a pig in their pen, too stupid to realize they lived in shit. How could it affect him? The all-powerful Jackal! A man of indomitable will. To feel this…soft, didn't seem real. A sigh turned into a sob. Fucking weakling! He swallowed his sorrow as best he could. He gripped the sheets in his fists. He couldn't stay in bed forever. He had things to do. He needed a reprieve from the pain Olivia's loss caused him.

What did he do before? When the desire to take her became so strong his hands shook? When the image of her lying on her bed in the pink room called to him, suffusing him with need and when he realized he wasn't quite ready to destroy her he had at least been able to visit his others. Pound his anger into their soft flesh supplanting Olivia's face and voice, their screams her screams, their pleas her pleas. There had always been the other girls. The ones he didn't hold out on. Only after he glutted himself on their fine skin would the desire subside. He could function again, wear the face others saw, never suspecting his terrible true one.

He shifted in bed. Was that the answer? To take another in her place? It would have to be. How could he hope to function otherwise? He thought of Jen. Between her and Lucy, she resembled Olivia more. The face. The way she cried and pleaded was almost identical to Olivia's. If he took her, played out his fantasies on her instead of Olivia, it might provide him room to breathe. But then he would be back to the problem of Olivia. He would worry about that later. Thinking about Jen, he became aroused. Depressed people don't get hard-ons. He grinned while considering Jen. Her despondency troubled him. Near the end, before she had been freed by Olivia, he noticed Jen would escape into her mind whenever they entered the room. She would become so detached it was like fucking a flesh mannequin. He had considered her for the provisioning room and she would have been there shortly if Olivia hadn't intervened. His erection throbbed. He could break her out of her funk. Nothing like terror to sharpen an otherwise dull mind. Might be time for a visit.

Where might she be? At home? He had failed to keep an eye on his other girls because he had been mourning his loss. Olivia dominated his thoughts since she had escaped him. Still, it wouldn't be hard to find her. The news archives would help. And Lucy? She made the talk show circuits. Not into hiding that one. It almost seemed like she didn't worry about him. Silly girl. She would be fun to break. The refocussing of his goals energized him. Now, he had something to look forward to. Planning, hunting and the taking. All of it culminating in a night of delight and plaintive screams. His erection ached. He slipped out of bed. Time for a shower. Time to find release. Which one to take first? Jen appeared to be the more broken of the two. Ready to accept her death. Maybe she had been waiting for it all this time, waiting for him. In that regard, it would be downright rude of him to not make a house call.

-22-

Olivia and Harry decided to move to the house in the city, near downtown Hamilton and the police station. Initially, they almost passed on it. Harry couldn't do the work needed on the place to make it habitable and to hire out someone else would be too costly. Harry would have to ask Frank to help and the thought of it stressed him out and he almost quashed the whole idea then. It shouldn't have. Frank was his brother for crying out loud and they did get along, for the most part. Truth was, Frank was singularly the most selfish person he knew and if he wasn't his brother, he didn't think Frank would be someone he liked. Sadly, the inverse was also true. The tension caused him to wipe at his upper lip more and more. Olivia made sure he went to the meetings by going with him and her supportive presence was welcome. It also kept her from being home alone at night. She didn't like the night. Harry kept inviting Frank to dinner for the purposes of asking for help and Frank kept declining citing work responsibilities. Harry told Olivia that Frank suspected coming by would end up costing him. She thought Harry was correct but she also thought it more simple than that. Frank's work did keep him busy and family had always been secondary to him, like something he had to deal with because it was expected of him, an obligation. They couldn't go ahead with the house unless Frank agreed to lend a hand. Let's be real here, unless Frank did most, if not all the work, they couldn't even consider the house downtown. Harry worried someone would snap up the house while they sat around waiting for Frank to show up. Because of the state of the house Olivia thought it unlikely. The house, although situated in a convenient place, possessed the derelict air of a squatter's abode. No doubt some homeless people would be upset to see it sold.

During this time, Dale and Olivia spoke to each other on the phone often. They were getting to know each other again even though it could never be the same. How could it? They were both such different people now. Funny, before her unfortunate incarceration, she felt the powerful one in the relationship. Not to say he would take her shit if she tried to take advantage of him. No, it was more that he would do more for her than she would ever do for him. That he loved her more than she loved him. Nothing would be inconvenient to him if it helped her. She remembered once, phoning him after a night out with her friends, drunk at a house party, asking him to come pick her up and drive all her friends home. He did it. No complaints about it or expectation of repayment. Even when her friend Heather puked in the back seat, he cleaned it up the next day before she could. By the time she showed up with coffee and bagels, the car was spotless. If that were her, she wouldn't have picked him up. She would have told him to call a cab and fallen back asleep before she hit the hang up button. Strange, to think such thoughts now, years later. She never thought she took him for granted. In retrospect, maybe she did.

Now she felt afraid and excited at the same time. What did he think of her? She had so much baggage now. Scarred, externally and internally. She refused to leave the house to meet him for coffee. She felt safe leaving the house with her dad and didn't feel comfortable with anyone else. He offered to chaperone her around and she turned him down with stuttering and inadequate words, unable to describe to him the terror the offer inspired. She just couldn't do it. Not yet. All those faces in the crowd and one of them could be *him,* the Jackal, and she wouldn't know it. Stalking her, waiting for a moment when she would be vulnerable to take her away again or just end her. Odd considering she could go to the meetings with her dad. Her dad just made the outside world appear not so scary, like he carried a staff of safety with him. Or it could be as simple as Harry being her dad. Olivia thought it better to stay home, in relative safety, with the alarm chain under her shirt ready to depress in a moment despite the gallant offerings of Dale's protection. And that's what she did. Stayed warm and comfortable inside while winter piled up beneath her windows, brightening up the night with a crystalline white carpet while contemplating the new house.

She studied the floor plans, dreaming of what could be done to it to make it more secure. She wanted it impenetrable to those unwelcome. They just needed Frank's help to make the place habitable first. When he agreed to come over for dinner, it took them both by surprise.

Harry and Olivia prepared a roast dinner with Yorkshire pudding, one of Frank's favourites and intended to stuff him into a stupor so he would readily agree to assist them in restoring the house at a significantly discounted price. Free would be ideal but knowing Frank, unlikely.

They fed him, both Harry and Olivia drinking Coke and being unusually accommodating and nice to Frank. One of them was always ready to top up his plate with roasted potatoes, fork more meat on his plate and be up in a flash if he needed another drink. This served to provoke a squint-eyed suspicious gaze from Frank. Frank, leaning back and dabbing at his mouth with a napkin, said, "That was wonderful. Now that I've been fattened up, can you two schemers tell me what this is all about?"

Harry said, "Schemers? What do you mean?"

Olivia feigned shock with a raising of eyebrows.

"For the past two weeks you've been trying to get me over for dinner. Even I know I'm not that likeable. And roast beef? Olivia hates it. She always has."

Olivia said, "I can't believe you remembered something like that."

"I'm a genius. I remember everything. So, what's this all about?"

Olivia said, "Proclaiming yourself a genius doesn't make it true."

Harry shot a reproachful glance at Olivia, his neck apple bobbing, and said, "We want to buy a house."

Frank held up his hands, "Whoa. We talking a loan? You know the interest rates are fluctuating like crazy right now. The market isn't all that steady. I don't have as much ready cash as people think you know and I don't feel comfortable..."

Harry said, "Not a loan. I can buy the house. That's not a problem. The problem is it's quite a fixer upper and I'm not much of a fixer. But you, you're a successful businessman. A contractor no less!"

Frank rolled his eyes, "Your flattery is transparent and ridiculous. So what? You want me to fix it up for you? How much free time do you think I have?"

Harry said, "For now, all we want is for you to take a look at the place with us. Maybe we can knock a few more bucks off the price and then, you know, give us your opinion on what work needs to be done."

"What if my opinion includes knocking the house down and starting over?"

"Then we don't buy it and you save us a ton of cash. C'mon man, I never ask you for anything."

"Alright, alright! I'll do it. Make the appointment for tomorrow. You're lucky I have an opening in my schedule."

Harry said, "Perfect! Thanks Frank!"

Olivia said, "Looks like you earned yourself some pie, Frank."

"Apple?"

"Of course. With french vanilla ice cream."

Frank grinned and rubbed his hands together. Olivia stood and his smile faded. He said, "Just curious. Would I have gotten pie if I said no?"

Olivia smiled and said, "Don't be crazy Frank. Of course not."

•　　•　　•

They all went to check out the house the next night when the temperature had the nerve to drop to -24 degrees Celsius. Harry ran out to the car, started it to warm it up and sprinted back inside like someone was chasing him. Once inside he said, "Damn it's cold! My nose hairs froze immediately!"

Frank sneered and said, "Pansy."

Olivia liked and disliked the cold weather. She liked it because she could wear a toque and mitts to cover her injuries and the purple toque and matching scarf was flattering to her skin tone. She disliked the cold because, well, because it was cold. But at least she was able to wear her knife around her waist without looking like a weirdo. Her bulky winter coat covered it nicely. She had cut a hole in the pocket just so she could reach it from the inside. She didn't tell her dad because when she did it she thought it was a little paranoid and maybe it was but hell, she felt better with it like that so screw paranoia. It made her feel better to be able to get at it with ease. She kept touching it, a physical guard against the terrors of the outside world.

The real estate agent wore blue eyeshadow. A lot of it. Her hair had been sprayed into a helmet. Olivia doubted a bullet could penetrate the shell of chemicals protecting it. What saved her from being full-on ridiculous was her smile. It radiated genuine warmth and Olivia could picture what she looked like as a child because of it. Following her aromatic trail of perfume and hairspray, Frank, Harry and Olivia toured the house. A bungalow featuring original hard wood floors and the cluttered, claustrophobic tiny rooms common in older homes, Olivia liked the place although it was apparent even to her eyes there would be a lot of work to do. The pictures on the real estate site exaggerated many qualities while hiding others. Since it was a single storey, she wouldn't feel the fear of being trapped upstairs. To her, there would always be an escape route and if she had to jump out a window like an action movie star, the ground would be a lot closer to meet her. They followed the real estate lady—Grace?—to a set of double doors. Beyond the doors, the backyard stretched out before them. A surprisingly large lot. Unheard of in the city. Usually people were crammed on top of one another you could reach your hand out a window on the side of your house and touch the neighbour's home.

Olivia loved the backyard. A perfect size for what she wanted to implement next. Frank studied the structure of the house, feeling for drafts at windows, flushing toilets, kneeling down to peer at the floorboards. A study in concentration, he examined everything with a frown, causing Grace to peer at him from time to time, intuitively knowing the sale depended on his say so.

Olivia knew Harry liked it too. He walked around wide-eyed with his cheeks curved upwards. What did Frank think? Hard to tell when he wore his professional, unreadable face like he did now. Did he hate it? She hoped not. She touched the handle of the knife through the hole in her pocket. In times of stress, the knife provided comfort. She wanted this house. It possessed potential, this little house on a huge lot. It would be nice to knock down a few walls and open the place up. She thought she could do it. Even without Frank's help, she found she wanted to do it. The idea of building and creating brought on a pleasant feeling. During the entire brief tour, which to Olivia lasted an eternity because she really, really wanted the place, Frank merely grunted, nodded or frowned. He scribbled furiously into a notebook while Grace expounded on the finer points of the older home situated conveniently within the city. He didn't speak to them until they were in the car and headed for home after promising Grace they would call her soon. Harry had to prod him, producing loud sighs as he drove and glaring at Frank expectant of some sort of comment. Frank kept quiet until Harry elbowed him in the arm while reaching for the radio, trying to sell it as an accident. Olivia smiled in the back seat.

"Hey! What'd you do that for?"

"Sorry. I was reaching for the radio."

"The radio is over there. My arm, which you dug your womanish elbow into, is right here."

"Womanish? Can an elbow be womanish?"

"Yes. Yours is distinctly feminine."

"Hmm. Yeah. So what'd you think of the house?"

"Oh. You should definitely buy it."

"Really?"

Olivia straightened in the back seat and leaning closer to hear, felt the seatbelt tighten on her shoulder.

"For sure. What it'd cost to repair you'll more than get back from resale. All in all, it's not bad off. Some rewiring needs to be done, some plumbing, and there are quite a few areas with water damage. Have to get in behind the walls to see if the wood is rotten but relatively inexpensive for what you'd get back from it. Oh, and the roof looks suspect."

"Relatively inexpensive? Is that because you're giving me the family discount little brother?"

"Huh? Discount?"

"Yeah. A significant discount."

Frank's mouth tightened as though he had bit into a lemon. He said, "Well, I don't know. It's winter. Not many jobs going on. It'd be good to have income coming in."

"Are you telling me you are intending on charging me full price?"

"Well, maybe not full-full price."

"What? Like five percent off?"

"I was thinking two-point-five percent."

Harry's hands kneaded the steering wheel. His lips disappeared into a line. Olivia knew the look. It was the look she got when she arrived home late from a high school party or the time he found a joint in the pocket of her jeans. Harry was going to blow his stack. Frank could see it too and he shifted in his seat, positioning himself further from Harry.

"Are you fucking kidding me? I know you can be a bit of a robot, which is probably why you're so successful but this is too much. I never wanted to bring this up. I never thought there'd be a situation in which I would have to. But Frank, you're going to do this for free. I'll pay for the supplies, at cost, for what you get them for and you're going to do the work for free. You owe me, Frank."

"But that's—"

"You owe me! Who gave you the money to start your business, huh? No bank would give you the money, remember that? It was me Frank, me working two jobs, going to school and I gave you all my savings. Did I charge you interest on it? Did I complain about it even though I went into debt on the student loans? I didn't work two jobs to go into debt, Frank! I worked two jobs to pay for your school! I did that for you! Now, here I am, asking for help and you sit there, wanting to make a fucking profit off me! No way, man! No fucking way. You're gonna do this. And by God, you're gonna like it!"

They drove in silence. Olivia could see her father shaking. Harry didn't get mad often so when he did, he released a few years worth of anger. Frank kept his face turned towards the passenger window. The streetlights flashed in his hair.

Frank said, "Okay. I can do that."

Mollified, Harry's shoulders dipped down. He said, "Good."

"Well, when you're right, you're right."

The wheels turned underneath them and the winter wind pushed against the windows. Olivia exhaled, glad the tension had passed and ecstatic they were going to buy the house.

Frank said, "Did you say, 'by God, you're gonna like it.'?"

"I might have."

Olivia said, "You definitely did, Dad."

Frank flashed teeth and said, "Do I really have to like it, Harry? Really?"

Struggling to keep a straight face, Harry said, "Damn right you do."

-23-

Jen's reality had been knocked loose of its moorings while in captivity. Being returned home, free from torture didn't return her to her former self. That person died in their house. At home now, she would pass hours in a fugue. Sitting in the kitchen, a coffee forgotten in her hand, her breakfast untouched before her, she would be aware of her family moving around her. They would speak to her, ask her questions yet their voices took forever to reach her. She answered her mother's question, of whether she wanted toast with jam for breakfast to realize her mother was no longer in the kitchen, the question having been asked hours before. She didn't wonder if she had lost her mind. She knew it. She had lost it in the pink room where all her illusions of safety and the privacy of her own body were stripped from her by men in animal masks. Voracious men with salacious and limitless appetites. Men who made a meal of her flesh. How to return from that? You can't. Every time the stump of her hand entered into view it reminded her of the room and those men. Physically, she came home and was welcomed with tears and hugs from her parents and her two sisters. Mentally, she never left the cotton candy room.

She knew her parents worried about her. She heard them talking in the night, wondering what to do. She wished she could tell them something, anything to relieve them of their pain. Jen found it difficult to differentiate between the real world and the bunkhouse of her inner mind. The place she created where she could disappear from the men. The floaty plane where at times, it seemed she hovered above her own body, witnessing transgressions against her flesh that her mind couldn't dredge any sympathy for. As though she were watching it on TV and the director failed in developing empathy for the main character.

Her sisters had been overjoyed to see her. They talked to her as though she were the old Jen, using jokes and sarcasm to communicate. She wasn't the old Jen and their words didn't reach her and they were young and did not have the patience or ability to break through the shell she constructed and soon found themselves back to their old routines, hanging with friends, going to parties, essentially doing all the things they did before, and during, Jen's disappearance. Jen, cognizant of her siblings distancing themselves, couldn't do anything to stop it nor could she summon the energy for the effort. Better to float along passively than to participate in the rest of her life.

Her parents didn't know what to do so they did nothing but do their best to make her feel loved and safe. They were stunned and overjoyed to have her back and had been convinced she was dead and they were still getting used to her being home and alive. For years after she disappeared her parents would lie in bed comforting each other, whispering kind platitudes about their daughter being alive while believing with dread certainty their daughter mouldered in a shallow grave in a field of nowhere. It was a new and welcome experience to have her home and safe. Most of the time, her mother spent the day sitting beside Jen, nearness being the only company her mother craved.

It had been two months since she had been freed from her nightmare and although she hadn't been captive for as long as Olivia, she did endure over two years of cruelty under both their hands and she felt dirty, guilty and not yet part of the normal world.

Jen loved having her mother near her. She wanted to tell her that but by the time the words passed her lips she would see shadows pooled in the room and she would be alone, her mother having left hours ago.

She had seen the Jackal in her hallway once wearing nothing but the mask and winter boots wet from the snow. An illusion. She knew it to be so because more often than not, the Gorilla would be right behind him, grunting while squeezing his erection in his fist. The Gorilla couldn't be there. Olivia had killed him. Even the cops said so. When they appeared from her imagination to stand before her, her eyes would widen and her remaining hand would caress the hard and puckered skin of her stump. She would blink and they would be gone. Not even the wetness from their boots remained on the floor.

Sometimes, at night, she would hear breathing from her closet. As she watched, the door would creep open on noisy hinges. The clothes jiggled on the hanger and then the head of a Jackal would emerge from the darkness with red eyes glaring at her from behind the mask. She would whimper, go to the place in her head and in a flash of time, it would be morning and her stump would be red and chafed from where she rubbed at it all night. The visions would come upon her at any time. She had no control over them. How could she ever feel

110

safe or get past what happened when at any moment her tormentors appeared before her? She needed help. This couldn't go on forever or she would visit the room in her head one time too many and never return from it, comatose and unresponsive to the loving administrations of her parents.

In the back of her house past her backyard the trees crowded together, their leafless branches holding hands to form a dense line. Snow provided a white floor with the scattered detritus from the trees marring the otherwise pristine surface. The land behind their home was owned by the government and was intended to remain a green-space, never to be developed. It was the main reason her parents bought the place years ago. They declined putting a fence up along the back so they could walk from their back door and into the woods. She loved the woods before she had been taken. Spent many hours tracking through it, following paths, squatting down to examine animal tracks. A few square kilometres, it would be almost impossible to get lost inside. If you just walked in a straight line you would end up on a road or walking into another suburban area. She felt at home in there at one time. Not anymore. She couldn't even conceive of leaving the house. Not without her parents. Even then, she would shake and tremble as her eyes darted everywhere, examining every dark corner and shadow waiting for a vision or the real Jackal to appear and strike her down. Better to stay home. Jen spent most of her time in her bedroom staring out the window, overlooking the woods. In those dark spaces beyond her window, she saw the Gorilla and the Jackal the most, their shadows emerging from the outline of the trees.

Too often she would catch sight of them, along the edge of the forest their heads craned up to watch her, unmoving. She would gasp, close her eyes and open them and sometimes they would still be there even though they weren't real. She wished her mind believed it. They had done terrible things to her. Said hurtful and evil words. After a time, the urge to fight them faded. Instead she created the special place to escape to and let them do their thing while she exhibited the participation of a corpse. Terrible as it was, the minuscule defiant part of her railed against this thought but she couldn't push it away. She began to believe she deserved what they had done to her. They did their best to convince her of it. A mixture of harsh words and kind tones and in a sick way, after a time their words made sense to her. How could this happen to anyone if in some way they hadn't earned it? They broke her down. She knew it, she had seen enough movies and read enough books about domestic violence to understand it. Their constant barrage of degradation wore at her armour. And once she decided she deserved whatever they did to her, it became easier to submit. Participate? Never. Stop fighting them? Absolutely. The ghosts of their cruelty haunted her and appeared to her in her house, in her closet and most often from the woods. They had no corporeality. The only substance they possessed is what she gave them in her mind.

Sitting in her bedroom, the TV droning on her dresser, wrapped in a fleece blanket, she glanced at the woods and saw the Jackal walking through them approaching her house. She dismissed it although her heart beat faster in her breast. Her mother turned on the vacuum downstairs. Usually someone stayed home with Jen. Her mom and dad rotated the duties, changing their holidays at work and burning through their sick bank to be with her. Could her mom see him? If she looked outside would she see him striding through the trees? She shook her head. Remember Jen, it's not real. She exhaled, closed her eyes, opened them and still he made his way to her house. She gasped but knew it couldn't be real. He manoeuvred through the woods, wearing a dark coat, dark jeans, boots and gloves with the Jackal's head tall and proud on his shoulders. She frowned. Almost every time she imagined him, he wore the mask and boots. Never clothes. Sometimes the Gorilla would show up trailing the Jackal. Sometimes, like now, just the Jackal appeared. He walked through the tree-line and stepped into her backyard with a determined and confident stride. She pulled the alarm chain out from under her shirt. She let it dangle on her chest and rubbed at her stump, pressing her fingers along the hardened skin.

She forced her eyes to take in the TV. Some talk show. She concentrated on their words and the crease in her brow softened. She peered into the backyard. No one stood there. No one walked there. She sighed, staring into the forest and then at the snow in her backyard. Were there footprints in the snow? So what. She had imagined their boots dripping on the floor didn't she? Sure, she thought, but when they were gone, the floor was dry wasn't it? If that is true, and she goddamn knew it to be true, then why were there still footprints in the snow? Could mean her delusions were becoming more advanced. Constant practice can do that. Practice makes perfect.

A thump sounded from downstairs, heard over the vacuum. After a few seconds, the vacuum motor died off. Silence from downstairs. Jen clicked off the TV.

"Mom?" Jen said, or thought she did. She scratched at her stump.

A creak sounded. She knew what stair that was. Fourth from the bottom. Mom had been on her dad to fix that for years. Someone was on the stairs. It had to be her mom. Maybe her mom did hear her. Unlikely though. Even if she had spoken she was too soft to hear unless you were in the room with her. Her hand drifted to the alarm around her neck. Her thumb ran along the top of the button.

She cleared her throat and said, "Mom?"

No answer except for another creak, near the top. That step moaned under the weight of her father. The girls and her mother were too light to disturb it. Someone big crept toward her. A dream? A vision? Had she spoken or, like so many other things, did it occur only in her head? No…she had spoken. A vein jumped in her neck. She stared at the open bedroom door, afraid to blink.

The Jackal appeared, framed in her doorway. Light reflected off the eyes deep in the mask giving them an otherworldly glow. A knife dripped blood onto the hardwood floor. She could hear it. More detailed than any previous illusion. The thump from downstairs, the blood on the knife. Did something happen to her mother? This had to be a dream then. She would wake up to find her mother alive and well, covering her in a blanket and telling her everything is fine. The police said it would be very unlikely she would ever see the Jackal again. He wouldn't risk it, they thought. This couldn't be real, could it?

His chest heaved under the dark coat. He stepped into the room, his tread heavy with intent. She could smell him. He stank of outside and sweat.

She said, "Are you real?"

"Time to take you home, my sweet Jen." The voice was muffled, echoey, from behind the mask.

"So you're real, then."

She held up the alarm on the chain, making sure he saw it. He lunged for her. She pressed the button.

She whispered, "Cops are coming."

He said, "Bitch!"

He clutched the chain in her fingers and wrenched it from her. How long would it take them to get here? No way to know unless he waited for them and he was not going to do that. Pressed for time, he couldn't make a quick escape if he took her with him and the realization quelled the brewing storm behind his eyes. No need to panic. Time to get creative.

He said, "Change of plans, then."

He grabbed her chin in his left hand and squeezed, holding her steady. Fear and acceptance rattled inside her frame. Afraid of death yet relieved her damaged self wouldn't have to struggle any longer. Easier to give in, to quit, than to fight. Better to submit. He raised the knife and she stared into his eyes with bovine placidity. In one swift movement, he swung the knife and buried it deep in the top of her head to sink into the softness of her brain. Blood sprayed out her nose and she sank into darkness with a gurgle.

•　　•　　•

The Jackal had to get out of there. He hadn't expected the alarm and knew how lucky he had been she hadn't pressed it earlier. He could be in cuffs right now, the Jackal mask ripped off him for all the world to see him, to know him. Luck like this couldn't last. Still, he had one last thing to do. It came to him with sudden inspiration. It was a struggle to get the knife out of her skull. He wiggled it back and forth and pulled it free, a squirt of blood following it out. He went to work with it. He rushed through it, wanting to move fast, wondering when the cops would get here and if he should even be doing this extra work at all. But he started and when he started something he hated to quit before he was done. He thought he worked fast but it felt like forever before he was finished. Time moved slow under stress. When he eased out the back door, the sirens were still some distance away. He set off through the woods. When the trees enfolded him, he removed the mask. He took off the reversible jacket and turned it inside out so now it was red. Blood red. After putting his gloves inside the mask, he stuffed it inside against his body and zippered up his jacket. He pulled a toque out of another pocket and put it on. Now he was just a dude going for a stroll in the woods. When he came upon the small river he walked in the slow moving water with ice building along the shoreline. He made it to his car without seeing one policeman or police cruiser. He felt pretty good. Although it didn't work out like he planned, under the circumstances it turned out better than he had any right to expect. And now he knew about the alarms around the necks. He would have to work a way around those. He still wanted a girl in his pen. And Lucy was out there, running free. She wouldn't be easy to get to. After the mess he left behind there would be a lot more security for the remaining survivors. He would have to expect increased police presence and who knew what personal protection they would employ? Interesting times ahead. He would wait them out. Wait until they lost interest like they did for Jen. And given enough time, they would do it again. Or he could go take Lucy and Olivia now, before the cops got organized. He rejected the thought before it fully formed. He wasn't ready yet. Not for her. In a very positive frame of mind, he contemplated the mentally rejuvenating effects of murder. He certainly felt better. Hell, he felt magnificent! He drove home listening to an angelic voice sing *Ava Maria.*

-24-

Part of Olivia's day included watching the news. One channel, CP24, reported the news all day. They would rerun stories in a smaller window and the rest of the screen would be filled with sports, scores and the weather. A nice drone in the background while she made the rounds of the house, ensuring all windows and doors were locked before settling down on the couch with a steaming tea beside her and the iPad in her lap. The tension she felt upon escaping the pink room was fading with time. Before, she would jump at the house settling or a strong wind rattling the window frames. She would examine the snow around the house, peering through the window to see if any new footprints appeared overnight, certain, at some point, there would be. Olivia used to crouch under windows when she passed them convinced the Jackal hid outside, watching, waiting for a glimpse before he rushed in and snatched her. She had ground her teeth till her jaw hurt and clenched her muscles until they spasmed from unending fear of the Jackal returning for her. Free in body, prisoner in mind.

As part of Olivia's morning ritual, she still checked the snow outside the house for footprints but she was no longer certain there would be any. Even though she double checked every door and ensured the alarm panel's green light indicating operation still blinked cheerfully the oppressive air didn't weigh as heavy. She didn't feel eyes on her all the time. She no longer twitched when the furnace click-boomed in the basement to push warm air through the vents. With time, she might even become normal. Her hand rose to her ear. Well, as normal as she could ever be. She frowned and resumed her battle on the iPad with Candy Crush, determined to advance. Between listening to the news, playing Candy Crush and sipping on her tea, Olivia looked forward to the move with fear and excitement. After Frank committed to helping them (which still surprised Olivia) they moved ahead with buying the place. The purchase was conditional upon the sale of the house they now lived in but no one considered it an issue. On the weekend, she and her dad were going to clean the place up, splash some paint around and get rid of the clutter to prepare the house for viewing. She wondered what she would do when people came to the house for viewings. Weekend or evening viewings would be best. She didn't like leaving the house without her dad and she wouldn't leave the house with anyone else. Not Dale, not Frank, not anyone but her dad. Maybe she didn't trust Frank and Dale as much as her dad and thought it unfair and might have to work on her trust issues. She thought of Dale often and wondered what type of relationship, if any, they could have with each other. They were two very different people now. They related to each other through shared remembrances and she suspected they were already beginning to drift apart. He didn't want to bring up what she had been through, which was good because she didn't want to talk about it. Not to him and not yet and instead, they ended up talking around it.

He would discuss what he had been doing the last five years and since they both knew where she had been during that time, their conversation drifted to movies and music she hadn't seen or heard. Nothing to relate to with each other. She appreciated his concern, knew it to be genuine, though their conversations soon grew awkward and filled with long pauses. She felt him drawing away from her and found no reason to stop it from happening. The once pleasant intimacy from high school didn't exist any longer. They were both very different people than they used to be. Alien to each other, to be honest, they were on different planets. He wanted to maintain their friendship. She knew that. He admired her and told her he thought her stronger than he could ever hope to be. Circumstances drew out a strength she didn't know she had and she wouldn't wish what she had gone through on anyone. She had strength, sure, but the cost had been too great.

Deep in her own thoughts, her remaining index finger moving the candies about on the screen, it took a moment for the news on the TV to register. When it did, her mouth hung open and she dropped the tea on the carpet. Unconcerned about the tea, her eyes riveted to the TV as though pulled by some inexorable string. What was being reported didn't make sense. Jen had been murdered? Jen's mother had been killed? She slipped the knife out of the holster at her side and held it, the way a child would hold a teddy bear for reassurance. When the phone rang she screamed. She pressed the button on the cordless and held the phone to her ear before realizing she could be making a terrible mistake. What if it was *him* calling? But then he wouldn't call. He had never spoken to her. Her dad's voice flooded her ear. He would be home soon. He had heard the news too.

• • •

The detective arrived as Harry and Olivia sat down to dinner. Olivia didn't want to eat. The idea she may have to eat something never occurred to her. Her dad insisted and made grilled cheese sandwiches and set two glasses of orange juice on the table. Olivia's hand strayed to the knife at her hip. The tactile hardness of the handle felt cool under her fingers. She twitched and cringed at the sound of wind pulling and pressing against the windows and the vinyl siding of the house. All the progress she had made over the months evaporated in a moment. She had been reduced to the quivering mess she had been when she walked out of the dungeon. The news of the murder rattled her father. He kept wiping at his lip. She could tell he wanted to drink real bad. She wanted to tell him to call someone from AA but that would take him away from her and she didn't want that. She needed him here and knew it to be selfish but right now she didn't care. Maybe later, when her insides weren't pinched so tight. When she had time, she could feel guilty and go to an AA meeting with him. If she could summon the courage to leave the house ever again. And that was a big if. The detective knocked on the door as Harry raised the sandwich to his mouth. Olivia had expected someone from the police hours earlier. Considering she and Lucy were the likely next targets of the maniac, she thought the detective would have been out here trying to quell her rising fears. After the news had aired, two patrol cars arrived and parked out front of her house. Not long after, media vans swung to the curb. One officer, a young female with dark rimmed glasses, knocked on the door to tell them a detective would be out later. She didn't think later meant hours later, after it got dark.

Olivia stood as the detective entered the kitchen. Mid-thirties with an air of competence, he appeared slim and well groomed. His gaze missed nothing and although she sensed compassion in his eyes, there was a bit of steel there too. He wasn't the one she had met before. No outdated moustache on this guy's face. She frowned, "Who are you?"

"Detective Constable Davis."

"What happened to the other guy? The one with the terrible moustache."

Davis blinked, smiled and said, "I'm the new detective assigned to the case. The other guy is now the file coordinator. And yes, the moustache is terrible. Word is his wife won't let him shave it. Says it makes his chin look weak, whatever that means."

She stared at him.

He swallowed and said, "Well, I'm not exactly new. I've been working on this for a bit now."

"You're new to me."

"Uh, yeah."

She folded her arms over her chest and said, "And you're only introducing yourself to me now?"

"I had a lot of material to review. Video interviews, witness statements, physical evidence…it takes some time to get through." His hairline beaded with sweat under her scrutiny. He said, "Is it hot in here?"

Olivia said, "I'm quite comfortable."

Harry said, "Would you like a drink of something detective? Something cold?"

"No. I'm fine. Thank you."

Olivia's fear commingled with her irritation. Fear of the Jackal and irritation at not being told of a new investigator. When did this guy get assigned? She thought the police would involve her more considering she had been a prisoner of the freak they were investigating for five years. She didn't think she deserved to be treated this way, like some lame cast off character in a gruesome thriller. And waiting all afternoon for this guy to walk in all casual and cool as though her life wasn't at risk? It stunk and it pissed her off.

A sneer curled her lip as she said, "Better have something detective. You're going to be here awhile. You're gonna tell me what the fuck is going on and what you intend to do about it. I want to know your theories, if you have any, and I want to know what you're going to do to keep me safe. I've waited all afternoon for you. You're not going anywhere until I'm satisfied you've told me everything. Do we understand each other?"

Even though he was older than her, he deferred to her with the respect he would a demanding teacher in grade school. He nodded and said, "Yes ma'am." To Harry:"I'll have some coffee please. If you have it."

•   •   •

Harry set coffee before Detective Davis and made tea for Olivia. Davis pulled a camcorder from the bag he brought with him and after fiddling with the tripod for the right height he attached the camera to it. He pulled out a large notebook and taking a sip of coffee and nodding his appreciation to Harry he said, "The reason I brought the camera here is to ask you some follow up questions. Questions that I thought of when reviewing your previous interviews. Before we get to that I'm going to fill you in on the investigation and why it may seem to you the police may have dropped the ball. Before all that though, I'd like to say a few things to you first. Things you may have heard before but I think they are very important, okay?"

Olivia nodded. Harry sat beside her, a glass of water in hand.

"Okay. Good. First, I want you to know none of what happened to you is your fault. None of it."

Taken aback, Olivia muttered, "I know it."

"Good. I'm glad. I just want that to be clear. Nothing you said or did or didn't do caused this to happen to you. Some demented fuck-sticks got it into their head to do horrible things to people for their own benefit. No matter what you think you may have done, no one deserves what happened to you. No one. I find sometimes victims tend to apportion blame onto themselves. I want there to be no confusion here: you did nothing wrong."

Olivia's eyes shined and she said, "Thank you." She understood what Davis meant. Years in the prison she had thought some of the awful things done to her were her fault. If she did what she was told, acted a certain way, maybe they wouldn't have taken her toes. Maybe she would still have an ear. Deep inside, she believed they would have found a reason to mangle her and torture her because it was in their nature to do it. They got off on it. Believing it didn't lessen the feeling of being at fault. It didn't help that the Gorilla told her she was to blame for her own mutilation over and over again. Now, this detective told her what she already knew yet it helped to have someone else reaffirm it, someone who knew she needed to hear it. Maybe, in time she could believe it and assign the blame where it belonged. On the bastards who did this to her.

"No problem. Now, I'm going to tell you everything I know. You deserve nothing less."

•   •   •

After Davis left Olivia closed the door and locked it behind him. She felt exhausted and leaned her head against the door, her head swimming with information. He did indeed tell her everything. He gave her a candid run down of the investigation and what he told her had scared her. Maybe it would have been better if she remained ignorant of certain things. Too late now. Once learned she couldn't unlearn.

"Would you like another tea?" Harry said.

"No. I'm good. I think I'm going to bed. I have a lot going through my head right now."

"I bet." Harry put a hand on her shoulder and gave it a squeeze. "What'd you think of Davis?"

"I have more faith in him than the other guy. Determined for sure. Which is good for us."

"Yeah. I like him too."

"Goodnight Dad."

"Alright hon. If you need anything, let me know."

"I will."

Olivia climbed the stairs to her room rubbing the handle of the knife at her hip. She turned on her iPod attached to small twin speakers and flopped onto her bed, too tired to remove her clothing. The music proved a soothing backdrop to the turmoil of her thoughts as she reviewed her conversation with the detective. Davis laid out the entire investigation to her. She had a lot of questions at the end and more continued to travel the synapses of her brain on a highway to nowhere.

Everything started with her escape. The Guelph Police investigated her abduction but that soon hit a wall and all leads were exhausted and the file was forgotten and untouched. Until she escaped, the police had no idea women were being abducted and murdered. When they did find out, they had to investigate in reverse. When Olivia killed the Gorilla and helped the other girls to escape, she did it in the town of Erin. The Ontario Provincial Police were the responsible agency for the town. They were the primary investigators of the murders. They pulled resources from across the province to assist. Detective Davis, a seasoned homicide investigator was assigned the lead. These investigations were complex and required a vast amount of resources to conduct. They generate a mountain of information that needed to be sifted through to determine importance. The forensics officers spent over two weeks in the house. They recovered DNA and fingerprints. They recovered and identified the two poor women in the freezer. The found body parts of other women they couldn't identify. Victims generally don't have their DNA or fingerprints on file and there were no dental records to pursue. How to match an arm to a description of a missing girl? Or a femur for that matter? They were asking family of reported missing girls to submit DNA for comparison. It was a shot in the dark, but they took it. Anything to know, to end the pain for someone out there waiting for news. For now, the police could do nothing to give them closure.

The Gorilla, Shawn Grady, left evidence of himself all over the house. Why wouldn't he? It was his place according to the bank records and the land registry office. The Jackal left DNA and fingerprints too however he wasn't on file anywhere. That meant he had never been charged with any offence requiring DNA or fingerprints. If they did end up identifying him, they would have all the evidence they needed to convict. But in order to do that, they needed to find him. They exhausted all connections Shawn Grady had with anyone, anywhere. Grady fit the typical serial killer type. He was a loner and social enough to fit in but no close friends. He had been well liked in his job as an electrician. No one had a bad thing to say about him. Only the income he generated didn't cover the expense of his paid off house and his shiny new truck. A forensic audit of his financials couldn't trace the money back to any benefactor leaving the police wondering where the money came from. All it proved was Shawn Grady owned the house he converted into the prison where she had been kept. It did tend to support a theory the Jackal may be financially independent or well off. But other than that tidbit, there were no other avenues to pursue to determine his identity.

Then the police started backgrounds on the victims. How did these killers find them? Why were they chosen and how were they picked up? Olivia had been abducted in Guelph, Jen from Barrie and Lucy from Burlington. The two dead girls were last seen in London. Four different police services with different records and policies on how to investigate. Olivia's disappearance was treated as suspicious from the beginning and so a lot of time and resources was spent on the investigation.

Lucy's disappearance was suspicious but with no leads it had been soon investigated into a dead end. Jen had been fighting with her parents a lot and had run away from home more than once before. Barrie Police thought she had run off again. They didn't treat it as an abduction. A standard missing report was submitted with minimal follow up. Even if located she was over eighteen years old and the police couldn't make her go home. They could only determine her well being. The girls from London were escorts, advertising their services on the internet, meeting strange men in motel rooms. Sad to say, those girls vanished all the time. No one investigating these disappearances thought they had a serial rapist and killer running loose and the police services didn't communicate to each other other than putting the girls' names on the police computer database as missing.

This sort of thing happened before with Bernardo and Homolka. Bernardo, a prolific rapist operating out of Scarborough, met and was encouraged by Homolka to escalate to torture and murder. Although, Davis had said, Bernardo didn't need the encouragement. After that had happened the police put a system into place to track similar incidents across Canada. That way, if a guy like Bernardo committed crimes in Burlington, Scarborough and Brampton, the information would be collected in one database and the police agencies would be notified of the similar incidents and then pool their resources to find the perpetrator. This system, called ViCLAS, collected incidents of a certain nature. The abductions involving Olivia, Jen and Lucy were so unremarkable and dissimilar they didn't fit the criteria for a ViCLAS submission. No one had a clue they were connected until Olivia fought her way out of the basement.

Imagine trying to collect five-year-old evidence. Track down leads and re-interview people about years' past events. All trails to the victims were occluded by time. If there happened to be video, it would be long erased and gone. After having this explained to her, Olivia could appreciate the difficulties. Davis wasn't complaining. He wanted her to understand and know even though the likeliness of the evidence even existing was marginal, they still looked for it in the hope something would lead them to the Jackal. She knew he wanted to find him and wouldn't stop until he did. His determination swam behind his eyes.

During the video interview, Davis kept asking questions about her strange relationship with the Jackal. He wanted her perspective on why he treated her differently than Lucy and Jen. He smiled when she said, "How would I know that? He's fucking crazy. I don't know what makes crazy tick. I don't even wish I did."

He turned off the camera, concluding the interview and Olivia said, "You spent a lot of time on my thoughts on the Jackal. Can I ask why?"

Folding up the wires he said, "Absolutely. I waited to tell you this. I didn't want it to influence your interview. It's pretty messed up."

"I can take it."

He said, "I know. You've proven it the hard way. Probably the hardest way there is. So here it is. Jen got it pretty bad. He did things to her. We think it happened after, you know, he killed her, though I think it was either a message or even worse, a compulsion."

"What did he do?"

"He cut her up. He took her ear, two fingers and three toes."

Olivia's heart stalled in her chest. Little nodules of skin appeared on her arms as a chill overtook her.

She said, "Like me. He made her like me."

Davis packed away the gear, clicked the hard case shut and sat before her. He placed a hand on her mangled one and didn't flinch. Not even a little. She liked him for that.

"You're the key, Olivia. I don't want to scare you but you need to know these things to protect yourself. I think those other girls were practice. I think the Jackal wanted you from the start, from a long time ago. That's why all the girls looked like you. The Gorilla? Just a game to him. All you girls were less than human. Playthings in a twisted doll house. To the Jackal though, you were someone special. Someone he fantasized about and if he took you or killed you, the illusion he built up around you would shatter and then what would he have? I believe the Jackal knew you and wanted you for years and took up a partner to mold and intimidate for the express purpose of one day owning you. The Gorilla was a buffer. A straw man to the Jackal. You were always the prize. I know at some point in your life you've met the Jackal. It wouldn't surprise me to learn you know him, when we catch the asshole."

Sweat dotted her brow. Know him? The Jackal? Why is that so absurd? Didn't she have these very same thoughts before? Why else the extra care the Jackal spent on her?

Olivia said, "Wait. Is that why you were asking about the guy from the recreation centre? The guy I'd seen at the university the night I was taken?"

"I want to know who he is. I want to know why he was there. And I'm going to talk to everyone that ever swam in that pool or walked in those halls until I know who he is."

He stood, "I gotta go. Here's my card and my personal number. Call me anytime. If you have a thought you think is silly, call me anyways. I want to know. After spending so much time with the Jackal, you have insight I think would be stupid to ignore." Davis nodded at Harry and said, "Look after each other."

"You can bet on it."

Davis left, creating as much mystery as he dispelled. Did she know the Jackal? The idea she might already know the Jackal, maybe spoken to him before, maybe even bumped into him made the hair on her arms stand at attention and let her know fear has no limits.

She fell asleep on top of her blankets with her iPod still playing. She dreamed of the Jackal that night. He snuck into her room and sat on her bed. In her dream, she awoke to him stroking her hair. Her head lay in his lap and she looked up at him. She asked him to take off his mask. He did. Before she could see his face, she woke up, sweat making her clothes cling to her body.

She drank from the tap in the washroom and returned to her room. She put on pyjamas and lay down. She didn't turn off the iPod. She liked the background noise when her thoughts strayed. Olivia slept with her knife in her hand. After all that happened, she needed it. It was her shield against the night.

The investigation plodded on. Davis contacted Olivia once a week to update her and to see if she were ok. It was different from the last time. Before, the police practically ignored her after interviewing her. Now, Davis called her weekly with updates. She felt good about that. Once again, after some time, the media vans left without a word from Olivia or Harry. The police stopped maintaining their daily vigil and opted to increase patrols in her area again. If she stood at her window, she would see a patrol car swing by twice in an hour. It was good to see but a lot could happen in the time the police weren't there. Just ask Jen.

After Davis imparted his belief she knew the Jackal, Olivia brooded over it. Picked at it, like a scab that wouldn't heal. It seemed absurd to think the Jackal might be Dale. He would have been so young when the first girl had been taken. And how could he control and intimidate a much older and violent Shawn Grady? It didn't seem possible. She had never witnessed Dale get angry or hurt anyone. Shawn didn't seem the type who would ever take orders from anyone he thought to be inferior. A young teenage boy like Dale would fit that criteria.

Davis thought the Jackal financed the torture house, paid for it and let Shawn be the figurehead. Dale's family did have money. How could he access enough of it to buy a house, convert the basement into cells and put in a walk in freezer?

She discounted Dale as the Jackal and moved onto the mystery man at the recreation centre, trying to remember what he looked like. She never saw him with anyone. Most times, he would be by the pool, a book open in his lap just like most of the other parents waiting for their kids to finish their lessons. She didn't remember seeing him talk to anyone. Never saw a partner with him. He roamed the halls, ending up near her somewhere, perched on a bench with a book and sometimes a coffee. Tall, strong, the features of his face blurred in her mind. As though she were trying to focus a camera lens yet unable to bring out the details in what she wanted to capture. He wore a hat, most times. A black cap with a yellow 'P' on it. She should share that with Davis.

Olivia called him and told him. He said, "Pittsburgh Pirates."

"Excuse me."

"The hat. The hat is for the Pittsburgh Pirates. A baseball team."

"Is that helpful?"

"Absolutely. Another detail to use. Good work. I appreciate you calling. Please continue to do so."

The compliment filled her with a warm glow and she tried to remember more. She didn't want to push it too hard. She didn't think much of him back when she worked at the recreation centre. He happened to be one of the guys she would see a lot. It appeared menacing in retrospect. Especially considering she had seen him in Guelph on the same night she disappeared. She wanted to be objective about him, like a good detective and recall facts. Coincidences like those were hard to ignore.

At first, the news of Jen filled her with despair at her own chances of survival. Did she think the Jackal would let her escape from him? He would wait, bide his time and appear like a demon in the night to whisk her to a new hidey-hole to use at his leisure. The thought brought on violent shivers making her teeth clack together.

Harry did his best to distract her with thoughts of the new home. Attempting to entice her into conversations about what walls to take down and what new tub to put in the washroom. It failed. After the news vans left and the police moved from their static post to periodic checks, she revisited phase three of her 'how to get healthy' plan. She wanted to institute it when she moved into the new house. In order to move into the new house, they had to sell this one. She needed to get moving on it. She decided to spend more time getting the house ready to view. Busy hands, busy mind. Olivia still startled at noises and a light sheen would appear on her forehead when a moving shadow would entice visions of the Jackal. She walked around the inside of the house gazing out the windows for new footprints and sometimes, when the sun hid behind a cloud and darkness descended seemingly in a blink, she would drop under a window and shiver, expecting the tall animal ears on the mask to walk by her window. She hated darkness. It hid so much.

Despite these setbacks, the clutter disappeared, furniture rearranged to accentuate space and walls were coated with fresh paint. Their home was ready to view.

•　　　•　　　•

"We sold it!"

"What? Really?"

Olivia knew something was up when Harry walked in the door from work. He didn't say a thing. He lifted the bag of *Swiss Chalet* takeout in his hand and a smile stretching his cheeks threatened to engulf his face. It wasn't until he set the bags on the table did he spill the news.

"Yup."

"Did we get what we asked for?"

"Double yup."

"That's wonderful!" She hugged Harry and for a reason she couldn't explain, crying overtook her, reducing her to putty. Her small frame shook in Harry's arms.

He began to recite the expected platitudes, words she hated to hear because they *were* expected. "Hey now. It's okay. It's gonna get better. We just need time."

She didn't hate the words today. Even though all the terrible things she had been through put lie to those words. How can anything get better? Jen's dead, the Jackal's still out there, maybe watching her, waiting for the right time. Despite all that, at that moment in her father's arms she dared to believe them.

-25-

Moving day arrived with surprising speed. She remembered packing boxes, labelling them and setting them aside and then her dad was pulling on her shoulder, telling her to get up and get started, his sleep tousled hair standing straight up on his head. Harry rented a U-Haul truck for the move and they estimated two trips to get it done. All in all, it took three. Frank showed up to help and so did Dale. To Olivia's surprise Dale's parents also pitched in to help. Dale's mom, Angela, teared up at the sight of Olivia and pulled her into a hug. Olivia swallowed a lump and didn't yield to the temptation to cry. She had done enough crying. Angela smelled of peanut butter cookies and it brought back pleasant memories. Dale's dad, Carl, patted her on the arm and seemed to want to shake her hand but dropped it and awkwardly hugged her and with a quick one-two pat on her back, let her go. Dale's parents looked the same, only older. They were both fit from time at the gym and Angela boasted a winter tan no doubt earned from frequent visits to a tanning bed.

Frank lasted one truckload before he received an opportune phone call from a client demanding his immediate attention. The most surprising addition was the police showing up to her house. Davis and four of his cop friends showed up to help on a day off. So before three in the afternoon they emptied their old home of any evidence of their presence and filled up their new one, cluttering the house with cardboard boxes covered in tape labelled with black marker and furniture that hadn't found a permanent spot.

After they unloaded the last of their belongings from the U-Haul truck, Harry fed the workers pizza and soda. They all relaxed in the living room, some on couches and chairs amidst cardboard boxes and unassembled furniture. Others stood, leaning against the wall while balancing the pizza and drinks in their hands. Olivia set up the iPod to the Bose speakers and they enjoyed the food, drinks and each other's company while listening to music. Winter moseyed on towards spring. Between spaces of melting snow, spots of grass showed emerald. The sun hung around longer in the evening and like the new house, the season of renewal inspired hope.

The police, except for Detective Davis, left after pizza and Olivia and Harry thanked them for their help. Dale remained searching through the pizza boxes littering the table. Just one box had any slices left in it, the one covered with gross tomatoes and feta cheese. Dale crinkled his nose and Olivia caught it.

Olivia said, "Dad. What's with this pizza? Did you ask for the least appetizing toppings or something?"

"It's part of a deal. It's like greek style or something."

"It's something alright."

Dale and his parents left not long after the policemen. They had been discussing the renovations needed on the house and Dale offered to help when he could and even volunteered the labour of his dad.

Carl owned a trucking business and often drove the trucks himself for the long hauls State side. He didn't have to but he liked to do it. He said it reminded him of the early days when he had just started up his business. And he told them he enjoyed the peace of the road to which Angela rolled her eyes and said while leaning to touch Olivia's knee, "Peace of the road huh? You just want to get away from me for awhile."

"Now honey—"

"I'm not complaining. I like the peace and quiet from you too."

Dale said, "So how about it Dad? You wanna help out or what?"

He glanced at Olivia and holding her gaze said, "Sure. Why not? I am a handy fellow."

Dale said, "Yeah. Much better than me. I once screwed my shirt to a skateboard ramp I was building. It didn't turn out like I hoped."

Angela said, "You got that right. Didn't you fall up it?"

Olivia said, "Wait a minute. You fell up a ramp?"

"It's easier than you think when the bottom of the ramp isn't level with the ground. I chipped a tooth."

Olivia couldn't help it. She laughed.

"Now that my embarrassment's complete, I'll take my leave."

Angela stood and said, "It was great seeing you again, Olivia. I can't tell you how happy I was to learn you were alive and home again."

"Thank you," said Olivia.

Carl said, "Have Frank give me a call. Get this renovation thing going. Despite what Angela says, something like that would keep me close to home, just the way she likes it."

"Yes. I'm all aglow with excitement."

They left, with promises to call and see-you-soon.

The silence between songs was broken by the dripping of the melting snow from the eavestroughs. The day proved warmer than forecast. When everyone was still here, Olivia opened up the back windows to let a breeze in. The cool air was refreshing at first, but soon turned cold. Olivia suppressed a chill. She wanted to close the window but the full belly and exhaustion of moving left her without the energy to do so.

She glanced at her dad, "You feeling cold, Dad?"

"What?"

"Cause if you're cold, you could close the window."

"Do you want me to close the window?"

"If you're cold and you were going to anyways then sure, that'd be nice."

His eyebrows climbed his forehead. She wasn't very subtle. He groaned, stood and closed the window. Slumped on the couch, almost lying down, Olivia smiled, triumphant.

She moved her eyes to Davis, "You feel good about Dale?"

"You tell me. You know both of them, the Jackal and Dale, better than I do. What's your gut feeling?"

"Gut feeling? If I had any kind of gut feeling I would've sensed this madness and never would've been grabbed."

Davis shook his head, "That's not true. That'd be like trying to sense a lightning bolt. It's like that whole guilt thing I see victims struggle with. If I only did this then that wouldn't have happened. It did happen and you can't change the past. You can bet your dad suffered guilt from that day, am I right?"

Harry said, "Oh yeah. Over stupid things, too. Things I knew I couldn't change, just like you said."

"Like what?" Olivia said.

"I kept thinking I should've convinced you to stay home another year, or go to a school closer to home so you could stay here. I felt, a lot of times, me losing you was my fault and I punished myself for it."

Olivia grimaced, "That makes no sense. They were all my decisions. You couldn't have done anything to change it."

Davis said, "Guilt doesn't have to make sense. It just is. Maybe it's because we think we are in control when, in reality, we control so little. We are the star of our own movies and we all want a happy ending don't we? Except we are not the directors, there is no script and all we can ever do is the best we can. Day to day." He took a drink of Coke and said, "So, really, what do you think of Dale?"

Olivia shook her head, "Not him. I've thought about it. A lot. Dale is not as big as the Jackal and I don't know, not as mature? The Jackal just feels older. Something about the way he moved and acted. I keep thinking about the relationship between Shawn and the Jackal too. I'm positive the Jackal was the leader. I just don't see Dale as a strong enough personality to control and intimidate Shawn. Besides, I wouldn't let him help me move if I thought he was the Jackal. He would know where I lived. I wouldn't want to make it too easy on the prick."

Davis laughed and said, "You're an interesting person Olivia."

"How so?"

"Other than the obvious you mean? Let's just say I've dealt with and had the privilege to meet many victims. They carry the past on them like a back pack. Some people it weighs down, others carry it along, comfortable with it because it helped shape them to be the person they are. Those people realize they assign how much weight the backpack holds. They decide if it will bow their back or if they'll straighten up underneath it. The trauma you've been through? It should have crushed you. It crushed Jen and after meeting Lucy, if she'd been in there as long as you and Jen were I'm sure it would've ruined her too. You though? You fought your way out of there and, from what I've seen, you continue to fight. Like I said, you're very interesting. I'd hate to get on your bad side." He stood and stretched and said, "I better get going. Looks like you guys still have a lot of work ahead of you."

She followed him down the hallway and closed the door behind him. She liked him.

Her dad, sitting on the couch with a soda in hand said, "I think he likes you."

He was oblivious to his daughter blushing in the shadows by the front door.

-26-

The security company installed the alarm the next day. Olivia had to wait a week before they returned to install the video cameras. She wanted the cameras to cover all the sides of the house with the capability of recording. Olivia fiddled with the settings, learning how to adjust the camera angles and zoom features. They recorded in twenty-four hour intervals and the old footage was deleted to be replaced with the new. Olivia's routine, after her father left for work, included checking the doors and then sitting down before the computer and reviewing the footage from the night before. Satisfied no one had crept upon the property, Olivia busied herself with unpacking boxes and studying the layout of the house, thinking of ways to improve it. The windows were large and allowed plenty of natural light. Inside though, the rooms were small and cramped. Olivia wanted to open the place up. She would ask Frank about what walls could be safely brought down. She made notes about her ideas and when Harry returned at night, they reviewed them together.

They invited Frank out the first weekend. He declined. He said he would be out of town on business. Sunday evening, when the fading light brought shadows to the property, Olivia spoke to her dad about phase three of her plan. She was nervous about it. She was aware of Harry's feelings on the matter since she was a small child. She needed it, though, to feel safe and hoped she could convince her dad of it. It would go a long way to helping her heal.

Harry reclined on the love-seat with the top button of his pants undone after the second helping of dessert he didn't need, eyes heavy, watching Sports Centre. Olivia chewed a nail, with her iPad on her lap, a photo of the impending discussion on the screen.

"Dad?"

"Yeah, honey?"

"Remember how I talked about three stages to a plan I had?"

"Yeah."

"I want to start it. Phase three."

"Ok. What do you need?"

"I uh, want a dog. I want to train it. I want it to guard me."

Harry hadn't spoken of it much but she knew he nursed a healthy terror of dogs. She had pestered him as a child for a puppy and he had always said no. No arguments she used and no amount of tears could weaken his resolve. Intermittently over the years, when she would see a puppy jumping to lick the face of a child, she would ask Harry for a puppy. He would say no. She had asked him why, curious as to why he would deny her this when he denied her little else. He told her when he was a kid one of his friends had been mauled by a lab, the most gentle of breeds. His friend lost the use of an eye. Harry had seen the attack and ever since then the mere presence of a dog filled him with a nervous anxiety. He walked wide around them, even the little ones. The furry beasts terrified him. After she learned of it, she let it go. She never wanted to be the cause of her dad's discomfort and at the time, realized it was a selfish goal and not worth pursuing. The thought of wanting a dog had never crossed her mind since. After being taken and being shown how helpless she could be, her mind turned to ways in which to improve her safety. She considered taking judo or jiu jitsu. She had read those martial arts use the opponents weight against them and a smaller person such as herself, with good technique, could overcome someone larger and of superior strength. She would have to leave the house to do it, which was bad. And it took years to become proficient in the arts and with the Jackal out there she didn't think she had the time, which was worse. Thinking on it more, it didn't matter how good she became because her success would depend on her attacker not carrying a weapon of some sort. A dog though, a dog could be trained to attack those who would do her harm, a dog would love her and defend her and it would give her something to love and want to defend in return. The dog wouldn't have to go to work and leave for hours. Its job was to be with her and to be her friend. It wouldn't care about her missing fingers, toes or ear. It wouldn't care she had been raped and imprisoned. It would only care about her. Knowing her dad's terror, a part of her felt shame for even asking. He would be living here too, in terror, like she had been. She believed after living with a dog and seeing how well it could be trained and be a useful part of the family, he could overcome that fear.

Harry tensed. His eyes widened slightly and his throat moved making the struggle to digest the request visible.

"What kind of dog are we talking here? A chihuahua? A furry alarm that could fit in a purse."

Trying to make a joke? Whatever she expected, him attempting to make light of it wasn't it.

"No. A german shepherd. Like the dogs the police use."

"Oh boy," Harry said. He rubbed a hand along his lip. *Uh-oh*, thought Olivia, *I got him wanting a drink*. Guilt overcame her.

"You know Dad? Let's forget it. Stupid idea, you know?"

Harry coughed and rubbed his hands together. He said, "No honey. It's a brilliant idea. I think we should do it."

"Dad, c'mon. Look at you. You look like you want to vomit."

"I did. A little bit. I swallowed it back." He offered a shaky smile and said, "I'll get over it. It'll help keep you safe. I'll feel better going to work and not leaving you so alone."

"Dad. We can think of something else. I know too much stress brings on the urge to drink. You being sober is more important to me. You've done a wonderful job and I don't want to ruin it."

"You know what I learned in AA?"

"What's that?"

"I'll always want to drink. Always. I've got my own personal storm cloud hovering above me ready to rain down at any time, for any reason. This fear of dogs? It's in my head. I know it and I can beat it. Not every dog attacks kids and people. If that were the case, who the hell would bother to own one? I also know I can't lose you again. I'm not strong enough and if this will improve your chances of continuing to live a life free of fear, then fucking right we're going to do it. And we'll get the meanest, ugliest bastard of a dog out there."

"Okay. And thanks Dad. I think this'll be great."

He bared teeth. Although he meant it as a smile Olivia thought it strained. Guilt worried her stomach. She pushed it away. Her dad could overcome his fear and who knows? Maybe he would eventually love the dog. She would get a cute little puppy because who doesn't love a puppy? People with no soul that's who. With a little training of the dog and her dad, Olivia believed everything would work out fine.

• • •

Olivia did her research. It kept her busy and her nagging fears in check. A good thing, lasting until the sun's rays drew lengthening shadows in the backyard, a prelude to inevitable darkness. What she learned wasn't heartening. Pure bred dogs were expensive. A popular breed, the german shepherd proved to be exorbitant. Ranging from five to eight thousand dollars for an untrained pup! After buying the new house and the cost of renovations, Harry didn't have the money and she couldn't expect her dad to fork out more. She turned her questing fingers to perusing internet sites for rescue dogs. The prices were much more affordable. Still, in her mind she pictured a majestic german shepherd patrolling the property, keen senses probing for danger. In her vision she pictured it wearing a cape. German shepherds didn't show up on the rescue sites too often. She had trouble finding one. As the week passed her disappointment grew.

During this time, Frank and Carl popped in to take measurements or run ideas past her. Dale showed up with his dad at times, admitting to her all this stuff hurt his brain. He wasn't geared towards working with his hands and grudgingly admired Frank and his dad. They made the work look easy. Frank learned soon enough Olivia was the one making decisions and stopped bothering to call Harry when a question arose. He would talk to her and then to Carl. Olivia could see by Frank deigning to consult with Carl that Dale's dad knew what he was doing. Supplies were routinely dropped on the driveway and Harry was left with the task of bringing them in and putting them where Frank directed so they would be ready for installation at some date in the future. Harry would arrive home after work and groan at the stacks of wood or drywall on the driveway, rubbing at his lower back before the work could even strain his muscles. A sympathetic gesture for the burden his muscles would soon be subjected to. Olivia always helped him and couldn't help but tease him and his 'old man' back.

After one of the many onerous trips back to the driveway and into the house with a length of drywall, Olivia stumbled upon a photo of a dog at a not-so-local shelter. A pure bred german shepherd named Brutus. In the description the dog was of shy temperament and had been abandoned by previous owners. The picture showed the dog curled in a ball at the back of the cage. His brown eyes showed over the tops of his paws. So sad. Maybe it was the sad look in the eyes or the fact the dog appeared so lost and trapped in a cage, whatever the reason, Olivia's vision blurred and it shocked her to realize the simple image had evoked such a response. She would have this dog. She glanced at the posting. Brutus arrived at the shelter three days ago. Would he still be there? She shivered at the thought he may be gone. Three days is a long time. Especially for a pure bred german shepherd. She glanced at the time. 6:17pm. The shelter closed at 9:00pm. About an hour away. They could make it.

She dialled the number for the shelter, heart in her throat and she actually tittered when they told her Brutus hadn't been adopted yet. She said they could be there in an hour. Her heart swelled with excitement. This? This felt right. Perfect even.

Harry dropped the drywall behind her with a curse. It slipped out of his hands and he chipped the corner when it struck the floor. He was frowning until he saw the smile on Olivia's face.

•　　•　　•

When they arrived at the shelter, the man who greeted them behind the counter had a celebrity gossip magazine open in his lap and a can of Coca-Cola in his hand. He offered a smile and stood. Large, with a florid, friendly face, he extended a beefy hand and introduced himself as Mark. He paused, noticing her missing fingers but it was a slight pause making it easy for Olivia to deal with because it was over so quick.

Olivia said, "I called earlier? About Brutus?"

She half-expected him to say, sorry, he had been adopted in the incredibly long hour it took them to get there. Ever since being in the basement, it took an effort of will to nurse hope. Such a fragile thing.

"You the one who giggled on the phone? I thought you'd be younger," he said with a wink. He walked out from behind the counter, "Would you like to meet him?"

"Yes, please."

Olivia and Harry followed Mark through double doors past rows of cat cages and through another set of doors with larger cages for the dogs. The room smelled musty with fur and the stronger scent of urine and feces.

Olivia spotted Brutus with his back against the bars of the cage. His eyes darted from Mark to Harry and then settled on Olivia. The tip of his tail wagged a smidgen. Other than Brutus, two other dogs occupied cages in the room. A small Yorkshire terrier yapped happily and spun circles in its enclosure. Another dog, older, cracked an eye, saw nothing of interest, and went back to sleep. Her attention focused on Brutus and she knelt before the cage. The tail moved tentatively.

Harry said, "Does he bite?"

"Brutus? No. Not him. Mopes around mostly. His previous owners moved out of their house and left him behind. A real shock for the people moving in. No. If you ask me, he's heartbroken. Some people'd say that's nonsense, a dog being heartbroken. I know otherwise though, working in here."

Olivia held the back of her hand to the cage, an offering.

Harry said, "Maybe you shouldn't do that."

"Relax Dad. We're friends. Even Brutus here knows it. Don't you boy?"

Brutus' tail twitched in agreement. He edged his snout closer, nostrils flaring. His pink tongue darted out and licked her hand.

Mark said, "I would say he does."

Without taking her eyes from Brutus, Olivia said, "I'd like to take him home."

•   •   •

Olivia didn't know what she expected. Well, that's not entirely accurate. She expected to show up, pay some fees and take the dog home because she wanted it to work like that. It didn't. Not at this shelter. Mark explained the process to her. She nodded at him, brow furrowed and biting her lip. They wanted to make sure the dog, when placed, would stay there and to better ensure that end, she had to apply to be the adoptive parent of Brutus. Too many times, people adopted a dog with good intentions. They wanted to keep the dog, they wanted to love it and they wanted it to love them in return. Turns out, having a dog is a lot of work. A lot more work than films and quaint TV commercials portray. Dogs needed to go for walks regularly. The bigger the dog, the more regular the walks. They had to be fed, occasionally washed and given a lot of time and attention most people don't have. And then the crap! In the summer, this didn't present too much of a problem other than the general grossness of crap roasting in the sun. In the winter though, the snow tended to cover it up before you could get to it. Come spring, when the snow melted, the backyard would look like a minefield of brown soggy logs. All in all, dogs were a huge responsibility to the surprise of a great many people.

Mark said the shelter instituted guidelines for the application process. The adoptee would be interviewed and a form filled out. If satisfactory, an employee would attend Olivia's house for a home visit to see if the property were conducive to a dog. If all worked out well, then the dog would be placed into the care of the applicant. The whole process seemed overwhelming and at first, quite ridiculous. How did they expect to place dogs? Intimidating to say the least and it induced unexpected anxiety in Olivia. She had thought it would be simpler. After Mark explained that by using this process they drastically reduced the return rate of the dogs, she understood it and accepted it. Even so, it still felt a daunting and scary venture. What if they decided she were unsuitable? Worse. What if she got through to the home visit and after seeing the place they denied her Brutus? The possibility of rejection scared and angered her in equal proportions.

"Please. Don't look so scared. It's not as bad as you think." Mark said with a smile. "Let's go have a seat. I'll get my clipboard out and we'll get the interview done."

They were back at the front and Mark sank into his chair, lifted his magazine, opened a drawer or two and finding the clipboard and form, placed it before her. He said, "Fill this out please."

The form took little time to fill. General personal information like her name and age. She glanced at Harry when she got to the address line. She forgot the house number. New house or no new house, it was not something she would forget. It was an indication of her nervousness and her fear they wouldn't let her have Brutus. She handed the completed form to Mark. He checked it over, nodded and stuck another sheet of paper in the clipboard.

With the pen all but disappearing in his hand, he said, "So. Why do you want a dog?"

She surprised herself by saying, "I want a friend."

When it came out of her mouth and she heard the truth of it, she grinned.

Mark smiled warmly, winked, and said, "Good answer."

•   •   •

The interview went well. Mark told her to be prepared for a home visit. He didn't expect any problems considering they had a fenced backyard. Harry chided her for her nervousness. She asked to see Brutus before she left and Mark appeared pleased by the request.

She knelt before the cage and told him to expect to come home with her soon. He canted his head and his tail wagged at her voice. She liked to believe he understood her. Who knows? Maybe he did.

The home visit took place two days later. The stress made Olivia irritable. She followed Harry around and wiped the table as soon as his dishes left it glaring at him for daring to leave such a mess. She brushed imaginary crumbs off his chair once he vacated it accompanied by a harried sigh. She wanted Brutus. Wanted him so much it made her wring her hands and wander the house looking for something to clean. She wanted the home visit to go perfectly. Late at night, while passing cars lit up her ceiling with flashes of light, she wondered if Brutus really was for protection. Maybe what she said to Mark made more sense. She wanted a friend. One to love her despite her scars, the ones on the surface and the deeper ones beneath. She believed Dale to be her friend but he wasn't around all the time and what she wanted was the kind of love only a dog could provide and the security attached to that love.

The detective, Davis, proved to be an interesting and intelligent person. He had been kind to her and as far as she could tell, very forthright with the case. She liked the quiet confidence and his eyes that seemed to read everything. She knew the attraction couldn't be reciprocated. Damaged goods, mangled, who would want to be with her? She convinced herself Davis was being nice to her because it was his job. It would look very good on him if he were to catch the Jackal. There could be no other reason for his kind words and charming smile. It was his job to care. He wouldn't like her, not in that way. She was damaged. Physically and emotionally.

There would be no expectations from Brutus. He would want food, water, exercise and her love. She had plenty to give and wanted to share it.

The very idea a home visit could affect the adoption filled her with dread. She worried her nails until she tasted blood. One minute she would think everything will work out, she was due for something good by now wasn't she? A person couldn't go through their whole life with shit luck could they? Then she would think, why not? Plenty of people get fucked by life everyday. Why not her? A karmic arrow pointing right at her letting her know fate wasn't done with her yet, oh no, not by a long shot. A few more dollops of misery have yet to be doled out.

When Mark called to make sure she would be home for the visit she spoke in a light, care-free tone while her guts twisted inside. Mark ended up being the home visitor, showing up at the front door with a clipboard and pen. Olivia couldn't picture him without them. He grinned at her surprise and she invited him in. Olivia had cleared away most of the boxes and put them in the garage. She hoped he wouldn't check in there. He might be crushed by an avalanche of boxes if he opened the door.

She relaxed a lot when Mark said, "This part is just a formality. Most people who thought they wanted a dog are usually scared when the process is explained to them. Too much work you see. The people who go through with it all are those ones we like to release a dog to. You can tell they want the dog, otherwise, why go through all this stress?"

"It is very stressful."

"Only because you care. In my book, that makes you a great applicant. Okay. Show me the rest of this place so I can sign off on Brutus."

And that was that. She got the okay to adopt Brutus. They could pick him up anytime. She called her dad and told him to expect to go on a road trip when he got home from work. Olivia rested on the couch, positioned so she could see Harry pull in the driveway. Once he got home, they were going to get Brutus. Time never moved so slow. She would be convinced a half hour had passed and would glance at her watch to see five minutes elapsed since her last check. The TV babbled in the background, the iPad sat forgotten on her lap and a cup of tea huffed steam while being ignored on the table. She wanted to get going. Her body hummed with the urge to go. Not until she had Brutus in the car would it be real to her. When headlights swept the living room, she stood and hustled out the door with her coat in her arms and her boots not quite on. She hopped in the car to see a surprised Harry watching her.

"No time for dinner?"

"Nope. No time."

"Did you lock the door and set the alarm?"

"Fuck!" She said in exasperation and shock. Those are things she had never forgotten to do before. She checked them repeatedly. It was like if she didn't move fast enough someone would come in and scoop Brutus from her. Ridiculous. Yet the power of this thought shoved all other considerations rudely aside. She yanked on the handle and Harry stopped her with, "I'll get it."

Harry fast-walked to the front door, disappeared inside and emerged a short time later. He locked the door, gave her a thumbs up and trotted to the car.

"Ready?"

She nodded.

"Can we get something at a drive-thru on the way?"

"I suppose so. If you must."

"C'mon honey. What's the rush? It's not like the dog will be gone when we get there."

She exhaled heavily, "I know."

•   •   •

Mark greeted them with a smile and a handshake. He handed Olivia the paperwork for the shots and licensing and recommended a good vet near them. Olivia, flushed and excited, handed the papers directly to Harry. She kept forgetting his fear of dogs and wondered how he was holding up. He hadn't wiped at his lip. A good sign. He may have been, in consideration of her, trying to conceal his terror. Feeling great affection for him, she put a hand on his arm and said, "Thanks for this, Dad."

"No problem."

Olivia turned to Mark and said, "Okay. I'm ready. I mean, we're ready."

"Perfect. Do you have your collar and leash?"

Olivia said, "Fuck." Her face burned a bright red.

She apologized to Mark and her dad for swearing and felt like the world's biggest idiot for forgetting to get a leash and collar. She hadn't even bought a dog bed, bowls or food. All the essentials for dog ownership slipped her mind. And Mark had reminded her to bring them at the home visit. She rushed her poor dad into the car, debated on even letting him stop for food when they should have stopped and did some shopping for the dog items.

Mark waved off the swearing and gave her a slip leash until she could get a collar and leash for Brutus. All of her self-recriminations and doubts faded when Mark walked out of the back room with Brutus on a leash. Brutus gazed at her with amber eyes, furtive but she did notice the swish of his tail upon seeing her and thought it a good sign.

Mark handed her the leash and she clasped it. Her heart thrummed. Her eyes burned and she swallowed. When she found her voice she said, "Thanks. For everything."

"No need. I'm sure Brutus here has found himself a great family. I'm glad for him. And for you."

She offered the back of her hand to Brutus. Like last time, he sniffed and licked it. She scratched the top of his head, between the ears. He closed his eyes and his tail flicked with enthusiasm.

"Yup. I'm sure you two will get along fine. Now your dad there? He might take some time getting used to Brutus."

Olivia turned to see Harry pale with a line of sweat on his brow.

Harry laughed, nervous and said, "I'm sure it'll be fine."

Mark recommended a good store on the way home for dog supplies. He provided a list and Harry took it and stuffed it in his pocket.

Olivia said, "Ready Brutus?"

Brutus' tongue darted out, licking her pants.

"I'll take that as a yes."

They walked to the car and Harry chuckled. A high tittering sound, lined with anxiety. He said, "I forgot he'd be riding in the car with me. Stupid thing to forget. I mean, how would we get him home otherwise?"

"Like forgetting a leash and collar? Not so stupid Dad. I'll sit in the back with him. Just don't look in the rearview mirror too much. With luck, you may even be able to forget he's there."

She opened the door and Brutus climbed in with his tail between his legs. She got in beside him, put on her seatbelt and Harry drove them home with their new furry family member.

-27-

The Jackal always liked the preparation prior to an abduction or murder. The planning built anticipation. It juiced his veins and electrified his heart. It allowed him to visualize how he would carry out the plan, and what he would do to the unfortunate once he had her. It never failed to give rise to a painful erection. Despite his planning, he had been lucky with Jen. If she had pushed the stupid alarm button any sooner, he would be in jail right now, rotting in a cage. He had no idea she was wearing the alarm. He should have known. He had never seen Olivia wearing it so, in retrospect, he couldn't have foreseen that. Relying on luck was a terrible way to do business. Luck had a disturbing tendency of running out. More research, more planning. One had to be careful about the process. It wouldn't do to be seen hanging around a certain place around a certain person. People remember the strangest things and he shouldn't underestimate that.

Jen's murder had sated him for some time. He wished he could have taken her with him to enjoy at his leisure. To draw out her terror and drink it in. A satisfying tonic. Would Jen have given him the satisfaction he sought? Curious. She had been dissociating herself for quite some time. In her pink cell, he sensed in her eyes a drawing away, her mind drifting some place where the horrors couldn't reach her. Even at the moment of her death when her eyes grew wide as dinner plates and pulsing with fear, it had been tempered by relief. She wanted it to end and she enticed him to do it. He didn't like that. She had manipulated him. Control belonged to the Jackal and not the victim.

He shrugged it away. It was something to learn from and move on. He had killed her and left an unmistakable message for Olivia. He intended to do the same with Lucy. He had a way to negate the alarm around the neck. He would have to test it first. Make sure it worked. Then he would take her, use her and dump her where she would be found, bearing the same disfiguring scars as Olivia. His penis pressed against his pants. Painfully pleasant.

He had recorded the interviews Lucy gave to the talk shows. He watched her on the screen, vibrant, full of life, so different from Jen. His heart ached with want. Although Jen bore more resemblance to Olivia, Lucy possessed more spirit, more defiance. He loved to beat that out of them first. All except for Olivia. He never beat her. He did help hold her down so Shawn could cut pieces of her away but he never was the one to hit or cut.

He would get to Olivia. It was as inevitable as the earth orbiting the sun. He had been kidding himself when he thought he could let her go. He would take her in every way possible and destroy her. He groaned in his chair at the thought of her under him.

Once he took Lucy, the security would be intense around Olivia. Maybe it wouldn't go away, like he knew it had with Jen. From his surveillance he knew the police were already losing interest in parking around Lucy and Olivia. He was surprised when he saw the sold sign on Olivia's old house. He hadn't known they were selling it and had no idea when they would be moving or to where. It didn't take much effort to find out and when he did, he saw the police were already in the area. But after time, their patrols past the homes were occurring less and less. They didn't have the time or the resources to keep up a sustained watch. If he took Lucy they might change all that. They might hide Olivia from him. He had his ways to find her though penetrating the security while maintaining his anonymity would be all but impossible. He would have to re-evaluate his plans for taking Lucy and Olivia. If he waited awhile longer, maybe he could figure out a way of getting them both at the same time and end his longing. He touched himself through his pants as he watched Lucy's interview on the TV. Lucy smiled on screen and it was like she was smiling at him. A dazzling symbol of youth and beauty. He might cut her lips off first. Something so powerful about destroying a beautiful thing. And all it took was a knife and the will to do it. He undid his pants. He needed some release.

-28-

Detective Davis stared at the chart on the wall of his office at home. It contained photos and small notes of the case referencing page numbers in the Major Case file, heavier than an Old Testament bible, sitting on the corner of his desk. He liked to have a paper copy as well as the electronic one on his computer. His gaze roved over all, trying to see something he missed. Frustrating, this case. It kept him up some nights, morose and sullen, feeling like an unintelligent slob. The stress accumulated on his shoulders. The pressure from outside was beginning to wear on him. The press, his bosses, the public, Lucy and Olivia were all looking to him to solve this thing so they could stop worrying about it. They saw Jen's death as a huge stain, questioning the police's ability to deal with the matter. All the reporter pundits offered their own insight and criticism on how the police could be doing a better job. The stress from them didn't bother him. His bosses repeated words and phrases like "public perception" and "optics" as though these were the most important considerations in the world. Davis didn't give a fuck about that and didn't feel the pressure their words and stern gazes were meant to give.

Davis understood public perception and the importance of it. Police derive their powers from the public's support of them. So yeah, they were definitely accountable to the public and should be. His bosses and their politician words didn't apply the pressure. The pressure came from himself.

To Davis, stress is internal and to a certain extent, we control our reactions to outside events and dictate how they affect us. Sometimes this isn't true. Sometimes an outside trauma can be so horrific or against our own belief of reality, it gets inside, churns about and consumes you from within. Not quite at that stage, Davis could feel it growing. An impending menace, hurtling towards him. His stress came from the death of Jen and her mother. Based on all that he knew from the investigation, reading reports, reviewing interviews, how could he not anticipate the Jackal going after her? Or any of them? Could he have

145

foreseen it? No. He told the survivors to protect themselves and take precautions because that's what you're supposed to say when the bad guy gets away. But he didn't believe the bad guy *would* come back. The bad guy took great pains not to be caught and identified so Davis didn't think he would show up again. He thought the Jackal was gone. Like all the other guys, he thought the Jackal upped and vanished, never to be seen again around here. To go after any of the girls went against this premise so no one believed he would do it. Davis believed he would act again, somewhere new, in some town far away but there was no way he believed for a second he would go after Jen. Suicidal to do so. He was almost begging to be caught. But he didn't get caught did he? He walked into her house, murdered her mother, killed and mutilated Jen and left without a trace. No witnesses, nothing.

Intelligence officers were watching both of the girls now. At first, they had been there twenty-four hours a day on rotating shifts. The cost of the surveillance mounted fast so it had been reduced to twelve hour shifts. The bosses were considering pulling it altogether if this didn't get wrapped up soon. They were convincing themselves the attack on Jen was a petulant, vengeful act. Sad truth of the matter was that money dictated so much of policing. They wanted to believe the Jackal got it out of his system and would leave the other girls alone. The Jackal would have to be insane to continue the attacks and not get caught. Davis believed otherwise. Didn't the Jackal's acts prove his insanity? After Jen, Davis knew the Jackal wouldn't be going away. He would be waiting for his opportunity. The Jackal had two other girls to kill and Davis felt certain Olivia would be the last one. His arrogance was too large for him to let Olivia and Lucy go. Davis wished he had deduced that before Jen was murdered. He couldn't let the brass pull the surveillance. Not before he found the bastard.

Olivia was the key to it all. He felt it in his gut. He had interviewed all her teachers from high school and all her friends. He questioned her fellow workers and her boss at the recreation centre and got nothing. He got a good idea of Olivia the person before the abduction. From all accounts, they described her as a kind and conscientious person. Nice sentiments but not very helpful. None of it would lead Davis to the Jackal. She appeared to be an investigative dead end.

Then he and his team worked on a different angle. Where did Shawn Grady get the money to buy the little terror house? They traced it back and got nothing but more accounts owned by Shawn. The Jackal used Shawn with incredible skill, hiding behind him to become all but invisible. It was clear the Jackal possessed better than average financial resources but where to start based on that?

The creeper at the pool, the guy who showed up at the university the night Olivia had been taken needed to be found. Security video? Long but erased. He had spoken to almost all of Olivia's co-workers and learned nothing helpful. He requested the recreation centre provide him a list of all the people registered to use the facilities during the time Olivia worked there. Over five-year-old records. No one he spoke to knew where they were kept or who kept them. He assigned one of the junior officers the task. As far as he knew, she was still working on it. He would have to go through the list and see if anyone remembered the vague description of the male provided by Olivia who had last seen the guy over five years ago. *Fuck my life,* he thought.

He scanned the wall, looking for something, anything to give him a place to start. He couldn't fail Lucy and Olivia like he did Jen. They had been through more than enough shit to last them two lifetimes. He smiled, thinking of Olivia. What incredible will. To bite into a person's neck, break out of a cell she had been in for five years and instead of running off screaming into the night, she rescued two other girls. Amazing. He liked her. A lot. Only she was a victim and a witness and he had to be hands off. Wasn't professional to start dating a victim of a crime you were investigating. Maybe after it was all over? Shit. Like she would be interested in some old guy like him. Well, he wasn't that old. He was maybe five years older than her? Not so bad.

Jesus. Stop being such a moon-eyed teenager. Focus on catching the Jackal. After that, who knows? Maybe he should call her. He hadn't give her an update on the investigation in awhile. The thought made him smile and then he shook his head, thinking, be professional. This is a courtesy call. You told her you would call on a weekly basis and you're fulfilling that obligation. Yeah, right. He called her, and when he heard her voice, he couldn't help but grin.

-29-

Olivia learned to relax. Brutus taught her how. A routine arose without contemplation. She would wake up and Brutus would groan, yawn and follow her out of the bedroom leaving an indentation behind in his dog bed. He would sit by the food bowl, eyes following Harry and Olivia as they worked on coffee and breakfast. She would feed him and let him out in the backyard, not as concerned with the shadows as before. He sat at the door when he wanted back in and he would stay near her for the rest of her day. Wherever she happened to be, he sat close by and her hand would stray to scratch behind his ears. She loved him immediately and Olivia felt loved by Brutus.

Harry tolerated Brutus for Olivia's sake and his fear dissipated from the constant exposure. If Brutus barked or growled, it would have been harder on him to cope. Hell, if the dog barked Harry might have screamed or crapped himself. If it came to that, he was sure he would rather it be the former. Harry thought the dog must have sensed his discomfort because for the most part, Brutus gave him space. He never sat between Olivia and Harry even though he always remained close to Olivia's side. It got harder for Harry to dislike the dog. A grudging respect for Brutus grew because his effect on Olivia was noticeable. Before, even in a reclining state, Olivia wore the worried frown and searching eyes. With Brutus around, her features smoothed out and it seemed to Harry she breathed easier. After a week, Olivia convinced Harry to go outside with her to take Brutus for a walk. A big step for Harry and for Olivia. Even though she went out to the AA meetings with Harry and to the dog shelter to get Brutus, she preferred to stay inside and for her to want to go out and walk the block or wherever was a sign of her healing. He did his best to keep clear of Brutus in the house and now Olivia wanted him to walk by the dog's side? Well, maybe he could walk on the other side of Olivia, furthest from Brutus. Still, the idea lifted his hand to swipe at his upper lip. Harry wanted to see his daughter go outside. It would be nice to see her grow the confidence to venture away from the house and who knows, after awhile, she may go on without him. For that reason, he couldn't say no to the dog walks after dinner. He would feel like a bad parent to deny her the simple request. She wanted to walk Brutus everyday but was still at the point of being fearful of the outside world without someone by her side. While talking with Olivia, he kept a wary eye on Brutus. Brutus, for his part, ignored Harry. He never pulled on the leash or yanked her to the side to investigate a smell. He would pause and glance at Olivia if he scented something he wanted to investigate and if she noticed this, she would let him lead her to what his nose found so interesting. Brutus plodded beside her, nudging her on occasion to invite a pet or, if that didn't work, he licked her hand. He sniffed other dogs and allowed them to smell him with calm acceptance. All in all, Harry grudgingly admitted to himself, Brutus was an exceptional dog.

●   ●   ●

Olivia loved the walks. She could feel her tight back muscles loosen. She checked over her shoulder less and less. She would watch the rolling shoulders and hips of Brutus when he walked, mouth open with his tongue swinging out like a flag and wondered if she would ever get to the point where she could enjoy the moment without the weight of the past and the present shadow of the Jackal. They walked every night after dinner, sometimes making their way to a Starbucks or a Tim Hortons. In this fashion, they walked out of winter and into spring.

The air lost its chill. The cold breezes sliding down your neck became warmer and the winter coats were replaced with lighter jackets. She and Harry talked about the house and remarked on its transformation under the hands of Frank and Carl. Dale's contribution included breaking drywall, screwing in boards lopsided and causing Frank constant aggravation. At Frank's angry-eyed request, Dale stopped helping and provided Olivia with company. They spent many afternoons sipping tea and coffee while Frank and Carl worked around them.

Frank showed up almost everyday which surprised Olivia until Frank told her he wanted to get it over with and move on. The house began to take shape. Carl spent a lot of time there as well at the insistence of Dale and his wife Angela. Frank was the only one who outwardly disliked Brutus. He walked in after they had had him for three days, carrying a toolbox in his hand and setting it on the floor. Brutus left Olivia to see who walked in. He sat in the hallway, his head canted to the side. Frank noticed him as he took off his coat. Carl crowded in behind him, peering over Frank's shoulder. Brutus growled.

"Olivia?"

"Yeah?"

"There's a growling dog in your house."

"His name is Brutus! Say hi!"

"But...it's a dog!"

Olivia appeared by Brutus and scratched him between the ears.

"Yeah. I know. He's my dog."

"I don't like him."

Olivia said, "You don't have to."

"How am I going to get any work done with that around?"

"He won't get in your way. He hangs out with me exclusively."

"What does Harry have to say about you having a dog?"

"He doesn't know. I hide him in my room when he gets back from work."

"Really?"

"No. Jackass. He's fine with him."

"Huh. I'd like to see that."

"Stick around for dinner some time and you will."

Frank turned to Carl and said, "Can you believe this nonsense? Do you like dogs?"

"I don't like or dislike them."

"Way to take a stand there, Carl."

Carl shrugged.

Frank sneered at Brutus and disappeared with his tools into another room. The only time Brutus growled was when a stranger walked by the house or when Frank or Carl showed up. Even after a few weeks, Brutus would greet them at the door with a growl and then saunter back to Olivia's side. She had heard Frank mutter once after Brutus growled, "Yeah, well. I don't like you either." Olivia smiled.

Carl attempted to pat the dog's head and Brutus rebuffed him by baring his teeth. Olivia thought it was nice of him to try which was more than Frank ever did.

Olivia's confidence grew. Brutus' quiet demeanour and constant presence soothed the turbulence inside. The noises outside the house no longer startled a sweat from her or caused her to gasp. The night time shadows lost some of their menace. She loved nothing better than to sit on the couch, a blanket wrapped about her legs with a tea in her hand, a book in the other and Brutus beside her. She would pet him, taking comfort in his soft fur and the rise and fall of his back under her hand. For the first time in forever, she thought of the future. She contemplated registering for online courses and getting her bachelor's degree, what she had started to do so long ago.

Davis called every Sunday evening. She counted on his calls. She sensed genuine concern for her in their professional conversation tinged with a flirtatious tone. It boosted her self-esteem. If someone as attractive as the detective could like her scarred and mangled self, there was hope for her. She would never have to explain to him what happened or even talk about it if she didn't want to because he already knew. Maybe she was getting carried away here? *It's his job to care*, she thought, *and besides, you look like an ogre. Davis is showing professional courtesy and that's all.* She hated it when those old thoughts surfaced. Habits she formed in a pink dungeon where she questioned her worth and believed the cruel comments of her tormentors. She stuffed them down. She remembered what male attention felt like in those long ago days prior to living in a pink prison. She knew what flirting was. She had once been a master of it. Detective Davis definitely flirted with her on the phone. Yeah, definitely. She smiled thinking she didn't even know his first name.

That afternoon, she sat on the porch in the backyard with the sun heating her skin and she turned her face up to it. Brutus investigated smells along the fence, his tail wagging like a flag in the wind. The sounds of Carl or Frank (she didn't know who and didn't much care at this point) working on the closet in her bedroom could be heard through the open window. Summer arrived and she intended to take advantage of it. In a month, when the short season of hot weather arrived, she would be sipping on lemonade from a glass sweaty with ice. By then, the work on the house should be done and she could get a break from both of the men. They worked on it as much as they could and since they both weren't being paid for it, she shouldn't be too annoyed with them. She spent most of five years being alone and even though she were free and could talk to whoever she wanted to, she preferred the solitude. Strange, before her captivity, she had been quite an extrovert.

Olivia marvelled at the work done to the house. Frank and Carl had taken down a wall, put a support beam in and opened up the entire first floor. She could see the living room, dining room and down the hallway to the bedrooms from their kitchen. Bright and airy. Very different from when they moved in and every room needed a light on to remove the corner shadows. Even during the day, the house would be dark before they had done the work. In Olivia's opinion, they did good work. It was hard to get used to having them around all the time when all she wanted was to be alone with Brutus. Carl wasn't so bad. He kept to himself. But Frank? He was the type of person you could take in small doses. With luck, he would be gone soon enough.

Glorious sunlight induced lethargy and she felt herself drifting until Brutus growled beside her. She cracked open an eye. Brutus sat staring at something behind her. Fear's fingers played along her skin. She craned her neck. Frank stood in the doorway looking at the fence.

"You need anything Frank? You want a drink or something?"

"No. Just taking a break. Checking out the backyard."

She turned back to face the green space, peppered with mounds of dog crap. She should pick that up soon. Before she and Harry started sitting out here more regular.

"What about Carl? He thirsty or hungry?"

"I don't know. Why don't you ask him?"

"I'll do that." She stood and stretched. Brutus growled beside her.

-30-

When the Jackal noticed the undercover officers, it made his butt pucker up tighter than a drum. What was worse than the cops was the damn dog Olivia had adopted. A german shepherd no less. One mean ass dog and reputedly loyal and protective of their owner.

He had been on his way to see her and every time he did he learned something new causing him to revise his plan or consider abandoning the whole idea of a double abduction. The dog had been the newest wrinkle. He had been thinking of the dog and what to do about it. Concerns about the police had long since vanished since he noticed they no longer patrolled by her or Lucy's place. He thought it would be safe. Driving towards her house on a side street, he slowed the car approaching a stop sign. He noticed a blue sedan parked against the curb. He had to straddle the middle of the road to safely pass it. Glancing inside, he saw a man playing on an iPad. Nothing too unusual there. He turned his gaze back to the road and then his head snapped back, his eye catching the shape of the police radio on the seat beside him. He forced his eyes forward and stomped the brake realizing he had almost driven right through the intersection without stopping at the sign. In the rearview, the cop lifted his head and then returned to the iPad in his lap. The Jackal drove on. The cops were still watching Olivia. That man was definitely a cop.

He thought they had vanished. Surveillance cost a lot to maintain indefinitely if that's what they thought they had to do after Jen. It might be cheaper to put them in witness protection. He couldn't see Lucy agreeing to that. Too independent and proud. He wondered what Olivia would do. Did they even offer it to them? He should have considered the possibility of undercover surveillance. To be fair to himself, he did consider it but believed it to be abandoned by now. It had been a few months since the murder of Jen. When would they pull it?

Even though he had become more famous than Bernardo, he never sought fame. Anonymity secured longevity and he had enjoyed the years when no one even suspected people like he and Grady existed. Now the secret was out and the Jackal was synonymous with the Bogeyman. A feeling of pride bloomed in his chest. He liked being recognized for his work, but not enough to get caught. Hell no.

The fact is the police presence scared him and he didn't like being scared. He was the scary one, the Jackal, the cannibal prince. His fear turned to anger and he bared his teeth like an animal backed into a corner. Did they know who they were messing with? He had already made them look the fools with Jen and her mother. He would do it again. He would just have to exercise patience. He could wait for the surveillance to be terminated. Then he would swoop in, steal them from right under their noses. He would watch the news about it as he carved into Jen and soiled Olivia. He could do it without anyone finding out who he is. He had been working hard on his plan. Ironing out every wrinkle and thinking through every contingency. He had found everything he needed on the internet. Amazing what one could find out there.

He bought a pre-paid credit card with cash and had the items sent to a P.O box registered under a different name. He created layers of obscurity with ease. But his plan had hinged on the police being out of it. He would have to hold off a little longer, maybe near the end of summer and hopefully by then, the police would have relaxed and let their guard down. It would make it easy for him to don his mask and create a night of terror for the girls and delicious memories for himself. He would have liked to keep them someplace safe for some time before he killed them. He would like to toy with them like he had before. He wanted to snuff out the hope in their eyes over days, weeks and years. He didn't have a room or a place to keep them anymore. No Shawn Grady to act as a straw man. What he was going to do was risky enough. To keep them, like he did before would be inviting disaster. One night would do it. He could destroy them both and hide their bodies and the police would be so busy looking for them, they would spend less time looking for him. So he hoped. Either way, he would get Olivia out of his system and show Lucy there was no escape from him. Only a short reprieve.

Remembering Jen's terror calmed his quavering heart. The adrenaline drained from his system. His hands shook on the steering wheel. He steadied his breathing. He would have Olivia and Lucy. Planning, preparation and patience would ensure it. It will all be worth it when he could play with Lucy and Olivia minus his mask. Especially Olivia. He pressed play on his iPod and relaxed to *Ava Maria,* the song he and Olivia shared. He turned it up and drove away from Olivia's. He would see her soon enough.

-31-

Harry could not believe the change in Olivia. He had gotten used to the Olivia who clawed her way out of a basement. A wild-eyed person frightened of any errant noise or passing shadow. A young woman who cowered in her own home believing the horror would visit her again, expecting it to descend upon her any second, caressing the knife on a belt while her eyes forever roved, never resting, never feeling safe. She skirted the house with shoulders hunched and bent as though anticipating a beating at any moment. It hurt him to see her so damaged. He had feared she may never recover. The bright, confident and considerate young woman who left for university never returned. They had taken that from her and he wasn't sure she would ever get it back. She had proven to be a fighter but Harry had known that before all this mess. She had always been strong and very stubborn. She didn't have quitting in her and even though she struggled adjusting to her new life, she made plans and thought of the future. She got him to stop drinking, she got them into a nice place closer to his work, near a police station and she got herself a dog. Incredibly resilient, his daughter.

He would have to credit Brutus for the change in her demeanour. They were perfect for each other. Each complementing the others insecurities and imbibing confidence as a result. He never strayed far from her side, watching her with his amber eyes and licking her hand at every opportunity. The only time he went from her side was to do his business in the backyard. He would sniff along the fence looking for a place to go while pausing to look back at her, as though to make sure she hadn't left him. Harry wondered about Brutus. Did he understand his first family abandoned him? Is that why he appeared so concerned as to Olivia's whereabouts? In contemplation of Brutus's calm and conscientious demeanour, Harry's fear of the dog receded. He was getting used to the dog and against his instincts was starting to like him. It was hard for him though. He had been afraid for so long, he didn't know how not to be. He had to learn, for Olivia's sake. The first night, driving home in the car with Brutus he was so scared and nervous his shirt clung to his sweat soaked frame. He kept expecting those jaws to clamp around his exposed neck while he drove. It was stupid, he knew it, but the image was so strong he thought for sure it would happen. He couldn't wait to get out of the car. They stopped for supplies and Harry volunteered to go in and get them. Out of sight of Olivia, he stood inside the door, breathing in through his mouth and out through his nose. A technique he read about to reduce anxiety and return the heart rate to normal. It had been useful to him ever since he quit drinking.

He would get used to Brutus. Olivia smiled more and the tension that used to draw her shoulders up around her head grew less pronounced. As dogs went, Brutus was remarkable. Brutus possessed an almost human awareness of his discomfort and respected it. Harry anticipated that one day Olivia would have the courage to leave the house without him. As long as she took Brutus with her of course. He hoped she would someday continue with getting her education. She could take online courses and complete university that way. Get a degree while never leaving the house if she wanted to. She could get on with her life and maybe heal from the cruel interruption. She wished they caught that bastard Jackal. Maybe Olivia wouldn't be as scared of the night or strange noises if she knew he was in jail. Detective Davis believed he would make another appearance. Especially after carving Jen so she would resemble Olivia. What was the connection to Olivia? Why was she so special to this sick bastard? He wish he had some idea, even an inkling of why. With his shadow an overhanging presence, would Olivia ever have a normal life? What if he came for her? Would Harry be able to protect her or would he end up another victim, like Jen and her mother? It isn't fair for Olivia to have to live this way. It wasn't fair for her to have been taken. He sighed. Life was indifferent to fairness. It had taken a long time for Harry to learn that. All a person can do is try to be prepared. But how do you prepare for an avalanche or a meteor strike? That's what Olivia's abduction had been like. Violent and unpredictable.

He sighed, watching Olivia sit out back, Brutus lying by her side, her hand absently scratching him on the top of his head. She had the alarm around her neck, the house alarm with the video cameras, her knife and now Brutus the guard dog. She should be safe.

•　　　•　　　•

Summer arrived in July. According to the calendar, the first day of summer was supposed to be June 21st. The weather decided not to acknowledge the calendar and remained rebelliously cool until halfway through July. Then in typical Canadian fashion, it got so hot people complained about it forgetting a short time ago they were whining about the cold and bitter winter. Olivia never complained about the summer heat. For her, the hotter the better and she refused to turn on the air conditioner even if just breathing caused her to sweat. Harry would invariably arrive home, moan about the heat in the house and the hum of the AC would begin before he completed his complaint. To Olivia, summer lasted for only a blink before the cold air swooped down from the the north to remind everyone that, yes, they lived in Canada. Olivia decided to take advantage of the weather and spent most of her time outside, soaking in the sun, reading a book while music emanated from the windows of the house. The first summer in five years she could spend outside. She wouldn't waste it.

Frank and Carl finished the renovations. It took longer than both of them expected. Wood rot pervaded the house. They had to replace her closet and to her delight, it was considerably bigger than before. Olivia invited them both over to dinner for a thank you. Carl accepted. Frank declined citing the workload that had built up while he worked for them for free. He never tired of reminding her or Harry that he was renovating their house for free.

They were done and she felt relief to no longer have them around. She enjoyed being alone and thought she might be turning into a hermit. Do hermits live with their dads?

Her routine consisted of getting up with Harry, eating breakfast with him after feeding Brutus and quietly enjoying the rising sun brighten the windows. After he left she would set the alarm to monitor doors and windows, check the same windows manually and review the video from the previous night. Then she would catch up on the news hoping to hear the Jackal was either dead or caught, preferably dead, torn apart by a pack of ravenous dogs just for the irony of it. And the intense pain he would experience before he died. She checked every day although she knew Davis would let her know before the news people did. Once the news failed to relate the horrible death of the Jackal, she would take her tea, iPad and a book into the backyard with her. Brutus, tongue lolling, walked beside her. Some days after her tea she would mow the yard and pluck vile dandelions. After she picked up the dog crap of course. She had mowed over his droppings before and to see it spray out the exhaust in a brown haze and the accompanying smell had her tasting bile. She preferred never to do that again. Other days, she would zone out in her book until she would need a break and then toss the ball to Brutus. She kept the knife at her hip, attached to the belt on her shorts and continued to pat it in times of nervous contemplation.

She thought of Lucy often. She had Lucy's phone number. Davis had given it to her a long time ago on his business card. The card sat ignored on the stand beside her bed. What did Lucy think of what happened to Jen? Did she hunker down out of sight after she heard about it? She didn't seem the type to lie low. The hazy, lazy days removed any urgency to call Lucy and she kept putting it off. The summer lounging was too nice to lousy up with a stressful conversation on the Jackal. She wanted to move ahead and leave all the memories behind. That would be easier to do if the Jackal wasn't still out there. Besides, Lucy didn't feel the need to call Olivia.

Olivia sighed under the heat. The sun pressing down on her skin with a heavy hand induced a delightful indolence. Brutus suffered the heat to be near her and she felt bad about it. His tongue grew long out of his mouth and his panting took on a hectic cadence. She had Harry bring home one of those little turtle pools and she placed it at the end of the deck and filled it with water. Brutus showed how grateful he was by hopping into it and lying down. He would submerge his face in it and she would see his pink tongue darting out to lap up the water. Once satisfied, he hopped out, made sure to pad near her before shaking the water off as though wanting to share the refreshing glory of the pool. Brutus alternated between prowling the yard, dunking himself in the pool and napping beside her. She loved the mutt and could see her dad warming up to him. Taking incrementally tiny steps forward, one day, he may even summon the courage to pet Brutus.

The sun's arc crept into the other half of the sky. Olivia, realizing the afternoon had arrived and she hadn't eaten lunch, summoned the energy to go inside for something to eat. She sighed. The end of summer was fast approaching. September loomed before her. The days had passed in a blur and there was still no end in sight to the investigation and the identity of the Jackal. How long would she have to hide from the outside world? Would she be more eager to go out and join it if the Jackal were caught or dead? Hard to answer. She liked to think so but she would always have a fear, irrational or not, of being snatched off the street and disappearing. It happened so quick the first time. Rude eye opener to realize how helpless a person could be to surprise and superior strength. She patted the knife at her waist. Brutus' claws clacked on the floor behind her. She opened the fridge, turning her thoughts towards something more productive: like lunch.

She sang along with the iPod, content in the moment. She patted Brutus on the head and removed cheese from the fridge. Crackers and cheese plus lemonade. Delish! For the moment, she felt safe.

-32-

The Jackal packed a white panelled van with the gear he would need. He stole it from a work site and being a Saturday, he figured no one would notice or report it missing until Monday morning. And only if they happened to need that particular van so he had a good window with the van being safe to use. He liked the camouflage the white work van afforded. It aroused no suspicion. They were as common on the road as seagulls are at a beach. Not even the cops would pay him much attention. He couldn't believe the police still sat there, day after day. It must be costing them a fortune. He thought of himself as a patient and meticulous man and as such, going after them without the police watching was a bad idea. Going after them with the police watching was damn near suicidal. He should leave both of the girls alone and move on. Or at least wait until the police did go away. He had always believed himself capable of controlling himself enough to be able to move on without a backwards glance. He should be able to play this smart and just quit. He had had his fun. Years of it. No good thing ever lasts. He couldn't let go. The very idea that he could was a lie. It made him wonder who was in control. Him or Olivia?

He had read of other convicted serial killers and the repeating theme of them being caught was they were the victims of their own laziness, complacency and arrogance. A dangerous mixture. The Jackal didn't believe his affliction could be called laziness. No, the danger to him lived and breathed and called to him from her room. Olivia was the danger. He couldn't stop thinking of her. He couldn't stop wanting her. Is this what drug addicts go through? Attracted to and needing something clearly harmful to them? He even scoffed at them, upon a time but no longer. He was decided. Tonight was the night his torment would end. He would have both of his prizes, spirit them away as the police supposedly watched from their cars.

He went inside his house, the one his family didn't know about, and ate a steak dinner. The steak was good but it didn't compare to the flesh of his ladies.

Terror added a distinct flavour to flesh. He would have a taste of it again soon enough. After, he washed the dishes by hand, dried them and put them away.

He ambled to the back porch with a glass of lemonade. *Ava Maria*, on repeat, played in the background. It was their song, his and Olivia's. He sank into an outdoor recliner. The sun drifted towards the earth. This is what Olivia liked to do. Sitting in the backyard with the sun as a warm companion. He liked it too because it helped him feel close to her. It's what she had done all summer and he had to admit, it was peaceful.

Stars dotted the darkening sky. Finishing his lemonade, the Jackal stood and made ready to leave. Tonight he would be reunited with his lovelies. Joy tempered with trepidation, the Jackal anticipated an unforgettable night.

-33-

Harry sat in his Lazy Boy chair, the plaid pattern an eyesore to Olivia, and berated the Toronto Blue Jays on the TV. A once hot coffee sat forgotten beside him. He complained to her bitterly of the Blue Jays and their inconsistent performance. She feigned interest and needled him from time to time with phrases like, "Well if the owners cared…" or "That guy is always getting injured isn't he?" setting Harry off on another tirade of why individuals should own teams and not corporations. According to Harry, corporations cared about money first and the World Series as an after thought. They were in the last couple of weeks of the season and the Blue Jays would not be playing any post-season games. They were too low in the standings. Olivia grinned as Harry espoused his opinion on the sorry state of Blue Jays' baseball.

Baseball bored Olivia and the game could never hold her interest and she suspected it never would. Her dad loved it and so she suffered through it and tried to amuse herself any way she could. She would sit on the couch, her feet tucked under her with her latest book in her hand. Brutus dozed on the floor under her. She enjoyed these moments of normalcy.

The phone rang and deciding not to interrupt her dad's time with his ever-disappointing Blue Jays, she answered the wall mounted one in the kitchen. It surprised her to notice the darkness outside. Since her escape, she'd been obsessively aware of the dark. Today she hadn't paid it any attention. Another sign of healing? She hoped so.

"Hello?"

"Olivia?"

"Hey Davis. What's going on?"

"We got him. The rec centre guy. We're bringing him in now. I just wanted you to know, before I interview him."

Flustered, Olivia didn't know how to respond and so she remained silent.

"Olivia?"

She said, "Is he the Jackal?"

"Well, you know, right now it's all pretty circumstantial. What we mostly got is coincidence. But this guy is going to get the full treatment. Financials, background checks, freaking grade school records. We're going to get as much as we can. By the end of it, he'll think an enema is less intrusive."

"What's his name?"

"Darcy Bowles. Mean anything to you?"

"No. Nothing. Hey Davis?"

"Yeah?"

"Do *you* think it's him. Do *you* think he's the Jackal?"

"It doesn't look good for him, that's for sure. If you're asking for a definite answer I can't give you one right now. I need more information. We need to process his DNA, after we get a warrant for it, of course. I will tell you this though. You wanna know where we picked him up?"

"Yeah."

"A block from Lucy's place. Just strolling along, heading towards her home...we think."

"Were you guys watching him?"

"Just found out who he was earlier today. Once we knew, we had a few guys set up on him. We decided to bring him in when we saw him heading to Lucy's in case he was planning to...you know. Like I said, this guy looks good. But listen, I gotta go. I'll let you know more tomorrow."

"Just one more thing. Did he have a mask with him?"

"No. It could be in his house though. If he still has it. It'd be pretty ballsy to carry it around outside with him. We're trying to get a warrant for the house too."

"He still has it. He wouldn't get rid of that. It's who he wants to be. But I'll let you go. Thanks Davis. Thanks for the call."

She hung up. Harry stood near her. When did he leave the TV?

Harry said, "What's up? You look a little peaked."

"That was Davis. They think they got him...got the Jackal."

"That's good news, right?"

"Yeah. Definitely. Only, I didn't think it'd be this easy."

"This seemed easy to you?"

"No. Well, I don't know. I was kinda hoping he'd be killed, you know, resisting arrest or some such shit. He had that feel about him, suicide by cop instead of capture. I can't picture him going to jail, not willingly anyways."

"Cheer up. Who knows? Maybe someone will murder him in prison."

Olivia, shaking, began to cry. Harry pulled her into a hug.

"I don't know what to do. They think they have him but they can't say for sure. I don't know what to think. I should be relieved but I feel so anxious I want to scream."

Harry said, "Nothing's changed honey. We'll keep doing what we're doing until Davis calls back and says they definitely got him. Until then, we don't let our guard down."

She controlled her breathing, listening to her dad's heart in his chest and wishing she didn't feel so terrified all the time. There were times when lounging with Brutus, she forgot about the basement, about ripping Grady's neck open with her teeth and the taste and smell of his hot blood jetting down her throat. There were moments when she even forgot about the Jackal. How stupid of her. How naive. Those events forever shaped her. Those ugly and terrible men were a part of her, forever altering her thoughts of safety and how she thought of herself. She couldn't help but think the Jackal wasn't done with her yet. To believe him to be caught and sitting in jail didn't seem right. It did seem too easy. Maybe she built it up in her mind as something more because of what she went through. A towering event in her life ending not with a bang but with a quiet whisper.

Suddenly tired, she pulled away from her dad and told him she was going to bed. She walked down the hall to her room, patting the knife at her belt. Brutus padded behind her.

She settled in her bed and put the knife under her pillow. She hadn't done that for awhile but it felt right to do so tonight. She slept in her track pants and sweater. Harry had turned on the AC the minute he walked in the door. She couldn't decide if the AC caused the deep chill inside her or the talk about the Jackal. Either way, she climbed in her bed and pulled the covers up to her chin. She reached over to turn off the bedside lamp and paused with her finger at the switch. She retracted her hand and thought tonight she would sleep with the light on. Her mind burned with rampant thoughts. Brutus lay on his dog bed, eyes watching her with doggy concern.

"I'll be alright fella."

His tail twitched.

Sleep arrived unexpectedly, amidst heavy worry.

-34-

Lucy was arguing with her parents when Davis called her. Mostly arguing with her dad. She wanted to go out and didn't want to be driven around by her dad, which he insisted on doing, to act as a surly, squinty-eyed bodyguard, terrorizing people who dared approach her. It wasn't her fault she was taken and it wasn't her fault that he felt so much guilt because of it. She wanted to go out and meet a friend for coffee. A boy, a cute one who was interning at CBC news. He had been backstage giving her the eye wearing one of those head-mic's talking to whoever, flashing her a smile now and then. After her interview, she put on her coat and he walked up to her, gave her his card while holding onto it a little too tight so he could touch her hand and she liked that, a lot.

She called him and they started flirting and it was progressing until Jen got herself killed. Maybe that wasn't accurate. More like the Jackal killed her. Point being, her dad went ballistic and insisted on driving her everywhere and being her annoying shadow. And that definitely put a crimp on her social life. How do you go on a date with your dad following you around? Short answer: you don't.

So the intern, Trevor, was losing interest. And, Lucy thought, why wouldn't he? Phone convos and clever texts are fine for a while but not forever. She needed that human touch. And judging from Trevor's texts, he needed it too. And her dad was ruining everything! And he didn't care!

She was holding a phone in her hand, waving it at her dad to accentuate her point, saying, "I'm going to live here forever aren't I? Become some old cat lady. No husband or boyfriend, just a houseful of stinky fucking cats! You know I hate cats! I don't want to be a cat lady!"

"You're overreacting. I'll drop you off. I'm not going to stare at you, but I'll be close by and when you're done, I'll give you a lift home. What's the big deal?"

"The big *deal*, Dad, is—"

The phone trilled in her hand and she jumped, staring at it with her mouth open.

Her dad said, "Are you going to answer it or eat it?"

She glared at him, nodded and said, "Yeah, but this…is to be continued."

Lucy slid her thumb along the answer button and said, "Hello?"

Davis told her the same thing he told Olivia. She interrupted him when he said they arrested the guy just down the street from her house. "Just outside? You're kidding me?"

He wasn't. Olivia understood it was possible they didn't have the Jackal in custody. Lucy chose to believe they caught him. To her, they got the guy and she could finally go out without her dad breathing down her neck. The Jackal had been caught and she was gloriously fucking free! She hung up the phone, beaming which caused immediate suspicion from her father.

"What?"

"They got him. They got the Jackal."

"Really?"

"Yeah. That was the cop."

"Well. Who is he?"

She waved her hand dismissively, "Darcy something or other."

"You don't remember his name?"

"Yeah, I said it was Darcy didn't I?"

"When can we know more?"

"He said he'd call later with the details. Right now they are interrogating him."

"Hope they beat the fucker."

Her mother from the other room yelled, "Dear! Language."

He rolled his eyes and said, "Sorry, honey. But did you hear? They got the prick!"

"What? That's great news!"

"So Dad?"

"Yeah?"

"Can I have the keys now or what?"

-35-

Davis studied Darcy on the TV monitor. He wore the expression of a man who had been bonked on the head, a perpetually stunned face. Davis frowned, all but sure the man sitting in the interview room wasn't the Jackal. If he is, then he is the world's best actor. A few years back, an investigator once told him there were no such things as coincidences and the saying had proven true to Davis. But sometimes, very rarely, a coincidence was in fact a coincidence. And this man, sitting on the chair, offering stuttering and vehement denials, had the distinct odour of innocence to him. A scent Davis detected early in the interview.

Darcy was a broken man. Busted apart by events beyond his control. The story he offered had checked out in every way and the more concerning part was, it made sense. He did not project the air of a man capable of the acts the Jackal had done. He didn't have the arrogance to skillfully manipulate a man like Shawn Grady to his will. The presence wasn't there. Darcy wanted to disappear, disperse into the background, escaping notice and being spared the uncomfortable action of conversation. Physically, he appeared to be a match. Tall, lean and strong. That is the only way he compared to the Jackal in Davis' mind. Darcy avoided eye contact. Not in the way a guilty person would, where the eyes would slide away whenever a tough question needed to be answered. No, Darcy didn't *like* to look people in the eye. It made him very uncomfortable because it was too direct. Davis believed it would be how he talked to anyone and not just because he was in a police station being questioned as a suspected serial killer.

"What do you think? He our guy?"

His direct supervisor, Sergeant Ben Arturo, stood with him, watching Darcy stare into his lap. Ben held a coffee in his hand. Davis could smell tobacco smoke on him. He must have just come in from outside.

"From the interview? I'd say no. But I've been fooled before."

"Did he consent to giving a DNA sample?"

"Yeah."

"On video?"

"Yeah."

"Sweet."

Consent could prove tricky to deal with in court. They wanted to know if the consent was truly voluntary and if the person giving it understood their right to refuse and the potential consequences. For big cases, Davis didn't believe in using consent to get his evidence. He would rather go by way of warrant. And he did this time too.

"I still applied for the warrant. I told him I would be getting one for his DNA and he offered it right then. No hesitation."

"And that worries you?"

Davis turned to Ben, "It doesn't worry you?"

He sighed, "Yeah. Yeah it does. Why can't shit ever be easy?"

"I know."

"What he'd have to say about being at the rec centre? And the university and Lucy's house? Can't all be coincidence, man."

"I'd normally agree with you, but…" Davis shrugged his shoulders.

"Shit."

"Yeah."

"What are you waiting on now?"

"The DNA warrant's been signed. Just waiting for a tech to get the sample. They're gonna put a rush on it. They could match the fingerprints, the ones we lifted from the house, right away. The DNA takes a little longer as you know. A couple of days at least. I gotta tell you boss, I'm not very hopeful. When we first got him? I fist punched the air, you know? I was pumped! Now though, I got a bad feeling. A real bad feeling."

"I remember those. They suck."

"Agreed."

"What's his story anyways? What'd he say about being at the rec centre?"

"Darcy'd been going there for years. He used to take his daughter, Lisa."

"Oh shit. I know where this is going. She's dead, isn't she?"

"No. But that's exactly what I thought when he started talking. He woke up one day, went to work and when he came home, his wife and kid were gone. She just took their daughter and moved back home to the States with her family. Their daughter was born there, so now he can't get her back. She won't even let him see her."

"What's this have to do with the pool?"

"Before his wife split with Lisa, he used to take her swimming all the time because she loved it. By the way, we checked and a Lisa Bowles was registered for swimming lessons there for two years. Right around the time Olivia worked there. After his wife left, he went to the pool, to sit nearby. He would close his eyes and listen to the kids' laughing. Sometimes, he could hear a laugh very similar to Lisa's and he'd pretend she was back. He said, for the time, it helped with the pain."

"Was Olivia there when he went back by himself?"

"Yes. See, Olivia worked there when he used to bring his daughter for the swimming lessons. She wouldn't remember him, then. Why should she? He was just like any other parent at the pool drying off their kid when they got out of the water and yapping to other parents about how special their kid was. But she would notice a man hanging out at the pool without any kids. It would be something people notice because it borders on creepy."

"And this all checks out?"

"Yup. Tracked down his ex-wife. They were never married. Kind of like-oh shit, you're pregnant so let's live together-type of deals. One of our guys spoke to her and the timeline is right."

"Damn."

"Yup."

"Did she say why she left?"

Davis smiled, "Said she couldn't stand Canadian weather. Hates the cold. Hates how in one day you can go through four seasons, snow, rain, sun and hail."

"Huh. She's right. Our weather can do that. Some parts of the States are like that too though. Why didn't she bring Darcy with her?"

"He was too nice."

"Too nice? Is that a thing?"

"I guess. He'd do anything for her and Lisa. He never got mad or miffed at whatever she asked him to do. She didn't think it was normal. She said she likes a guy with some backbone."

"A super nice guy? The guy we pegged as a serial killer is a super nice guy?"

Davis shrugged. He said, "You know what he does for a living?"

"No. What?"

"He's a contractor."

"That's good, right? He'd be able to build the basement like that. He'd know how to do it."

"Yes and no. He said he had a job in Guelph at the time of Olivia's abduction. Doing work for the university. Some students ruined one of the dorms and they hired him to fix it up. He just finished on the day the students were starting back at school."

"He can prove this?"

"Guelph University keeps records that far back. So yeah, we can and did prove it."

"Fuck."

"Exactly. Even if he is our guy, the defence has great reasons as to *why* he was where he was."

"If it's him, there is no excuse in the world that would explain why his DNA and fingerprints are inside that torture house."

Davis sighed and said, "I think, by now, we both know it won't be."

"Goddamnit."

They shared a moment of disappointment. Ben said, "What about walking to Lucy's house? What'd he have to say about that?"

"He lives in the area. He went for a walk. We spoke to a few neighbours. It's not uncommon for him to go out for walks."

"Turning into a real clusterfuck isn't it? We were all about to start kissing your ass, congratulating you on your awesomeness."

"That option is still viable. Here, I'll drop my pants for you. You can be the first to kiss it."

"I'll pass on your ass."

"You're a goddamn poet Sarge."

"A man of many talents. That's me. So, what's next?"

"We work on this like he's our guy until we're certain he's not. The fingerprints and DNA should prove it either way conclusively. I have no other leads to follow."

"Alright. I'll have to report this to the Inspector. She won't be happy."

Davis nodded and said, "I'll be here for awhile. I have a few follow up questions to ask."

Ben stepped out of the room and when Davis thought he'd gone, Ben poked his head back in and said, "So? You're sure he's not our guy?"

"I'll be sure when we get DNA. But I'd have to say, at this point, his story checks out. We've proven that much of it."

"Poop."

"Yes. Poop."

"Call if you need anything."

"Will do."

•　　•　　•

Sergeant Ben Arturo notified the Inspector of the disappointing news. The Inspector, Mary Fitch, had been preparing her statement for the media. They were aware the police had made an arrest and were salivating for details. The Inspector wanted to give it to them yet after speaking with Ben, she decided it would be prudent to be vague. She would offer the general nonsense, we're still investigating, person of interest, blah-blah, bullshit, bullshit. She closed her eyes and said, "Fuck."

She squeezed the phone in her hand, her frustration turning her fingers white. She should call Dave, the man in charge of the surveillance of Lucy and Olivia. After they arrested Darcy, they pulled the incredibly expensive security. She had been under enormous strain to keep justifying the expense. All she ever had to do to stifle their questions and quiet suggestions was to mention Jen but that wouldn't last forever. She asked them, could they afford not to have the remaining girls watched? The media and the public were openly critical over Jen's death. Mary thought they had every right to be but kept the opinion to herself.

She would have to get Dave and his men back on the security detail, especially after the shitty news of Darcy maybe not being their guy. It was late, almost four in the morning. Darcy had been in their custody for hours now. She didn't want to wake up Dave, but she had to. She called him. Dave answered, groggy, and with disappointment colouring his words, said he would get the team back out there.

She hung up the phone feeling positive about the decision. She crept back into bed beside her snoring husband wanting to squeeze in another hour before the alarm brayed in her ear. She fell asleep not knowing that she had made the call too late. They never should have pulled the surveillance.

-36-

The Jackal almost shit his pants. Not quite, but something might have touched cotton. He had driven over to Lucy's place, doing laps near her home, looking for the cops he thought might be there like they were at Olivia's. Lucy wasn't as fearful as Olivia. He hadn't had enough time to teach her to be. The Jackal knew if Lucy went out her dad would follow. Especially at night. He didn't care about the dad. He looked soft, weak. A jiggle gut and a rounding back, the Jackal didn't think he would pose a problem. He would have to kill him, to have more time before the cops discovered her gone. If they found out before, the police would go into full panic mode and it would ruin his chances of taking Olivia too. He had considered taking Olivia first but in the end decided against it. He wanted to leave the best for last. The Jackal was nervous though. This was sloppy and so much could go wrong. He would be lying to himself if he didn't admit it excited him as much as it scared him. If they got him, he would never get out. It would be an ironic end to him considering what he and Shawn had done to the girls. But no, he couldn't go to jail. He wouldn't last the week. Even though he kept his girls in little more than cells, he couldn't see himself in one. Couldn't even picture it in his head. It didn't seem possible.

He parked on a side street, turned off the van and moved to the back out of the driver's seat so it would appear unoccupied while he still had a view of Lucy's house. He didn't know how he would do it, not like he did with Jen. Hers had been all planned out. Lucy's abduction would depend on her leaving the house. If she didn't, he didn't think he could pull off creeping in her window and snatching her. It could be problematic. Unless he crept in and killed the parents first. He could punch a knife in their throats, let them bleed out and then snag Lucy. He trembled at the thought. A night of blood.

In the van watching the yellow lights in Lucy's kitchen wink at him from behind the curtains, he ran through his options and that is when he saw the police. Two of them crept past his van. They were crouched low, duck-walking along the hedge and staying in the shadows and the Jackal ground his teeth, thinking *this is it, they got me* with his guts gurgling and the need to crap twisting his insides and he was making ready to jump in the driver's seat and drive off with squealing tires and then the two police sprinted away from him. A black sedan flew down the street and squealed to a stop. Two more cops, with Police emblazoned on their backs in reflective yellow, jumped out of the car and tackled a man on the sidewalk. Four cops piled on top and the Jackal could see the man's arm at the bottom flailing about. More cops spilled onto the street from marked and unmarked cruisers, blocking the road. All of this was occurring less than a block from Lucy's front door.

The Jackal, watching, muttered, "What the fuck?"

The man was picked up, hands cuffed behind his back and led to a black and white OPP cruiser. The Jackal couldn't pick out the man's features but from the way he swung his head back and forth, twisting in the officer's grip, he was confused and scared. He was stuffed in the back of the cruiser and it drove away with its befuddled package in the back, a long line of cars following behind.

Two unmarked cars remained in the street and four plainclothes officers stood in front of their headlights talking. One of them pointed to Lucy's house. Two of them high-fived each other and then they all piled into their cars and left. The neighbourhood returned to quiet in an instant. No one stood on their porch watching. No one had noticed the drama on the street. It had happened too quickly for a crowd to gather.

The Jackal frowned. What were they doing here by Lucy's house? Why did the one cop point to Lucy's house? It never occurred to him that the police thought the man they just arrested was him, the Jackal. His ego wouldn't allow it. Instead, he pulled out the binoculars and pointed it at something he saw on the sidewalk. He focussed the lens until the object became sharper. A black hat with a yellow letter 'P' on it.

He checked his watch: 9:43pm. He would settle in and wait. Maybe Lucy would come out on her own. If she didn't, he would go in and get her. And kill anyone in his way. It could prove to be a very interesting night. He would wait a while and watch. He had time.

-37-

Lucy's parents pestered her with questions she didn't have the answers to. In hindsight, maybe she should have asked Detective Davis more questions but she was too excited and wanted to take advantage of the Jackal's capture by going out without her dad following. They got him, right? Wasn't that the important part?

They wanted her to call Davis back and ask more questions but she could tell when he called her he had been busy and wanted to get off the phone just as much as she did. She did try calling him back, just to get her parents off her back and when his voice mail message came up for the fifth time, her parents shook their heads, muttering about the lack of communication with the police. They let her be after realizing there was nothing new to learn and her dad reluctantly handed her the keys to the car. She texted Trevor but he didn't reply. Did he finally give up on her and was even now out on a date? A woman without a psychotic, over-protective father wanting to go along? Lucy knew she was cute but how long could she expect a guy to wait for her? Catching sight of her reflection in the kitchen window, knowing she looked good, she thought Trevor should have waited a little longer. She was worth it. Oh well. She didn't want to pass up the night of freedom so she decided to go to Tim Horton's, get a coffee and something sweet, like a cherry danish. By then, Trevor, if he wasn't on a date, might see her texts and get back to her.

She sighed. A waste for someone as pretty as her to be going out alone on a Friday night. She should be partying it up with friends, doing shooters at the bar and picking out the man with the best abs to dance with. Although on the surface it wasn't obvious, the time she had spent in the basement had changed her. There was no doubting it. And her friends felt it when she returned home and they came by to see her and talk to her. It was different. Her oldest friend, Gwenn had asked her about the basement with wide eyes and a smile threatening to tilt the corner of her mouth, like she were hungry for it and wanted to slurp down all the delightful humiliations Lucy suffered at the hands of the men. Gwenn had tried to hide the smile, tried to stuff it down but Lucy saw it and it killed something inside her. Lucy saw through the feigned empathy and was disgusted by it. Was that how she used to be? Or still was?

Lucy's captivity to her friends was something to gossip about, something to revel in behind false smiles while they drank in the torment of another. Callous and shallow, they could not see past how Lucy's abduction affected them or how they could garnish reflected fame from it. They didn't see how cruel their fake empathy was or, even worse, didn't realize that they were fake. The mirror of introspection never penetrated past the skin.

She lived every day and night in fear of a visit. She would hear the door open and see the two men enter with their horrible masks. Sometimes they would show up and disrobe and other times they would walk in wearing nothing but the masks before they went to work on her. She didn't fight them. She learned early on the futility of it. She thought the Gorilla man had dislocated her jaw with one punch the time she had the nerve to resist. Under their violent tutelage, she became a realist. If she played nice, she got to keep her teeth. They would pinch the tender parts, pull on even more tender places and if she offered up the proper squeal, they would let her keep her nose. She thought, considering her choices, it was a fair trade.

But how do you tell your friends that? And worse, to know your friends, who haven't had to learn such harsh lessons, could never relate to such an experience? To them, it was something *interesting* that happened to someone else. She soon realized she didn't like her friends. They represented who she used to be and Lucy no longer had time for vacuous gossip mongers. Not anymore.

She learned life could be snatched at anytime and she intended to live hers to the fullest and without regrets. She refused to hide under a rock and let the threat of the Jackal keep her in a prison of her own making. Fuck that. That was no way to live. She scooped up the keys to her dad's car and checked her phone. No texts from Trevor. She sighed. Tim Horton's it was, then. At least it was in a public place. The Jackal would have to be an idiot to nab her in such a place. Especially wearing that mask. She chuckled at the thought. What the hell was she worried about? They got him, right? She hoped he would get his ass raped in prison. With a broken broom handle. And crushed glass glued to it. Yeah, that would be about right.

"Bye mom! Bye Dad!"

Her dad said, "Be safe honey!"

She rolled her eyes, "I will."

She stepped out into the night with the keys in her hand. There was a white van parked at the curb in front of her house. It was running. She frowned. The orange sodium street light illuminated the front seat area. There was no one inside. She slowed her walk, her heart moving from a walk to a sprint and then a voice behind her, a voice she knew so well called to her from the shadows.

"Hey Lucy-goosey. Daddy's back."

Lucy turned, opened her mouth to scream but he reached out and pain shot through her. She couldn't control her body. Her legs wobbled and the ground rose to meet her. Her head cracked off the hard ground and she lost time, confused, and then she was slung over his shoulder and he was off with her. He yanked open one door and inside was darkness.

-38-

Olivia's eyes popped open. Her pulse jumped, startled into action. She turned her eyes to the alarm clock. The green digital glow read 3:15am. Why was it dark in her room? Harry must have turned it off before he went to bed. He had done that before. But what had awakened her? Then she heard it. Brutus growling. She gripped the handle of the knife and slipped it from under the pillow. She sat up, peering at Brutus' bed on the floor. After her eyes adjusted to the dark she realized he wasn't in it. The growl sounded again, a low warning noise from deep in his chest. She turned to the noise and saw him sitting in front of the closet. He stretched his nose towards it and emitted another growl. There was someone in the closet, no, not someone, the Jackal. He was the bogeyman. He was the red-eyed demon in the closet. There was no escape. Olivia's mouth dried out, as arid as any desert and she sought control against the growing tide of panic. Think! No alarm went off. What does all that mean, dear Sherlock? She whispered, "It means, Mr. Watson, there's no one in the damn closet. There can't be because no one can get in the closet without first getting into the house. Yes, elementary."

So why wouldn't Brutus stop growling at the closet?

"Brutus? Hey Brutus!"

Brutus acknowledged her with a twitch of his ears. He didn't turn his head. Olivia frowned seeing a ridge of hair standing up on Brutus' back in the moonlight. There was no way anyone or anything could get into the closet. Must be some animal under the house, scratching their way in to where they could smell food. Any other alternative wasn't possible.

"Is that what it is, boy? You smelling an animal in there? Maybe a raccoon?"

That must be it. It couldn't be anything else. Her hand loosened around the blade of the knife. She lay back down, determined to get back to sleep but it wasn't so easy. This is the first time since Brutus came to live with them that he had acted this way. He wouldn't even look at her, standing sentry over an empty closet. Why? Sweat drew a line along her temple. Goddamnit! Would this feeling of fear ever go away? Brutus was probably growling at a damn mouse, as dogs liked to do and instead of turning over and falling asleep like a normal person she imagined monsters in her closet, waiting for her to close her eyes and her breathing to deepen so they could creep out and consume her with wide salivating jaws. Olivia couldn't equate herself with a normal person anymore. What happened to her forever changed her, physically and internally and what used to be a young, carefree girl, concerned with good grades and cute boys no longer lived within her.

She was damaged goods. She would be forever hiding her hands lest her missing fingers show. Or wearing her hair down in public to avoid eyes drawn to her missing ear hacked off by a maniac. Hell, she couldn't even wear open toed sandals to the beach. She could never forget or put this shit behind her. The mirror wouldn't let her. Any time she picked up a fork or knife, her missing digits would scream at her, *remember me little lady? Don't even pretend you're normal, don't even pretend you belong.* She couldn't see herself sitting at a table in a coffee shop while people around you talked of their 'first world' problems like they mattered. Like they *were* problems. They couldn't comprehend what she had been through and they wouldn't want to because it would disrupt the illusion of safety they had created. And Olivia knew safety was just that; an illusion. She reminded them of the ugly side of life, a side that would swallow them whole, a place where you crawled out of using murder to do it. They didn't want her around as much as she didn't want to be around their insipid mutterings. But oh, how she would love to be one of them. Then she could go back to sleep and ignore the growls and the strange posture of Brutus. She wanted a return to normal. Not this manic, anxiety ridden woman who had seen too much and had done too much to ever fit in. There were no do-overs in life. She couldn't go back to before the time in the basement. This is who she was. Time to quit fucking around and get up to do what you know you have to do if you ever want to get back to sleep.

"Fuck it," she muttered.

She placed her feet on the floor and with her knife in hand she padded out of her room towards the office where they kept the security monitors and controls. She would have to play back the night and watch it to convince herself nothing crept upon her while she slept.

She flicked on the light and sank into the chair in front of the screen. She turned on the monitor and the split screens revealed the outside world. Nothing moved except for the odd car. She reached down to pet Brutus. He wasn't there. The realization caused a trickle of fear to skim across her skin. He always came with her. Even when she got up to use the washroom, she would hear the click of his nails on the tile behind her.

She exhaled and clenched her hand around the haft of the knife. It was a damn raccoon or something. No need to freak out. She exhaled and then fiddled with the controls.

Olivia went back two hours into the night on the video and let it run at 1.5x speed. She will see nothing and return to bed a little tired and let's be honest, very annoyed with Brutus. It bugged her that he didn't follow her to nuzzle her hand with his nose and coax some affection from her. It felt wrong.

She clicked her nails against her teeth with one hand as the other was poised on the mouse button ready to pause it if something appeared out of place. The screen had been divided into four views. They covered all sides of the house with overlapping views so no spot on the property would be missed. She had been very specific about what she wanted. A good system, fairly inexpensive. She took her glance from the screen to peer down the hall. No Brutus. Was he still sitting in her room, growling at nothing? She had read somewhere dogs could sense the supernatural, like ghosts or demons but that was just hippy nonsense to her. Even if ghosts did exist, what did she have to fear from the dead? The living were the ones with the sharpest teeth and the pointiest claws. In her experience, the living were the ones to be feared.

On the screen, a shadow emerged. What was that? Her heart stuttered, as though it had been stun punched. She grimaced and she pulled the knife towards her chest like it were a pillow. She did see it though, it wasn't a damn illusion. A shadow. Moving from the fence and disappearing at her house. She rewound the feed. She let it play, but this time in slow speed. She leaned forward, the glow of the screen bright on her face. Her breath came in sharp bursts. The pulse at her neck jumped under her skin. Please let it be an animal. Please, please, please.

On the other side of the chain-link fence stood a thick brush. She had long wanted it gone and thought of cutting it down in the middle of the night because it hid too much. Problem was, she was afraid of the night and she didn't think her father would approve because the bush wasn't on their property. It was the one spot without a clear view. It offered shadows and darkness. She had rid the rest of her property of obscuring foliage. The bush she couldn't get rid of grew a man. Just below the bush was the sidewalk and then the street.

The bush was on the top of an incline. So even though it looked like the man sprouted from the bush, it was just him walking up the hill, growing taller than the bush with every step. But going up the hill meant he was walking towards her property. The man hopped the fence, *her fence*, and approached the side of the house. He moved with confident stealth. He passed under Olivia's bedroom window, close enough to reach up and tap on it if he wanted. Then he disappeared. She could feel her pulse in her eyes. She breathed out realizing she held her breath the moment she saw the man. He wasn't wearing a mask but that didn't matter did it? The Jackal wouldn't walk the streets with it on would he? She rewound the video and watched it again wanting to catch a glimpse of his face. The streetlights shone on the back of him so his face was a dark hole. She continued to watch and noticed he didn't pop up on the other camera. He had disappeared.

Olivia said, "Where the fuck did he go?"

The sensor light on the side of the house didn't even go on. She looked at the time stamp. The footage was twelve minutes old.

Brutus yelped from her bedroom. A sound of terrible pain, similar to a scream. She didn't know dogs could scream.

•　　•　　•

Even though the Jackal knew this night would entail all manner of risks he would have found unacceptable in the past, he still had made a plan. He expected police surveillance around both his girls' homes and they had been there, just as recently as yesterday. He spotted the cops and wasn't impressed. They appeared bored and disinterested and although they changed their positions with regularity, they were still easy to spot. You had to know what to look for and the Jackal had learned it well. He believed with some strategy and a little luck, he could take Olivia right out from under their nose. Wouldn't that be a pie in the face? He got hard thinking about it. The headlines would be ferocious. They would be more critical towards the police and would spew terror from every TV and newspaper in the country. He would be a superstar! He would be right up there with Bundy except for the getting caught part. He would be the Jack the Ripper of this generation. For years people would wonder who he was.

To slip in and out with both his girls and escape detection, he needed to note the position of the police before he parked his van and made his approach.

When he got to Olivia's, he couldn't find them. No government issued sedans with bored men in ugly ties trying to fight off sleep. He checked all the places they were before and…nothing. Where the fuck did they go? Were they onto him? Following him right now with Lucy trussed up in the back?

He checked his mirrors as though he could pick out the police by their headlights. He scanned every street he passed, careful to drive the speed limit. Sweat dotted his forehead and upper lip. Paranoia choked him. Tendrils of fear filtered through his veins. Had they somehow figured out who he was and were they waiting for him now to park so they could surround him and tear him bodily from the van? He knew dumb luck could ruin anyone. You can be extremely careful yet the stupidest thing can bring you down. A parking ticket did in the Son of Sam. Not every variable can be accounted for. Some things were out of your control no matter how much you may wish it to be otherwise. At least when he had the house, the chances of discovery were significantly reduced. If only that fucking Shawn Grady followed the rules! They were there for a reason! He wouldn't be here now, driving the dark streets looking for police, waiting for them to swoop out of the sky and nab him. Remembering the man arrested outside Lucy's house, another idea sprang to mind. Is it possible? Could it be? Did they pull the surveillance? Did they think they had arrested the Jackal? Could the explanation for no police around Olivia's house be that simple?

A smile flittered on his face, as tremulous as Jell-O as he was still unsure. It seemed too good to be true. He cruised the streets around Olivia's house. No cops. He saw the flickering lights of TV's in darkened windows with unimaginative people watching the screen and ignoring each other and wondering how much a divorce would cost them after the dust settled, or gossiping about their neighbours and worrying about their lawns. Or busy creating mini-versions of themselves so they can repeat the family cycle of get married-buy house-have kids-retire-die.

He wondered what they would do if he walked in their house, grabbed a knife from their own kitchen and went to work on them. Gutting them and cutting them down till the carpets squished crimson. Would they even run? Would they scream? Would they try to save their own lives? He didn't think so. They would be too shocked to react and by the time they'd think to, he'd be working on them with the knife. He had to admit, he was curious. And it'd be one hell of a diversion for the police and it would be entertaining, to say the least. From driving around though and not seeing one cop in the area, keeping an eye on Olivia, he could see he wouldn't need a diversion because there was nobody here.

He spent another thirty minutes searching the side streets before he decided to get on with it. He knew, at some point, the police would stop protecting Olivia. Security like that was too expensive to keep going forever. Still, he expected them to last a lot longer than they did. Amazing. The police were going to get fisted by the media after he took Olivia. He gripped the steering wheel and bared his teeth and thought, *not my problem*. He parked his car on a side street making sure he could park without getting towed or a ticket but close enough to drive over and carry away his prize. Lucy lay motionless on the floor. Tied up as she was, she had no mobility. He had stuffed a rag in her mouth and taped it on so even if she screamed, it be hardly loud enough for anyone passing by to hear. Not that anyone would be passing by at this time of night. He grabbed his back-pack from the floor behind the seat and opened it. The eyes of his mask greeted him. He ran a finger over the brow. He moved it aside and double checked that he brought the equipment he needed. Yup. All there. A tingle started in his guts. Like he was nervous, as though he was going on a first date. This wouldn't be his first date with Olivia but was sure, at the end of it, he would be going all the way. He slung the backpack over his shoulder and hummed *Ava Maria*.

-39-

"Fuck this," muttered Olivia. She fished the alarm out of her shirt and depressed the button. Her hands shook, picturing the signal reaching out to the dispatcher at the police station, someone, maybe an older woman chewing gum with a headset on, recognizing the priority alarm and sending officers to her home, their sirens piercing the night. How long would it take? How close was the nearest cop? Would Brutus die before they got here? Her teeth chattered. She clicked the alarm on the chain again her ears straining to hear the faintest sound of a police siren.

She peered out into the hall, her breath hot and choppy. Her fingers hurt from clutching the knife so hard. She stared at Harry's closed door. Should she call out to her dad? Would she want him waking up and stumbling into the hall, eyes heavy with sleep? Brutus whined from her bedroom. His pain squeezed her heart. The Jackal was here. Somehow, he got into the house and he was waiting for her in her own bedroom, wanting her to come check on her dog. Using poor Brutus as bait. Fuck! She hoped they had caught him when Davis called but at the time, didn't she know? Didn't she say as much to Harry? He couldn't be caught like that. It was too easy. How can this be happening! Poor Brutus. A pawn in the sick fucker's game. Was he bleeding out on her floor while she sat here?

Just calm down. The cops have to be here soon. No need to go all hero right now. From her bedroom, the song of *Ava Maria* issued. Although she knew the Jackal was here, in her home, the song cemented the belief and made it firm in her mind. She ground her teeth and gripped the knife. She toyed with the idea that this was some strange fucking mistake. Something that reason could account for and explain away the shadow creeping outside her house and the terrible sounds of pain from Brutus. The Jackal couldn't be here, in her home, could he? The song, though. That fucking song removed all doubts. He was here in her house. He was in her bedroom, maybe smelling her pillow or whatever sick fucking thing that got him off. Tonight, she would be fighting for her life. Where were the goddamn cops?

"Olivia?"

Shit. Her dad's shadow popped into the hall.

"What's wrong with Brutus? And what's with the music?"

Brutus whined at the mention of his name.

The light from the office shone golden in the hall while the dark of night claimed everywhere else.

"Olivia? You in the office?"

Shut up, Dad, she pleaded. *Just shut up! Go back to your room. The cops will be here any minute.* She peered out. Harry was a dark outline in the hall. She waved a hand towards him motioning him back, to get away, but his gaze was on Olivia's door.

Harry took a step out of his room. His weight creaked on the boards.

Go back to bed! Please!

His hand reached out for the hallway light switch. The light clicked on and he squinted from the brightness. In the moment he blinked to acclimate to the light, her nightmare moved into the hall. Swathed in black clothing he moved with incredible swiftness. The long ears of the mask brushed the underside of the doorway as he closed the distance to Harry. The Jackal's broad back filled the hallway. Harry jumped back against the wall. Harry's eyes bulged, standing there in a white T-shirt and boxer shorts with penguins on them. He had time to raise his hands before the Jackal was upon him.

The Jackal straight-armed Harry in the forehead with his left arm and in his right a knife blade caught the hallway light before it arced in under Harry's outstretched arm and plunged into his soft middle. One, two, three times it sank into flesh. Ruby drops splashed the floor when the knife came out. Red bloomed on Harry's shirt as he stepped back and then his hands caught the Jackal's wrist as they struggled in the hall. Blood from Harry's wounds gushed to the floor and the pattering drops sounded like rain. Olivia's mouth unhinged and a shrieking wail burned her throat. Dimly aware of the sound, recognizing that it was her making it, she watched her father slip on the blood pooling under his feet and with the weight of the Jackal on top of him, he hit the floor, hard. The back of his head bounced off the hardwood floor, a clunking sound, like a bowling ball bouncing down the lane thrown by a careless hand. He stopped moving.

"Dad!"

The Jackal's head turned to her. His back heaved under the coat and his breath sounded forced through the mask, the only evidence of his struggles with Harry. Where was her strength now? All this time, she had wondered what she would do if the Jackal turned up suddenly and now she knew. She would freeze and watch in horror while he tore her world apart again. Is this how it would end? With her dad dying on the floor and Brutus, a dog she rescued just to get him killed, sacrificing himself for her?

She ground her teeth. Tears burned her eyes. Her nose burned and her lip lifted in a snarl.

Olivia said, "Fuck that!"

It wasn't happening that way. He wouldn't take her from here. He wouldn't touch her in any way ever again. The sounds of *Ava Maria* stoked her anger. He meant to scare her? Petrify her into submission and make it easy for him to take her away and dump her into another hell hole? He wouldn't kill her like he did with Jen. His mercy didn't extend to her. For some warped reason he believed there was intimacy between them. He would spirit her away so he could renew his vows of cruelty. No one would ever see her again.

She wouldn't be locked in a cage to suffer that ever again. She wouldn't let him do it. If the cops didn't get here soon, she would finish it for them both, one way or another. She clutched the knife in her fist and crouched at the entrance to the office. Perspiration dampened her skin and her muscles trembled. If he wanted her, he would have to come to her.

The Jackal stood. Blood shone on the arms of his coat and darkened the legs of his pants. He stepped towards her.

She held up the alarm for him to see and said, "The cops are coming dick-wad! Better get the fuck gone!"

He shook his shaggy head and with the knife-free hand, he reached into his pocket and pulled out a device. A red light flashed, an eye blinking in the darkness.

"Cool. You have a remote control. Amazing. Now fuck off!"

He stepped closer, his boots leaving red prints on the floor. That was her father's blood on his boots.

He waved the knife back and forth, like you would wag a finger and held the device up again.

What's so fucking important about it?

"You know, if you opened your mouth and spoke, I might know what the hell you're trying to communicate here." But as soon as she finished the sentence she knew.

He had showed her the device right after she held out the alarm, telling him the cops were coming. Why would he do that and not run off? Because he knew the police weren't coming. The Jackal had thought of everything. That thing in his hand, the black box he was so keen to show off to her was a signal jammer. It had to be. That stupid thing had blocked the alarm from being sent. She had read about them on the internet when she was researching her alarm system. She craned her head, hoping for the sound of a siren or catching a glimpse of flashing lights indicating the police were on their way and hoping she was wrong and the Jackal was just another crazy asshole the world seemed littered with. He was crazy, only a different kind of crazy. Not the gibbering, salivating insane person who doesn't know right from wrong or what the consequences could reasonably be from their actions. The type of person who might cut off their mother's head because they believe she had been replaced by an alien. No, the Jackal knew what he did was wrong and took great pains to hide himself from view. He blended into the background, a tree in a forest of trees. Knowing this, she knew the Jackal brought the jammer to get into her house and out with his prize with no one being the wiser.

She grabbed the alarm and depressed the button frantically, wanting to be wrong about the jammer. She wasn't wrong. The clicking of the button competed with *Ava Maria* in the relative silence of the house.

He stopped a short distance from her and although the mask hid his face, she knew he smiled under it. She could feel it and was overwhelmed by the hate it arose in her. Acid in her veins commingled with the fury pumping her heart. An ugly grin distorted her normally kind features. Behind him, Harry's stomach rose and fell. Slow though, too slow for Olivia's liking. Blood pulsed from the wounds with every exhale.

Her grip tightened on the knife. She would love to run it through the bastard who stood in her hall, taunting her as her dad lay dying on the floor and her dog, poor Brutus may already be dead in her room. He was a destroyer, this masked maniac. Relentless. He would never let her go. Not as long as he was alive. Fuck him. Fuck him and his stupid games!

"This fun for you, you sick, small pricked bastard! Is that why you never touched me? Didn't want me to laugh at your tiny cock? Would I need a magnifying glass to find it? Maybe some tweezers?" She stood and he stepped back. She had made him step back. Was it fear he felt? Do monsters feel fear? Whatever it was, it satisfied her right to her core. Made her cheeks stretch into a smile lacking any humour. She stifled a giggle and a thought flittered through her head, *this is what crazy feels like*, and you know what? It feels good. Real good. She charged with a growl.

•   •   •

All thoughts of safety and self-preservation left her. She wanted the Jackal's head on a pike and if there was any justice in this world, she would have it. She could mount it on her wall above the dinner table and she and her dad could laugh about how silly the stupid man had been, thinking he could take her. She wanted to kill him and without hesitation she ran at him, knife raised, an animal snarl vibrating bass in her chest. She didn't see the Jackal remove something from his pocket, a black tool fitting into his hand perfectly. If she did, she would've been alarmed and maybe even stalled her flight to gut him. She did halt, somewhat, maybe the atavistic, primitive part of her brain alerting her to danger made her pause when he moved towards her and not away. It wasn't a knife he held. It was something else. Her knife reached him first. It slit a tear along his right arm and dug a furrow in his flesh. Then the tool he held hit her in the chest and she heard a clicking noise, like a breaker in a fuse box and pain infused her, invaded her. It stalled her muscles, tore into them with hot current and her legs failed her as she collapsed at the Jackal's feet. A Taser. The fucking bastard brought a Taser. The knife fell from her hand and clattered out of reach.

In practiced movements, the Jackal turned her over, held her wrists together and secured them together with a zip-tie. He moved down to her feet and sat on her legs. Her body began to respond to her commands again yet felt clumsy and disconnected. She tried to separate her feet and his weight settled on her hard, crushing her knees against the hard floor. The ties secured her ankles together causing the bones to grind together. Once done, he stood and pushed her over onto her side using his foot. He knelt and his knees cracked as he lowered himself to her level. Trussed up with ease, it brought back the first time with the Gorilla in the back of the van when his weight had crushed her and she learned what helplessness meant.

She groaned, "Not again."

She craned her head up. The shadows of his eyes studied her. He ruffled her hair like you would a kid after they scored a goal or did well on a test. His heavy breathing echoed in the mask. God, she fucking hated him!

"Fuck you, asshole!" She spat at him.

From behind his back he drew the knife and put the point towards her eyes. She pulled her head back, away from him and squeezed her eyes shut. Pain flared in her scalp as he yanked her towards him by her hair, a thousand complaints tingling from her roots.

Cold steel touched the lid of her right eye. The touch turned into pressure and she gasped and pulled her head away but he wouldn't let her move. She imagined him plucking out her eye, gouging it out of her head so she could feel the scrape of the steel on her orbital bone before he dragged it out. She didn't want to plead. The words left her mouth without permission.

"Please! Don't do that. Please, please, please."

The pressure released and a cry escaped her throat.

He stood and grabbed her by the wrists. He dragged her along the floor, taking her back to the bedroom. As her face slid along the hardwood floor, every pull on her wrists intensified the pain in her shoulder joints as though they were separating from the sockets. Her cheeks burned with friction from the floor and she turned her head so her hair would act as a buffer. He grunted as he dragged her into her room with that stupid song playing on her radio. Did he bring his own iPod and plug it in? Of course he did. He was a dramatic bastard.

He released her by the closet. His heavy tread walked around the bed and the music stopped. Wouldn't want to leave his iPod now would he? Nope. Not that. The light from the hallway spilled a yellow rectangle on her floor. Brutus' body lay under the bed and a dark trail marred her carpet. Blood coated the floor under him. He must have dragged himself under her bed after the Jackal hurt him.

She cried. Sobs that wracked her chest and forced snot from her nose.

"Brutus...my poor Brutus."

His tail twitched. Feebly and without any real energy. How much time did he have left? Would he die here on the floor, alone, like her dad? Was her dad still alive? When would someone bother to check on them? She shimmied her way towards him using her hips and legs to squirm over until the Jackal stepped over her and into the closet. What the fuck? She heard a thump, like boots hitting dirt. What the hell was he doing? Brutus whined. She inched closer to him, she wanted to touch him, wanted him to know she loved him and so she said it, "You're a good dog, Brutus. I love you boy."

She peered into the closet, wondering where the Jackal went and what he was doing when gloved hands popped out of the darkness, grabbing her feet. He spun her onto her back and she gasped at what she saw. The light from the hallway didn't reach far enough to illuminate him in her closet but she could see enough of him to know that what she saw didn't make sense. He seemed as shadow mostly, a dark outline in her closet but the light carpet in the floor of her closet disappeared at his chest. The lower half of his body was in, no, under the floor! How could that be? His upper body moved further into the light as he reached up her body to drag her towards him. The shaggy head of his mask and the long ears gave him an otherworldly appearance, like a cruel Egyptian god dragging her to the underworld. She screamed and he yanked her towards him until she bumped into his waist. He lifted her legs and with a fistful of her hair drew her knees to her nose bending her in the middle so she resembled a 'v'. He moved back and then he dropped her into the dark. A breathless moment as she fell thinking this was it, there was a hole in the earth and it would swallow her up and then she hit the ground with her back. It knocked the air from her. The restraints dug into her wrists and her shoulder blades tightened the skin across her back, stretching and straining. Her feet still stuck up out of the hole. She saw the shape of them above her with the feeble light outlining her toes with a golden glow. Dirt puffed up when she hit the ground. She tasted dirt in her mouth and spit it out. She was under the house. She didn't know how it was possible but she had been dropped into a hole in her closet and hit the earth. She regained her breath and looked at the Jackal watching her. How had he done this? She would have heard him cutting into her floor at some point. None of this night was possible. The light from the hallway silhouetted him and she saw the long ears, the hair sticking up in crazy tangles and with a full body chill she understood. Monsters are real. That wasn't a mask he was wearing, it was his real face. And now he would take her back to his cave and she would disappear and this time there would be no escape and no one to save her. She didn't think she'd be able to save herself, not again. And even though she had escaped once, it wasn't when the Jackal had been there. No. He wouldn't have allowed that. The Jackal would have quashed the uprising with a cruel fist and a liberal use of his knife and gardening shears. Anger and despair swirled within her. She wanted to give up. Disappear into that inner world where he couldn't touch her. Push away the terror and the fear and give herself over to surrender. The idea held attraction for her. And then she remembered Jen. Her distant stare. The way she would be there and not be there, as though she lived on another plane, pushed there by a cruelty she couldn't fathom. The Jackal snuck into Jen's home, killed her mother and then murdered and mutilated Jen just so Olivia would know, all of them would know, that there was no escape. This monster who created Jen and emptied her of her inner self and pushed it into the corner like a terrified child had now invaded her home to do the same to her. Not the same though. He had tied her up to take her with him. He wasn't done with her. He had murdered Jen. She feared him, that's for sure, but she also hated him and wanted him to feel fear, feel pain and to die at her hands so that way, she knew he would never come back for her. She wanted to tear the stupid mask off his face and jam it down his throat with a knife. Olivia tasted blood in her mouth and it reminded her of the Gorilla and what it felt like to rip into his throat so she could be free. Why should she make it easy on him? Fuck him. Let him take her eyes, take whatever the hell he wanted but she wouldn't make it easy for the bastard. He would have to fight her all the way. She would make every inch a struggle for him and if she saw the moment where she could kill him, like she killed Grady by ripping out his neck with her teeth, then she sure as hell was going to do it. If he put a finger near her mouth, he would lose it. Even now, why the hell should she lie here and let him take her? She still had her voice didn't she? Let's wake up all the neighbours, hell, the whole world, with her screams. Let her feet kick and take him in the groin, shins, knees wherever but in no way should she lie down and give in.

And so Olivia screamed. Screamed so her throat burned raw with the force of it, could feel the fibres vibrate and when her air ran out, she sucked in another glorious mouthful and let loose with a yell a Banshee would envy.

The Jackal put his hands on the side of his head. Not up by the fake ears, but by the side of his head where his ears would be and Olivia thought, *just a man after all* and screamed some more.

He raised his foot and she saw it, clenched her muscles to prepare for it yet still kept up her screaming. He booted her in the stomach and she felt her ribs bend with the force. She folded, drawing her knees into her chest. Tears squeezed out of her eyes. Her entire midsection throbbed, thrummed with pain. She could still feel the imprint of his foot. Did a rib crack? Her voice cut off and she found herself struggling to drag in air. As she gulped, her mouth a round 'o' knowing she looked like a fish out of water, the Jackal removed another item and she heard a tearing and knew what it was. He brought tape. The fuck-stick was a regular boy scout. Prepared for everything. She couldn't draw a breath and she wondered what she would do if he sealed that tape not only over her mouth but her nose too. Would she buck on the dirty ground as he stood over her watching her with implacable indifference?

He dragged her closer to him and knelt so his head and neck protruded from the floor. He knelt onto her stomach and put his weight on her. Her arms and shoulders ached and her ribs throbbed. There didn't seem to be a spot on her body that didn't hurt. He was stretching the tape out to cover her mouth when she saw a dark blob merge with the Jackal's head and Olivia, squinting, tried to discern what it was. Light from the hallway gave it a faint outline. It was furry and it growled.

•　　•　　•

The Jackal stiffened aware something wasn't right, something had changed and before he could turn his head, Brutus' open jaws clamped around the Jackal's neck and his teeth crunched into flesh. The Jackal tried to stand but was jerked off balance by Brutus, using whatever strength he had left to tug and pull and shake the Jackal. Olivia tucked in her legs so her knees brushed her nose and guessing where his knees might be, she shot them out. *Crack!* He fell and he gurgled a scream. She never heard such a beautiful sound. Grimacing, she kicked out again and her foot sank into softness and his gurgling scream was cut off. Brutus didn't let go. He growled and although Olivia couldn't see it from her angle on the floor, she imagined Brutus pushing against the floor with his forepaws as he tugged at the flesh on the Jackal's neck. Brutus was doing everything he could to help her. She wanted to cry, she wanted to scream and get out of this hole to help him. Something wet and warm splattered on her face. She closed her mouth into a thin line. The smell of copper filled the small space. It was a familiar scent to her. Blood.

She didn't want any of his blood in her mouth. She wanted nothing of him to ever get inside her. She didn't know the moment when the breath returned to her but she found herself yelling, "Good boy, Brutus. Eat him up! Eat the fucker up!"

The Jackal punched at Brutus over his shoulder, tried to get his fingers in between his jaws. Brutus wouldn't let go and the Jackal's efforts grew weaker. Brutus growled and tugged. Blood pattered on the dirt and on her face and into her hair. Soon, the Jackal's hands flopped into his lap. Brutus let go and fell onto his side. She couldn't see him anymore but she could hear him and it scared her. His panting was so loud in the quiet aftermath.

She had to move. She had to get free and get help for her dad and Brutus.

Her eyes watered and she shook them clear. No time for that now. She bent her legs in tight to her body and shimmied her hands under her butt to clear the bottom of her feet. It was hard work. She grunted and her muscles along her shoulders stretched and bones popped in the joints. She cringed with the effort and the strain it put on her body. She was so close to the Jackal and the area she had to work in was tight. When she had her hands in front of her she got to her knees. She wanted the knife in his pocket so she could cut the ties off. She would have to search his pockets. Her hands hesitated on the front of his dark jacket. She peered at his mask. Too dark to see anything, just vague shadows, lumps of darkness. Brutus whined and she jumped.

"I'm hurrying boy. I'll get us help."

She fumbled her hands into his pockets, looking for the knife.

"C'mon, where is it?"

In horror movies, this is the part where the madman would grab her wrist and say something witty. She glanced at him, wary, because after all she had been through, the idea didn't seem ridiculous at all.

Nothing in the first pocket. She reached over him and searched the other. Her hand closed on a hard edge. She pulled it out. A red light blinked at her. It must be the jammer.

She ran her thumb along the outside, feeling for the off button. She found a switch and slid it to the side. The red light extinguished. Biting her lip, she reached for the chain on her neck and pressed the button, once, twice and a third time just for the hell of it.

"Help's coming buddy. Hold on."

She needed the knife. It would be so much easier to climb out of this hole with her feet and hands free. Her hands moved along his waist and she grunted as she tugged him a little forwards so she could get to the back. Her heart thudded in her chest and the smell of his blood was stronger, more cloying. She coughed and kept working. Her fingers found a handle. She grinned in the dark. She pulled it free and sat back, taking a quick breath before she turned the knife and worked at the ties. She would have to be careful. In the dark she could easily slice open her wrists. She giggled. Thinking how stupid it would be to survive all this only to die because she cut open her own veins trying to break free.

Harry. Brutus. Remember them? Quit fucking around. She inhaled through her nose and released out her mouth. She visualized the knife, imagining how to turn it so the sharp part of the blade faced up and she could saw through the ties. She frowned in concentration and pressed the blade to the hard plastic and sawed. A shiver passed through her. No, not a shiver, more like a body-quake. So violent, she fumbled the knife and almost dropped it. She gripped it tight and the Jackal grabbed her wrist.

She screamed, a quick bark and his grip ground her knuckles together. She held onto the knife and then the Jackal spoke. She kept a tight grip on the knife and was turning the blade towards him but he stopped her, holding her in place. He spoke broken words between breaths, "I love...you...Olivia. I just wanted...you...to know that."

His hand lost strength and slid off her wrist.

Olivia said, "Go fuck yourself!" And she plunged the blade into him. Again and again. Not in a furious motion. More like a piston. Plunging it in and twisting it out with rhythmic regularity, the knife becoming slick in her blood soaked hands. She stopped when she heard the wail of sirens.

She sawed through the ties on her hands and then stood, her knees cracked and her cramped muscles shot pain through her thighs. Olivia cut through the ties on her feet and when she was done she stuck the knife in the Jackal's chest with a grunt. The adrenaline dump shook her frame. Her shaking hands touched Brutus. His chest rose under her hand. A sob broke from her throat and she climbed out of the hole and said to Brutus, "I'll be back boy. I got to check on my dad." Her voice broke, "I'll be back."

Leaving Brutus behind as she hobbled into the hallway, she recalled the Jackal's last words and his voice. She knew that voice.

-40-

At the hospital, Olivia waited for Davis and the doctor. She wanted to know about her dad and no one had told her anything yet. Although the way the paramedics glanced at each other as they lifted Harry onto the stretcher spoke more than words could she still wanted to know, she wanted to hope. Brutus had been taken to an emergency vet. Driven there by a police officer, a young guy, looking panicked as Olivia yelled at him as he loaded Brutus into the back of his cruiser, telling him to hurry the fuck up and be gentle or I swear to god! His eyes round and his movements hurried, he got Brutus out of there real quick. After he was gone, another officer sat in the ambulance with her while another police car, lights flashing and sirens screaming, followed behind. When they got to the hospital, they said her dad had been rushed off to an emergency room. A doctor approached her and with her eyebrows raised said, "Who's blood is that?"

"Not mine. Well, not all of it."

The doctor glanced at the officer and said, "Has she been seen by a nurse or a doctor?"

The officer shook his head.

"Can you bring her to triage? She needs to be assessed."

Olivia didn't want to be away from her father and said, "Look. I'm fine—"

"You're not fine. You've been injured and your colour doesn't look good and really, I'm surprised you haven't collapsed from shock. Shock can be deadly if not treated."

Olivia opened her mouth to answer and she continued, "No. You need treatment. It's not a request."

So the officer escorted her to triage and the nurse, nice and efficient, called for a stretcher after reading the results of her blood pressure and she was transferred to a bed in another room and forgotten. At least that's what it felt like.

An hour had passed since she first arrived. In that time she put on a gown and the nurses did their best to get most of the blood off her. They scraped as much as they could from under her nails and she submitted urine and blood. She waited for news about Harry. She asked and she was told to wait for the doctor. Olivia frowned at them and demanded someone tell her about her dad. She yelled it and the nurse fled from the room. Olivia crossed her arms on her chest thinking if they wanted a fight she would give them one but no one came back to see her. Machines beeped and footsteps padded past her door. She looked at the call button on the cord and was tempted to keep clicking the damn thing until someone came. Someone would have to answer her. She fought off a serial killer, actually no, she had killed two serial killers! After that, nurses shouldn't present her with too much trouble. She thought of going out there herself to talk to someone and was mad enough to do it. She slipped the covers off her legs and was swinging her feet to the floor when the phone beside her bed rang. She answered it. It was the vet.

"You've got a brave dog, here."

Olivia said, "I know. Can you tell me how he is? Will he make it?"

"Yes. He'll make it. There was some nerve damage. He won't be able to use his right back leg and he'll be here for a while. I want to monitor the stab wounds near his intestines and make sure we got the bleeding controlled but I feel good enough to say he'll make it."

Olivia cried in response. The relief overwhelmed her and it took her some time to speak. She thanked the vet with a thickened voice and continued to cry. All the crying was hurting her stomach. She found she couldn't stop. Her wonderful dog was going to make it.

A passing nurse heard her crying and he poked his head in and said, "You alright?"

"My dog will live."

The nurse furrowed his brow and he presented a confused smile before continuing on to wherever. She guessed he thought she should be happy. And she was. Problem was, how could she celebrate without knowing about her dad?

It had been chaos at her house. Police officers rushing about, paramedics and firefighters clanking a stretcher against and then into the door frame with bags hanging from their shoulders rushing to help her and help the police officer doing CPR on her dad. Harry was covered in blood and she couldn't feel his chest rise under her hand like she could with Brutus. Under the lights, his skin was pale and waxy. She felt unbearable guilt.

It was her the Jackal had been after. If it wasn't for her, Harry wouldn't have been stabbed and bleeding out on the floor of his home. Her stomach cramped, watching the paramedics work on her dad and she didn't know if she was going to be sick or pass out. His limbs flopped lifeless and the compressions given by a burly firefighter looked violent enough to crack a rib. Harry didn't respond to any of it. She thought she would lose him and that terrified her. He was her anchor. The first person she thought of when she wanted to talk or when she needed help. He was the man who taught her to walk and ride a bike. The person who had always been there for her. Her father. They lifted him and put him on the stretcher while continuing compressions. They were using a hand pump to squeeze air into his lungs as they rushed him out of there. That was the last she had seen of him.

She swung her legs back onto the bed and pulled the covers up under her chin, exhaustion and tears burning her eyes. Learning that Brutus was fine had quelled her anger for the moment and now she was just tired. The TV on a metal arm muttered nonsense from the wall. The talking head spoke about her but she didn't pay the person attention. Her mind sprinted and she couldn't slow it down to listen to the inconsequential like what the idiot on TV reported on her life. Her brain wouldn't give her a break and she was inundated with images of her nightmare of a night. She kept seeing the thrusting arm of the Jackal plunging the blade into her father, in and out and the amazed look in her dad's eye as though he couldn't believe it could end like this, standing in his boxer shorts and a white shirt, fighting for his life in the middle of the night to the sounds of *Ava Maria*. A sob hitched her chest and she expelled the air. A tear spilled from her eye. She thought of her fight with the Jackal in her closet. And his voice. That so familiar voice. She couldn't stop thinking about it.

"Hey, bitch. How you doing?"

Olivia's head snapped to the door and there was Lucy in a wheelchair with her head bandaged up.

"Lucy! Oh my god, what happened?"

"They didn't tell you?"

"No. They're treating me like a mushroom. Keeping me in the dark and feeding me shit."

Lucy laughed and then grimaced, "It fucking hurts to laugh."

"I'm not much for laughing right now."

Lucy's smile faded and she said, "Yeah. Me either. The Jackal scooped me right out of my driveway. They say he tasered me. Whatever he did, it fucking hurt. He grabbed me before he went after you I heard. Ballsy bastard, that's for sure. We drove, we stopped, he left and then there were flashing lights everywhere and sirens. I started rocking the van and kept doing that until a cop flashed a light through the windshield and saw me. And now, here I am."

"Shouldn't you be in bed?"

"Probably. I can't sleep though. I got a headache from hell. There's a ringing in my ears that won't go away but hey, at least I'm alive right? Thanks to you again, I hear."

Olivia burst into tears. Lucy wheeled closer.

"Hey, hey, he's dead now. No more creepy fuckers waiting for us. Not anymore. You took care of that."

Olivia wiped the tears from her eyes and said, "My dad. They won't tell me about my dad."

Lucy's face hardened, "Oh they won't will they? I'll find out for you. Was he hurt bad?"

Remembering him on the floor, soaked in blood, skin as pale as paper, Olivia nodded as more tears choked her voice.

"Are you sure you want to know? Right now?"

Olivia nodded and said, "I have to."

"Hey! What are you doing in here?"

Olivia and Lucy turned to the voice. The nurse who passed earlier glared at Lucy with his arms crossed.

Lucy said, "Visiting a friend. What's it to you?"

"What's it to *me*? To *me*? I'm the one trying to keep you alive! You have one hell of a concussion and you need to rest. You need to be monitored. What you don't need is to be wheeling about the corridors at night. Are you crazy? I about died when I saw your empty bed!"

"Alright, alright. Keep your panties on."

"You know I'm a dude, right?"

"I'm not judging. And I didn't want to assume your gender." She waved a hand like queen ordering a servant and said, "Wheel me back to my royal bed, oh grumpy protector."

The nurse pushed Lucy out of the room and the door closed behind them. She wiped the wetness from her cheeks and blew her nose with the Kleenex on the nightstand. Olivia glanced at the TV. Her eyes burned and her body ached. When would they tell her about Harry? She just wanted to know although in her heart, maybe she already did. So tired. She closed her eyes to rest them, just for a second.

•   •   •

"Hey."

She twitched and in a glance saw Davis standing in the doorway. His sad eyes gave her all the answer she needed about her father. Now, faced with it, she didn't want to hear it. She didn't want to see his sad mouth open and utter the words that would destroy her world. To know instead of wondering was sometimes worse. To know erased hope. He took a step into the room and before he could speak she said, "It was Carl, wasn't it. The Jackal was Dale's dad, Carl right?"

He stopped, a stunned expression on his face.

"I've been thinking about it. Thinking about a lot of things. About my dad—" her voice caught at that. She swallowed and pushed on. "I woke up in the night you know? Brutus was growling at the closet. Just sitting there in front of it growling. It bothered me then but I didn't *think* about it. Brutus growled at Frank like that. But he also growled at Carl too, at both of them. It was Carl Brutus tried to warn me about. Like he knew there was a sickness in him and he could smell it and he tried to tell us but we were all blind to his evil weren't we? And then the closet. I thought Frank spent a lot of time working on that part of the house but I never checked on him. Could have been Carl…must have been. Frank did say the wood was rotten and needed to be replaced. I guess I thought he replaced it. But it was Carl. The fuck-stick built himself a little tunnel, didn't he? A way to get in without anyone being the wiser. I didn't supervise him and I guess Frank didn't either. Frank trusted him because we all trusted him. And Carl, according to Frank, did great work, enough to be left alone to do it. It must have been good work though, well concealed because I had no idea about it at all. I put my clothes in that closet and I never noticed a thing. And then, before the Jackal died. He spoke to me and he sounded familiar. I knew his voice! It wasn't until I got here that I had the time to think about it. He said he loved me." She growled, "What does a monster know of love?"

She took a deep breath and continued, "It must have made his day when we asked him to help out with the house, huh? We invited him into our home! Can you believe it? Dale used to say his dad was always busy. Out on road trips, business trips and whatever but he sure had the time to drop everything and help out poor little Olivia didn't he? Unless there never were business trips. Just something he told his wife to leave for the night or a week if he wanted. And he used that time to visit us, his *girls*. Jesus. What a sick fucker. I never suspected him at all. I used to see him all the time, when I dated Dale in high school. You'd think I would've gotten a feeling from him. Something, you know? Like the perv vibe you get from some guys when they are checking you out and staring right at your tits instead of your eyes. That was his gift though wasn't it? To hide in plain sight. Hide behind his family. I feel sorry for Dale. And his mother. It seems insane that they didn't know."

Olivia dropped her gaze into her lap. Her fingers clenched the sheets. She said, "I sometimes forgot he was there. In our house. Until he started clanging and banging. Probably creeping looks at me all the time. Enjoying being in the same house with me, his most beloved victim, and me not knowing at all. We don't really know anyone do we? I mean, if he could keep something like that inside, hidden from the world, from his wife and son, then there's no way we can ever know anyone is there?"

Davis moved beside her bed and sat down near her feet. He had no answer for her. Besides, he knew she spoke to herself more than she did to him. When the mask was removed, the shock of it had weakened his knees. They never investigated Carl. He was just the father of the ex-boyfriend, a successful businessman and a family man. They didn't bother to look into him. They should have, considering they had investigated everyone else.

Davis said, "You know, we looked at Frank. We always look at the family. I even spent a minute or two on your dad. And we went to town on Dale because we had to. You just broke up with him and so of course he was a suspect. It never occurred to us to look at his father."

Olivia used the sheet to wipe at her eyes.

Olivia said, "Was that box that he had? The black thing with a red light? Was that a signal jammer?"

"Yeah."

"Where'd he get something like that? And the Taser? Aren't they illegal in Canada?"

"The jammer? I looked it up. You can get it online. Pretty easy to do. And the Taser you can order from the States. They sell them there. We'll track it down, we'll track it all down. We still have a lot of work to do. And when you're ready, we'd like to talk to you. About tonight. But only when you're ready."

She was worried about Dale. Would he ever want to talk to her again? Every time he looked at her or heard her voice, he'd be reminded of his dad, a crazy-ass serial killer that fooled his wife and son for years and years. Could he get over that? Could anyone? And her dad…but she didn't want to think about that, not yet.

She looked at her hands in her lap. Her missing fingers looked ugly to her. But then, they always did.

"Davis?"

"Yeah?"

"There wasn't any surveillance or guards, were there?"

"No."

"They pulled them when they thought you got the guy, right? The guy from the pool?"

"They must have but they didn't tell me. I didn't know. I wouldn't have let them. That's why they didn't tell me."

The drone of the TV and the beeps of the machines filled the silence. She wanted to close her eyes and rest. Her eyes burned in their sockets. Every time she closed her eyes she would see the Jackal stabbing her father again and again? Would she hear the whispered voice of the Jackal proclaiming his love for her? She didn't think she would ever rest again. Davis looked into his lap and ran a hand through his hair.

"You were supposed to keep us safe."

"I know."

"Listen, Olivia, about your dad, Harry."

Her eyes sprung tears and she raised her hand, palm towards him and said, "I know, Davis. I know."

View other Black Rose Writing titles at www.blackrosewriting.com/books and
use promo code PRINT to receive a 20% discount when purchasing.

BLACK ROSE
writing™

Made in United States
North Haven, CT
20 August 2024

56338751R00125